KNAVES' WAGER

Loretta Chase

1949 –

RODMAN PUBLIC LIBRARY

Thorndike Press • Thorndike, Maine

Library of Congress Cataloging in Publication Data:

Chase, Loretta Lynda, 1949-
   Knaves' wager / Loretta Chase.
      p. cm.
   ISBN 1-56054-085-0 (alk. paper : lg. print)
   1. Large type books. I. Title.
[PS3553.H3347K6   1990b]   90-47662
813'.54—dc20   CIP

Thorndike Press Large Print edition published in 1991
by arrangement with Walker and Company.

Cover design by James B. Murray.

The tree indicium is a trademark of Thorndike Press.

This book is printed on acid-free, high opacity paper.

KNAVES' WAGER

1

It was late March 1814. On the Continent, Buonaparte's once-great Empire lay in smoking ruins about him, his Grand Army reduced to a handful of ragged, starved boys. Yet the Corsican clung stubbornly to his throne, even as the Allied net closed about him.

That was all far away, however. The stretch of English landscape through which Mrs. Charles Davenant travelled this day lay quiet. Yet snug and secure in her well-sprung carriage, the widow gazed into the grey distance as unhappily as if she too knew what it was to lose empires. She had, after all, been privileged to rule her own life these last five years. Now that precious sovereignty was slipping from her grasp, and in her sad fancy, she rode in a moving prison to her doom.

A small, wry smile tugged at the corners of her set mouth. Though her tiny kingdom seemed to be in ruins, remarriage was hardly Doom. Her predicament was a mere twist of Fortune, a hard tangle in the thread of one insignificant life.

Without, the darkening sky cast its chill shadow upon the spring countryside. The widow turned from the sombre scene to the more heartening one within the carriage: her niece, Cecily Glenwood. Here was the radiant sunshine of golden curls, the clear heaven of wide blue eyes, and the fair blossom of pink and cream complexion. Here was youth and promise, the endless possibilities of a life just beginning, for Cecily Glenwood was travelling to London for her first Season.

Like her sister and cousins before her, Cecily would succeed. She could scarcely help it. All the Davenants and their offspring, male and female, were blessed with abundant good looks. The majority were charming, as Mrs. Davenant's late husband had been. Some, also like Charles Davenant, had their failings. Selfishness, for instance, was a quality prominent among his siblings. Had these in-laws been otherwise — sensible and trustworthy parents, for example — neither Cecily nor her cousins (there were yet more approaching marriageable age) would have needed Mrs. Charles Davenant's help at all.

She had already guided three nieces through successful London Seasons and seen each happily wed. Though she loved this niece as dearly as the others, the widow could not help

KNAVES' WAGER

Also by Loretta Chase
in Thorndike Large Print

The Devil's Delilah
Viscount Vagabond
The English Witch
Isabella

**This Large Print Book carries the
Seal of Approval of N.A.V.H.**

but wish, this once, Conscience would permit her to leave the responsibility where it belonged.

Fortunately, she was suited to her chosen responsibility. She was but eight and twenty and of remarkably unexcitable disposition. In physique and character she was built for endurance.

Lilith Davenant was tall, slim, and strong. Her classical features — a decided jaw, a straight, imperious nose, and high, prominent cheekbones — had been carved firmly and clearly upon cool alabaster. Her eyes were an uncompromising slate blue, their gaze direct, assured, and often, chilly. In fact, the only warmth about her was the tinge of red in her thick, shining hair. Still, even that rich, dark auburn mass was resolutely wound in rigid braided coils about her head.

Her character was as uncompromising as her appearance. According to some wags, Mrs. Davenant bore such a stunning resemblance to a marble statue that it was a wonder she had a pulse. Some doubted she had. No one of the masculine gender (excepting her husband, who was reputed to have died, not of consumption, but of slow freezing) dared approach near enough to find out.

This was precisely as Mrs. Davenant preferred, though she'd hardly have said so, if

9

anyone had been audacious enough to ask. Her manner did not invite personal questions. Her feelings were sealed and locked, as secure in her breast as were her funds in the Bank of England. More secure, actually, for Mrs. Davenant was running out of money.

Her former man of business had lost most of it in mad speculations during the last year. His replacement, in reorganising the widow's affairs, had come upon an enormous unpaid debt — Charles's debt — a small fortune lost in wagers to his erstwhile companion in debauchery, the Marquess of Brandon.

Once this last debt was paid, there would remain scarcely enough to keep Lilith. Seasons for her remaining nieces would be out of the question. This prospect was as unendurable as the alternative: to wed again.

The widow had spent the better part of the journey wrestling with Duty and Conscience, as well as a host of other demons she had rather not name. Yet not even her dearest confidante (if she'd had one) would have suspected Mrs. Davenant was troubled. She sat beside her niece, as cool, assured, and marblelike as ever.

"Oh, I do hope he'll be dark and devilish-looking," said Cecily.

Lilith slowly turned to examine her niece, who had remained uncharacteristically silent this past hour.

"To whom do you refer, my dear?" she asked.

"Him," said Cecily. "The husband I am supposed to catch in three months. That is a frightfully short time. There is one fox Papa has been after for seven years, and Papa is a brilliant huntsman. I don't see how I'm to catch anyone in just three months when I've had no experience at all."

In the seat opposite, Mrs. Davenant's plump companion suppressed a smile. Emma Wellwicke was older than her employer, and more tolerant — as perhaps a soldier's wife must be in these tumultuous times. While Mrs. Wellwicke might find Cecily's outspokenness amusing, the companion knew as well as anyone else that plain speaking would never serve in the Beau Monde. It had best be gently discouraged.

"My dear," said Lilith, "one does not speak of 'catching a man' as though it were a hunt."

"Oh, I would not say so to *them*, of course," Cecily answered. "But I cannot pretend to myself that catching a husband is not what I'm about — and I know I must do it quickly. Otherwise, Mama says she and Papa will be obliged to find me one at home. I know that is a deal more economical way to go about it, but it is not a pleasant prospect. None of the local bachelors is dark and devilish-looking — and I am so tired of blonds. We are all fair. It is so monotonous."

"Looks are not everything, Cecily," said Emma.

"Yes, I know. But I daresay you have never met Lord Evershot, whom Papa is so fond of. Such an ancient man — past forty, I think — and such a red, blotchy face. And you have never seen anything so absurd upon a horse. Meanwhile, Mama drops hints about The Honourable Alfred Crawbred, and he has the tiniest little black eyes and the most squashed-down nose. I am certain his nurse must have dropped him repeatedly upon his face. Yet he believes himself an Adonis and is forever waddling after the maidservants."

Emma bit her lip.

"Cecily, please," the aunt warned.

"It is quite true. I once spied him chasing a housemaid — and he looked exactly like Papa's favorite sow, lurching to the trough at feeding time."

"That will do, Cecily," Lilith said quietly. "Though I cannot approve Mr. Crawbred's behaviour regarding the maidservants, neither can I countenance uncharitable observations upon his physical attributes. Nature is not so generous with everyone as she has been with my nieces and nephews."

Cecily gazed at her in surprise. "I did not

12

mean to be uncharitable, Aunt. I only meant I had much rather not become Mr. Crawbred's wife. Why, you know he will expect to kiss me — and that is not the half of it."

"Oh, my," said Emma.

Mrs. Davenant turned with an inward shudder to the window, in order to compose both herself and a suitably quelling yet tactful response. In an instant, all this was forgotten.

Hastily, she opened the coach window and called to her coachman to stop.

"What is it?" Cecily and Emma asked simultaneously.

"An accident."

The coach slowly came to a halt, and Lilith climbed out, adjuring the other two women to remain where they were.

Though somewhat in awe of her queenly aunt, Cecily remained where she was approximately seven seconds before clambering out. Emma followed, to urge the girl back. This was sensible on more than one count, for the rain which had threatened all afternoon had commenced, and the road dust was rapidly turning to mud.

In a ditch by the roadside lay what had once been a dashing black curricle. Cecily's practised eye told her the vehicle would never dash again; futhermore, neither would one of the horses. She clutched her aunt's sleeve.

"The poor animal," she cried. "Oh, do please have the coachman put it out of its misery."

"Yes, yes," was the impatient answer. "John will see to it, but I fear — "

"A man, missus," the coachman called out from behind the fallen curricle. "Not dead, I don't think."

Lilith ordered her niece back to the coach with Emma. As the girl reluctantly obeyed, the carriage which had been following with servants and luggage neared and halted. Summoning the stronger members of her staff, the widow led them down to the smashed vehicle. They stood patiently waiting in the rain as their mistress joined John.

The injured man lay partly under the curricle. Luckily for him, none of it lay upon him. He was bruised and filthy, and though not conscious, alive, as John had said.

Careless of the mud, Lilith knelt beside him. "Is anything broken?" she asked the coachman.

"Not as I could tell, missus."

"Try to be certain. I do not like to move him if it will cause damage."

Cold rain streamed from the coachman's hat down his neck. He glanced ruefully at the other servants, none of whom seemed any more pleased than he to be summoned to this scene.

14

"We could leave someone with him and go on to the next inn and send a party after him, missus," John offered hopefully.

He received an icy glance in answer. "Indeed," said his mistress. "I hope that was your intention originally. I noted you did not slacken your pace when we came upon this wreck — though it was not so dark then you could have missed it."

Returning her attention to the injured man, Mrs. Davenant took out her handkerchief and wiped the mud from his face. His eyes opened. They were a rare, arresting shade of green.

"Olympus," he muttered. "It must be. Hera, is it not? No — Athena. Death, where is thy sting? Athena, where is thy helmet?"

"He is delirious," said Lilith. "We had better risk it and carry him to the coach."

She began to rise, but the man grasped her hand with surprising strength.

"Have you appeared at last only to abandon me?" he asked weakly.

"Certainly not," she answered. "I would never abandon an injured fellow creature — but I cannot climb out of this ditch while you are clutching me."

He groaned softly and released her hand. Lilith gave him one brief, uneasy glance, then moved aside to let her servants do their work.

After some discussion and difficulty, the man was finally placed in a half-sitting, half-falling position on the carriage seat. Since Mrs. Davenant was at this point nearly as dirty as he, she sat beside him and tried to prop him up as comfortably as possible in a carriage grown exceedingly cramped. He was a large, long-legged man who took up a deal of room.

Though he managed to keep from tumbling onto the carriage floor, he was too weak to remain fully upright. Eventually he subsided into a drowsing state, his head resting on the widow's shoulder — and once or twice slipping to her firm bosom, from which he was somewhat ungently ejected.

More than an hour later, he was carried into an inn. It took nearly another hour — and all Mrs. Davenant's imperious insistence — to obtain a room for him.

It happened that a mill was to take place the following day. The result was a hostelry over-run with noisy, demanding bucks, and a staff run off their feet attending to them.

After attempting in vain to receive further assistance, Mrs. Davenant sent one of her own servants in search of a doctor. Others she dispatched for hot water, clean towels and diverse other necessities. In between giving orders, Lilith became aware of the excessive attention the inn's male patrons were paying Cecily.

Once again, the widow cornered the innkeeper. Not long after, a pair of noble gentlemen were persuaded to chivalry. They gave up their chamber, and Cecily took refuge there with her maid from the chaos, while Lilith and Emma managed matters for the accident victim.

"Really, Susan," said Cecily as her maid poured tea, "I cannot understand why Papa says Aunt Lilith is cold and strange. What is cold and strange, I ask you, about giving a lot of silly girls a whole Season in London?"

"I'm sure I don't know, miss," said the maid wearily. "But I do wish we was in London now. I never heard such a din, and I can tell you I been pinched more than once — and John says we'll never get there tonight, not in this weather. He says we should've left the man where he was, you know, and sent folks after him — "

"Which is just my point," Cecily interrupted. "If she were cold and strange, she would have done so, wouldn't she?"

"Yes, miss, and I don't like to be uncharitable, but I do wish she'd done just that."

"Well, then, I think *you* are cold and strange. He is dark and devilish-looking as

17

they come." Cecily sighed. "But I believe he's rather old."

"His injuries are slight," the doctor told Mrs. Davenant as he left the patient's room. "His trouble is that he was ill to start and had no business out of bed. I would guess he hasn't had a proper meal or decent night's rest in days. One of those too stubborn to admit he's sick, though I think he might admit it now that he's made himself weak as a baby. Travelling alone, in his condition," the doctor muttered. "What are these chaps thinking of? Or do they think of anything, I wonder? Wyndhurst you said his name was?"

"That is what he told my coachman," said Lilith. "I have not spoken with Mr. Wyndhurst since we arrived. I trust my servants have tended to him adequately?"

"I daresay they did the best they could. I've had more cooperative patients, I can tell you." With that and a few instructions regarding medicine and nourishment, the doctor left.

A while later, Emma appeared with a steaming bowl of broth.

"I will see to that," said Lilith recollecting the doctor's hints regarding the patient's uncooperativeness. She took the tray from her companion. "You need some sustenance yourself, Emma — and I have had more practice with invalids."

The patient, to Mrs. Davenant's surprise, was sitting up in bed. True, he was well propped up with pillows, but he did not appear near death, as she had expected. No dying man could have invested his green-eyed gaze with so much insolence. He boldly surveyed her head to toe, not once, but twice — quickly assessing the first time and lazily considering the second. Lilith's hands closed a bit more tightly upon the tray handles. This was the only outward manifestation of the acute tension which gripped her as she approached the sickbed.

Mr. Wyndhurst had begun as a muddy, injured mess requiring a great flurry of activity. Thus, beyond noting the rare colour of his eyes, she'd not had time to study him before. Now, washed and combed by her servants, he commanded attention.

His hair was black, curly, and luxuriant. The green eyes were fringed with thick black lashes. Their heavy-lidded look, the faint lines at the corners, and the sensual mouth intimated a depraved character. Mrs. Davenant was certain, moreover, that he had been looking down his long, straight nose at everyone his entire life. The strong cheekbones . . . the stubborn chin . . . everything about his hard, chiseled features bespoke arrogance. He was pale and ill, yet his entire frame exuded pure masculine power, utter self-assurance. He was devastatingly handsome. Regrettably, he seemed fully aware of this circumstance. He might have been the very model of a bored, dissolute scoundrel.

Lilith set the tray down on his lap and stepped back. "You can feed yourself, I trust?" she asked politely.

He eyed the steaming broth with a pained expression.

"If I could," he said, "I should also have the strength to hurl this mess out of window. Chicken broth? How could you?" he asked in aggrieved tones. "I thought Athena was wise and just, but she enters the room of a dying man only to poison him. Chicken broth," he repeated, shaking his head sadly. "Is it come to this? Then fall, Caesar!" He sank back against the pillows, his eyes closed.

"In your state, you will be unable to digest anything more substantial," said the widow, unmoved.

"Then bring me wine, oh wise and beautiful immortal," he murmured. He cocked one eye open and added, "Unless you've got some ambrosia about. Ambrosia will do as well."

"It will not do, Mr. Wyndhurst." Lilith drew a chair close to the bed, sat down, and took up spoon and bowl. "If you cannot feed yourself, I shall feed you — and you will swallow every last drop. You must do so sooner or later, or you will starve to death."

"A prospect too heartbreaking, I agree."

"If I had meant to let you die, I might have done so more easily by simply leaving you where you were, instead of inconveniencing myself or my servants." With the ease of long practice, she administered the first spoon.

The submissive air Mr. Wyndhurst abruptly assumed was undermined by the gleam of amusement in his eyes.

"You see?" she said, ignoring the mockery she saw there. "It is not as nasty as you thought."

"It is every bit as nasty," he answered after swallowing another spoonful, "but I dare not combat the goddess of wisdom. If, on the other hand, you could contrive to be Aphrodite — and I'm sure you could, if you liked — "

"I do not like, sir. I did not come to flirt with you."

"Did you not?" He appeared astonished. "Are you quite certain?"

"Quite."

Mr. Wyndhurst spent some minutes mulling this over while Lilith continued feeding him.

"I understand," he said at last. "When you

found me I must have been a most repellent sight. Naturally, you could not know what lay beneath the grime your servant so conscientiously — painfully so, I must add — removed."

He *was* vain, Lilith thought contemptuously. Aloud she said, "I am sorry if Harris was not gentle with you. He is more accustomed to grooming horses."

"No wonder my hide is raw. It is a miracle he did not try to brush my — "

"There are but a few spoonfuls left," Lilith hastily interjected. "You had best finish while it is still hot."

Though he accepted the remaining broth meekly enough, there was no meekness in his steady scrutiny of her face, nor in the occasional glances he dropped elsewhere. He was sizing her up, Lilith knew. Well, if he had any intelligence at all, he must realise he wasted his time. All the same, she was edgy. When at last the bowl was empty, she rose.

"Now I hope you will get some rest," she said as she took up the tray.

"I'm afraid that's not possible." He slumped back among the pillows once more. "Your company has been far too exciting for a sick man. You should not have agitated me so. I shall not sleep a wink."

"I fed you one small bowl of chicken broth,"

Lilith said with a touch of impatience.

"It was not what you did but how you looked when you did it. Such resolution in the face of ingratitude. Such militant charity." He smiled lazily. "And such eyes, Athena."

"Indeed. One on either side of my nose. A matching set, quite common in the human countenance."

"The Hellespont in a summer storm."

"Blue. A common colour among the English." She moved to the door.

"Really? They seem most uncommon to me. Perhaps you are right — but I cannot be certain unless you come closer."

"You are short-sighted, Mr. Wyndhurst?" she asked as she opened the door. "Then it is no wonder you drove your curricle into a ditch. Perhaps in future you will remember to don your spectacles."

She heard a low crack of laughter as the door closed behind her.

To Cecily's eager enquiries during dinner, her aunt offered depressingly unsatisfactory answers. Yes, Mr. Wyndhurst was well-looking enough, she noted without enthusiasm. He was also shockingly ill-behaved.

"Oh, Aunt, did he try to flirt with you? I was sure he would. He had that look about him."

"A look?" Emma asked with a smile. "You discerned a look under his impenetrable coating of mud?"

"He had the devil in his eyes," Cecily said. "I saw him open them when he thought no one was looking. He reminded me of Papa's prize stallion. The naughtiest, most deceitful, ill-mannered beast you ever saw. But when he moves, he is so graceful that one is persuaded he must have wings. Like a bad, beautiful angel."

Lilith put down her fork. "Whatever Mr. Wyndhurst may be, tending to him has been altogether wearing. I am not decided what to do tomorrow. We cannot leave him here, yet I cannot subject my servants to another night of sleeping in the tap-room — or wherever it is the poor creatures will lay their heads. I should have asked his destination. If it were near enough, we might have sent word."

"You've done all you can for one day," said Emma. "The decision can wait until tomorrow, when you're rested." She smiled ruefully. "At least I hope you'll be rested. I do think you should let me share a bed with Cecily. Having done by far the most work, you have earned the most comfort." She turned to Cecily. "I promise not to snore."

"Pray snore all you like, ma'am," Cecily answered with a grin. "I am a prodigious sound sleeper."

★

Though she was eventually persuaded — thanks to Cecily's threats to sleep on the floor — to accept Mrs. Wellwicke's offer, Lilith was wakeful long after her companions had fallen asleep.

She had no sooner thrust the obnoxious Mr. Wyndhurst from her mind than another gentleman pushed his way in: Sir Thomas Bexley, her erstwhile friend and, of late, patient suitor. His recent letters indicated he meant to repeat his offer of marriage in the very near future. Though her feelings had not changed since the last time, it seemed her answer must.

Poverty did not frighten Mrs. Davenant. She was disciplined enough to live frugally. She need not and would not in any case accept the charity of Charles's family. Unfortunately, poverty touched not only herself. Without funds, she could be of no help to her nieces.

She lay staring at the ceiling. The prospect of marriage was repugnant to her. There were reasons, but perhaps these were paltry. She would not be miserable with Thomas. He admired and respected her, and would exert himself to make her happy. Their tastes and personalities suited.

No, she could not be so self-centred as to reject marriage to a perfectly worthy gentleman — not when the consequence was a lifetime of wretchedness for those beautiful, fresh, innocent girls. Cecily, for instance, to be married to that repellent sot, Lord Evershot — or to that obese young lecher, Mr. Crawbred.

It was always the same: whatever wealthy and sufficiently well-born mate was handiest would do. Her in-laws took greater care in mating their precious horses. The children — whom they produced in such shocking abundance — they only wanted off their hands.

Well, it would not be, she told herself. Aunt Lilith would look after them: Cecily now, Diana next year . . . Emily next . . . and Barbara after . . . then it would not be long before Charlotte's girls came of age . . . and the eldest nephew, Edward, could do with some guidance — if he'd stand for it.

Thus, counting her beloved nieces and nephews instead of sheep, Mrs. Davenant finally fell asleep.

2

Despite inadequate rest, Mrs. Davenant was up and about early the following morning. She'd scarcely quit her room when Cecily's groom, Harris, who'd dutifully looked in on Mr. Wyndhurst, informed her the man had vanished.

The innkeeper expanded upon the news. "They came for him early," he told the widow. "Seems his lordship's relations were expecting him and sent someone to look when he didn't appear. Must have found the smashed rig and alerted the family because — "

"His lordship?" Lilith interrupted.

"His lordship the Marquess of Brandon, ma'am. On his way to his cousin's. Lord Belbridge, that is."

His patron's countenance grew stony.

The innkeeper went on quickly, "They came for him — the Earl of Belbridge himself and a pack of servants. As I said, it was early — maybe an hour or more before cock-crow — and Lord Brandon was very particular that

27

we wasn't to disturb you about it. He said to thank you for your kindness and apologise for his hasty leave-taking. I think that was how he put it," the landlord said with a frown. "Anyhow, he paid your shot, ma'am. Said it was the least he could do in return for all the — What was it he said? He laid such a stress on it, the word — ah, the *inconvenience*."

After uttering a few cold words of acknowledgement, Mrs. Davenant turned away, her heart pounding with indignation. The Marquess of Brandon, of all people. Her servants had braved the cold, filthy storm and the muck of the ditch, risking pneumonia. They had spent the night on floors — when they might have slept comfortably, warm and dry in their proper beds in her London town house. All this they had endured for the most foul libertine who had ever trod his polluted step upon the earth.

With her own hands she'd fed the man who had half killed her husband — for was it not Brandon who had mercilessly led Charles on an insatiable pursuit of the lowest sort of pleasure? Finally, when her husband was too ill for pleasure any more, this so-called friend had released what was left of him. Then Charles was hers at last — hers to watch nearly two years, while he crept slowly and painfully to his grave. Not once in all that long, weary time had this bosom bow deigned to visit him. A letter or two from abroad was all. Then, one curt, condescending note of condolence, two months after the funeral.

Now Brandon patronisingly threw a few pieces of gold her way — when she owed him thousands. She would pay him, Lilith vowed. She would sell the very clothes from her back if necessary. She would not be in his debt, not for so much as a farthing.

Mrs. Davenant stood staring at a small, poorly executed hunting print until she had collected herself. Then she returned to her travelling companions to break the news regarding their patient and urge them to a speedy departure.

She fumed inwardly the entire distance to London. Outwardly, she was as coolly poised and unapproachable as ever.

Even Cecily was eventually daunted in her efforts to penetrate her aunt's reserve. Questions about the Marquess of Brandon elicited only warnings: he was precisely the sort of man young ladies must scrupulously avoid; he had not been so near death as he pretended; if he could deceive an experienced physician, what hope was there for an innocent young girl — and so on. Cecily would have preferred to be told what she didn't already know.

As Mrs. Davenant's carriage was entering London the subject of her disapprobation was reclining upon a richly upholstered sofa in the cavernous drawing room of a massive country house many miles away. He was being wearied half to death listening — or trying not to listen — to his cousin's litany of woes.

Julian Vincent Wyndhurst St. Maur, Baron St. Maur, Viscount Benthame, Earl of Stryte, Marquess of Brandon, was a little tad this afternoon. He was affronted by the behaviour of the chill he'd contracted en route to Ostend. He had given it the cut direct. The ailment, instead of humbly taking itself off, had only fastened itself more firmly — and had apparently gathered equally boorish associates.

Though Lord Brandon was not so weak and ill as he had feigned for Mrs. Davenant's benefit, he was scarcely well. At the moment, he wished he had remained in bed. His inconsiderate cousin might have respected his peace then, instead of pacing agitatedly upon the thick Axminster carpet in a manner viciously calculated to bring on *mal de mer*.

"Do me the kindness, George, to sit down," Lord Brandon said at last. "That constant to and fro raises the very devil with my innards."

Lord Belbridge promptly flopped down upon the sofa by his cousin's feet. George was a rather stout fellow. The jolt of his heavy frame on the sofa cushions set off a wave of nausea.

"Damn," said Lord Brandon with a grimace.

"Sorry, Julian. Keep forgettin' you're ailin'. But I'm half out of my wits, what with Mother at me the livelong day — or goin' off in hysterics when she ain't. Even Ellen's overset — though it's the children she worries for, and how they're to hold up their heads — "

"Being attached in the customary way to their necks, I expect their heads will contrive to keep from tumbling off. Really, George, one would think no man had ever kept a mistress before."

"If he were only keepin' her, what should any of us care? But he's been *livin'* with her — near two years now."

"Of course Robert is living with her. You keep him on a short allowance. He cannot afford two sets of lodgings, now, can he?"

George's jaw set obstinately. "Well, I ain't goin' to give him any more. He spends every farthin' on *her*."

"I see. You would prefer your brother spent his vast sums upon drink or hazard, I suppose. Come, George, you are a man of the world. As I recollect, there was a ballet dancer or two enlivening your salad days while she lightened your purse."

31

"That was different. I had my fun for a bit, then got another. I didn't talk of *marryin'* the tarts, Julian."

Lord Brandon's half-closed lids fluttered open. "My ailment appears to have affected my hearing. I was certain you mentioned marriage."

"He means to marry her," Lord Belbridge grimly confirmed. "He's only waitin' 'til he comes into his money, in less than four months. Can't touch his trust fund 'til he's five and twenty, you know. Then he's little need of his allowance. Not that it's any great fortune — but it's respectable. He wants to make an honest woman of her and set up his nursery." George groaned. "Expects we'll welcome her into the family. Can you see my sweet Ellen callin' a fancy piece 'sister'? And a damned Frenchie at that. Gad."

There was a moment or two of silence while George allowed his cousin to digest this piece of information. Lord Brandon pressed his fingers to his temples.

"Robert cannot possibly be so imbecilic as to marry his mistress," he said finally. "He must know you would seek an annulment if he did. Furthermore, I do not see what prevents your dealing with her yourself. Fill her purse and she will take her charms elsewhere."

"Tried," George answered sadly. "Again

and again. She won't leave him. Why should she? She could get a wealthier lover, but not one fool enough to marry her. Not a lord, certainly." He uttered a heavy sigh. "That ain't the worst of it."

"Naturally not," his listener murmured.

"When she wouldn't listen to reason," George went on, "I took to threats. Told her we'd see the wedding never took place, whatever it took to do it. She only looked at me like I was somethin' pitiful. Then she told me about the letters."

"Letters," Lord Brandon repeated, his expression pained. "I might have known."

"Love letters," said his cousin. "She showed me one or two and told me there were a score more like 'em — all eggin' her to marry him. Callin' her his 'dear wife.' Sickenin', just sickenin'."

"Such epistles usually are, except perhaps to the recipient, for whom they undoubtedly must provide many hours of laughter."

"I went to my solicitor right after that. He hemmed and hawed for an hour before he broke the news. Which is, that if those letters end up in a court of law, they could be worth as much as twenty-five thousand quid in damages."

"Indeed," said Lord Brandon. "Robert quite astonishes me. He has fallen in love with his whore, proposed marriage to her, not once but many times, and all in writing, no less. If he marries her, there is a great scandal, his family is dishonoured, and he is ruined. If he doesn't marry her, she sues for breach of promise, there is a great scandal, his family is dishonoured, and he is ruined. How very neatly he has arranged matters. I must remember to congratulate him." Cautiously, he pulled himself upright. "I think I shall go to bed."

"Is that all you can say?" George cried, jumping up.

"I'm sure you will not wish to hear my feelings regarding being summoned from France — at Prinny's behest, no less — merely to be informed that my cousin is a besotted fool. This is the 'urgent family matter' so desperately requiring my assistance, now of all times? When, finally, Buonaparte is within our grasp, when all the wit and tact we possess will be required to return his obese Bourbon rival to his unloving subjects?"

"They wanted you home anyhow, Julian," was the defensive answer. "They said you was near collapse — and had done more than your share at any rate."

"As you say, I have done enough. As to Lord Robert Downs — my young cousin is so unspeakable an idiot that we were all best advised to cease recollecting his existence."

"But dammit, Julian, he *is* my brother — and think of the scandal. Think of Mary. Think of the children."

"I cannot think of anyone at the moment, George. My head is throbbing like the very deuce. Will you ring for a servant? One with a stout arm and broad shoulders, if you please. I shall require some assistance regaining the sanctity of my bedchamber, where I expect to expire gracefully within the hour. No mourning, I beg of you. Black is not Ellen's best colour."

"But, Julian — "

"Wash your hands of him, George. I assure you *I* do."

Not many days after her return to London, Mrs. Davenant met with her man of business. Mr. Higginbottom, possessed of the first good news he'd been able to offer his client in some six months, was buoyant. The debt, he told her, was cancelled. Lord Brandon had no wish to take bread from the mouths of widows.

The slate-blue gaze grew so icy that Mr. Higginbottom involuntarily shivered. Congealing within, he soon petrified, to sink into arctic waters as his client expressed not only profound displeasure that the marquess had been apprised in such detail of her private affairs, but also an adamant refusal to accept his lordship's charity.

It was futile to argue that gentlemen cancelled such debts every day for far more whimsical reasons. It was useless to point out that the Marquess of Brandon didn't want the money, most assuredly didn't need the money, and in fact cared so little about it that he had let the matter lie buried these last seven years. It was equally useless to point out that twenty-nine thousand pounds, sensibly invested, would earn such and such a return, that she need not sell both her remaining properties, that in a few years she might expect to see her income return to its previous level or very near.

Mrs. Davenant only coldly retorted that she was not on the brink of starvation.

"You will use the funds from the lease of my Derbyshire residence for the present," she said. "When the Season is done, we will discuss letting the town house. I wish the debt paid — with appropriate interest — as speedily as possible, though I hope your terms can accommodate certain matters of necessity. As you are aware, a family commitment requires my remaining in Town. Still, it will be as economical a stay as can reasonably be expected."

She paused a moment before adding — and

this was her first and only hint of emotion — "I will not be beholden to *that man,* sir, not for any amount." She handed the businessman a slip of paper. "You will add this to the sum," she said. "There was a misunderstanding with an innkeeper."

"Yes, madam," said Mr. Higginbottom, and "Yes, madam" was all he said to everything else. Only that evening, to his wife, did he declaim upon the inscrutability of the ruling classes.

Sir Thomas called, as he had promised, at two o'clock. Mrs. Davenant, as she had promised, granted him a private interview.

The baronet knew his offer was expected. He was not, however, confident of an affirmative answer. Though he'd been granted the signal honour of her friendship, he could not be certain he had as yet awakened any softer feelings in the widow's breast. To be sure, he required only sufficient softening to produce the word "yes."

Sir Thomas was a widower of nearly forty. He topped his prospective bride by a mere inch or two; his square figure was not so fit as it had once been; and his light brown hair, to his grief, was thinning. Though he was well enough looking — his jaw firm, his brown eyes alert and clear — he had never been sufficiently handsome to break hearts, or even win them without effort. Thus, he had very sensibly concentrated on the winning of hands, and did so for practical reasons.

Though as ambitious as ever, he was no longer the nearly penniless youth he had been at the time of his first marriage. Then, as now, he was content to do without love, though for different reasons. Of his first wife he'd required only money. Of his second, he required strong character, irreproachable reputation, and superior breeding. He wanted, in short, the perfect political hostess.

There was nothing, certainly, of Love in her response. Lilith acknowledged she respected him and was honoured by his proposal. So far, so good.

"I should be pleased to be your wife, Thomas," she continued composedly. "But before we make an irrevocable commitment, I must deal frankly with certain circumstances of which you are at present unaware."

Sir Thomas's smile faded into a puzzled frown.

"As you may know, I had a considerable fortune in my own right," she went on. "As my grandparents' only living descendant, I inherited everything. The property was not entailed. My grandfather's title was recent — and the bulk of the property was my grandmother's."

38

"My dear," he quickly intervened, "I am aware of these matters. All the same, in like frankness I must remind you of my own situation, which is such, I flatter myself, that your finances are irrelevant. Certainly they are and always have been irrelevant to my wish to make you my wife."

She hesitated a fraction of a moment. Then, her chin just a bit higher, she answered, "Nonetheless, I prefer to be quite open with you. My income is sadly depleted. Mistakes have been made — certain investments my previous financial advisor — "

Once more Sir Thomas interrupted. "I am sorry you have been ill-advised," he said, "but there is no need to weary yourself reviewing the details. In future, I hope you will allow me to see to your comfort — the very near future, if you will excuse my impetuousness, my dear. That is to say, as soon, of course, as your niece is set up."

"I am telling you," she said patiently, "that I am no longer a woman of means."

He smiled and stepped toward her. "And I am telling you, Lilith Davenant, it matters not a whit to me. Will you become Lady Bexley, and make me the happiest man in Christendom?"

If the answering smile was tinged with resignation, Sir Thomas was unaware of it. He heard the quiet "Yes" he had wished for these eighteen months or more, and his heart soared. He did, truly, believe himself the happiest man in Christendom. He had achieved another great ambition and won the hand of the regal Lilith Davenant.

So great was his appreciation of and respect for her queenly reserve that, instead of embracing her as he was fully entitled, he only planted one fervent kiss upon the back of her hand. He did not perceive the way she had steeled herself for the obligatory embrace, nor did he remark the relief that swept her features when he only bent instead over her white hand.

"The good die early," Mr. Defoe once observed, "and the bad die late."

Thus it could come as no surprise to any reasonably intelligent person that, despite his relatives' unflagging efforts to plague him to death, Lord Brandon did not expire. On the contrary, he recovered surprisingly swiftly.

"Small wonder," his aunt remarked with a sniff. "Even the Old Harry is in no hurry to have *you*. A more selfish, insufferable, obstinate blackguard of a nephew there never was and never will be."

"Auntie, your tender affection will unman me," the nephew replied. "Really, you ought not dote upon me so extravagantly at meal-time. I cannot see my beef-steak for my tears." All the same, Lord Brandon cut into his beef-steak accurately enough.

He had just come down to breakfast. It was proof of his aunt's determination that she had risen from her bed before noon, only to be on hand first thing to nag at him.

The Marchioness of Fineholt was a small, fragile-looking woman with a will of iron and a tongue, her relative reflected silently, like a meat axe.

"I had always thought your sire the greatest villain who ever lived," she went on. "Yet worthless reprobate that he was, my brother Alec at least knew what was due his name and family. Though why I expect you to care about anyone's name when you don't trouble with your own — "

"My dearest Auntie, my name came to me when I was born and has remained with me ever since without my bothering about it at all."

"Thirty-five years old," she snapped, "and you haven't got a wife — not to speak of an heir."

"I can understand your wish not to speak of him," the marquess answered sadly. "His mama was so misguided as to have been born in Philadelphia — to a haberdasher. I cannot imagine what she was thinking of."

"I don't mean those dratted Yankee cousins, and you know it, Brandon. You haven't got a son — not on the right side of the blanket at any rate, though I don't doubt there's a score or more of the other sort peppering the countryside, here and abroad."

"Wicked girl," said the nephew between mouthfuls. "Will you not spare my blushes?"

"Spare you?" she echoed wrathfully. "There is your poor uncle — a sad invalid these last five years — and even he took pen in his poor, trembling hand to plead with that unspeakable woman. While you, strong and healthy as an ox, spend your days lolling about upon the sofa, refusing even to discuss this debacle."

Lord Belbridge entered the breakfast room at this juncture.

"Now, Mother," he placated as he sat down beside her. "You know Julian's not been lollin' about. He's been gravely ill."

"And bound to send me to an early grave in his place," she grumbled. "I should have expected it. Not a male in the lot with an ounce of ingenuity. Or if they've got any," she added with a darkling look at her nephew, "They'd rather spend it coaxing the next trollop into their bed."

"You mean to say there are trollops about this fair green countryside, Aunt?" Lord Brandon turned to his cousin in reproach. "You might have mentioned it, Georgy."

"Julian, please — "

"Don't beg him, George. It isn't dignified, and you've made a sorry enough spectacle of yourself as it is. There's the tart showing you her letters, and what do you do but politely give 'em back."

"Mother dearest, I couldn't well bind her hand and foot while I searched the premises. Besides, she's too dashed clever to keep 'em all with her. Stands to reason she'd have 'em locked up with a solicitor, or someplace safe."

"Reason," her ladyship repeated scornfully. "When were you and Reason ever acquainted, pray tell? Oh, that ever I should live to see this day." Her voice grew tremulous, and a very dainty lace handkerchief was applied to very dry eyes. "My baby, caught in the toils of a French drab, and no one will lift a finger to save him."

"Now, Mother — "

"You have no conscience, Brandon," she went on, ignoring her son. "No feeling for your kin."

"I am positively bubbling with feeling, ma'am. Unfortunately, the situation is beyond mending."

"Fiddlesticks! You have made a profession of bending women to your will. You will not

43

persuade me you cannot wrap this baggage about your finger, clever though she may be. You are simply too lazy to trouble with any matter not pertaining to your own pleasure."

She rose to deliver her parting shot. "You are spoiled, vain, selfish, and far too clever and good-looking for your own good. I pray that one day — and may I be alive to see it — a woman will cut up your peace. Pleasure has taught you nothing. Mayhap pain will." With that, her small, rigid figure swept out of the breakfast room.

Lord Belbridge threw his cousin a reproachful glance. "I wish you wouldn't tease her, Julian. She takes it out on me after."

"Have you considered sending her to Wellington, George? Perhaps she might be employed to browbeat Napoleon into submission. I wonder no one thought of that before." Having finished his breakfast during the marchioness's verbal bombardment, Lord Brandon took up the newspaper.

George sighed, went to the sideboard, and filled his plate. When he sat down again, his cousin asked from behind the newspaper in a very bored voice, "Are you acquainted with a fellow by the name of Bexley? Sir Thomas Bexley?"

"Not intimately acquainted. He's a deal too political for my tastes. Still, one can't help

44

knowin' of him. One of Liverpool's protégés."

"I see. An ambitious young man."

"Ambitious, yes, but he's forty if he's a day. Looks older. Goin' bald," George explained. "Probably all those years in the West Indies did it. Bought plantations there, you know, with his wife's dowry. Made pots. Came back . . . well, I couldn't say when, exactly. Two or three years ago, maybe. After he lost his wife."

The marquess glanced over the paper. "Careless of him."

"She passed on, Julian," his cousin answered with a touch of vexation. "Dash it, you've got no respect, even for the dead. She passed on, and the poor fellow came back and I guess he buried his sorrow in politics. They say he's movin' on fast. Shouldn't be surprised to find him in the ministry one day."

George swallowed a few mouthfuls. After a moment or two, he asked, "If you don't know him, what makes you ask?"

"Boredom, I suppose."

"Somethin' in the paper?"

"Only that his engagement is announced."

George put down his silverware. "You don't say! He's done it, then. Well, there's a few chaps stand to lose money on *that*. Mean to say — it's Davenant's widow he's marryin', ain't it?"

45

Lord Brandon nodded.

"Better him than me. Feel an east wind blowin' just thinkin' of her. Cold female, Julian. But you knew her, I expect. You and Davenant were together a good deal." George returned to his meal.

"I never met the lady then. She was in Derbyshire. Charles was in London. He took ill and returned to the country shortly after I was required to take residence out of England."

"I recollect. Annoyin' that. And not a bit fair. Stupid female. Burstin' out from the wood, shriekin'. If it wasn't for her, you'd have only winged him. A wonder we weren't all killed. Duel's no place for a woman."

"Perhaps, having provoked the situation, Lady Advers felt obliged to see it through to the conclusion. At any rate, she taught me a valuable lesson."

"Yes. Keep away from married women."

The marquess laughed. "Good heavens, no, George. What I learned was never to let my attention wander, on any account."

Two hours later, Lord Brandon threw his relatives into transports of joy and relief when he announced plans to proceed to London that very day. He was bored with rustication, he said, and from all reports, Castlereagh seemed to be muddling along well enough

46

without his dubious assistance. Since he had nothing better to do elsewhere, Lord Brandon thought he might toddle off to look into this tiresome little matter of Robert's nuptials.

3

Lord Enders's opera box was rarely an object of interest to the audience. If he and his wife had company, it was bound to be the wife's brother, Sir Thomas Bexley, and he was sure to be escorting Mrs. Charles Davenant. Though Bexley was absent tonight, the widow was not, and her severely cut, sombrely coloured costumes had never aroused envy or even interest in her neighbours.

Lady Enders was equally unexciting. Hers were the same passable features as her brothers. Unlike him, however, she always appeared fussy, a veritable snowstorm of stiffly starched ruffles and furbelows heaped upon her gown, and the entire contents of her jewel-box mounded upon her throat and bosom.

Nonetheless, on this particular evening, the opera box received second, third — indeed countless — glances from a majority of the gentlemen present. This was because tonight a young lady broke the monotony. She was a jewel of a young lady, with her guinea-gold curls, her wide blue eyes, her dainty nose, and (here the sighs became audible) her pink, bee-stung lips. More than one masculine pulse accelerated at the sight of Miss Cecily Glenwood.

"I see we may expect a stampede at the intermission," said Lady Enders in an undertone. "I had not thought it possible, but the child is even prettier than her cousins."

One of her rare smiles softened Mrs. Davenant's features. "She is a dear, sweet girl as well," she said softly. "Those her beauty attracts will return on account of her nature."

"You have always been so fortunate in your girls, Lilith. Lady Shumway, on the other hand — Why, whatever are they gaping at?"

The enquiry was occasioned by a sudden stirring in the audience. The usual buzz of voices preceding the curtain's rise had swelled to a Babel, and every head was swivelling in the same direction.

Lilith followed the general gaze . . . and stifled a gasp. The Marquess of Brandon, in the company of one fair-haired gentleman and one brunette female — of obviously dubious character — had entered the box nearly opposite.

"Brandon!" Lady Enders whispered harshly. "I cannot believe my eyes. He has not been seen in Society in years. Why, he has scarcely

been in England, to my knowledge — not
since he killed Advers in that scandalous duel.
Seven years ago that was, when Brandon had
to flee the country. Wicked man! Do you see
how brazenly he stares back at them, the insufferable scoundrel?"

Mrs. Davenant had looked away as soon as
she recognised him. Like her companion, she
had observed how more than one head turned
away, abashed, upon meeting the marquess's
haughty stare.

Cecily had not missed this phenomenon.
"Why, Aunt," she said, "is that not the gentleman — " Then she fell silent.

Puzzled, Lilith slanted another quick glance
at the box. She'd not regarded the other,
younger, gentleman before. Now she perceived he was perfectly capable of attracting
notice in his own right, for he was remarkably
good-looking. Still, had not Cecily expressed
an aversion to blonds?

Lilith was about to point out that staring
was rude when she experienced a prickling
sensation at the base of her skull. Almost re-
flexively, she looked away from Cecily and
across the theater . . . and locked with Lord
Brandon's mocking gaze.

The marquess smiled and made an elabo-
rate bow.

Instantly, Lilith felt every eye in the audience upon her. Her poise held, however. She did not withdraw, in confusion or otherwise. Turning deliberately from the marquess, her own gaze swept coldly over the audience and finally came to rest upon the stage. To her relief, the orchestra started up.

Mrs. Davenant heard little of the performance. She could not have said afterwards whether it had been Gluck or Mozart. Lord Brandon's presence had spoiled it for her, tainted the very atmosphere of the hall. She was too conscious of him throughout, too tense with pretending he was not there. Nor did Rachel improve matters by relating in rasping whispers every outrage the marquess had ever committed.

By the interval, Lilith could not endure another word. She left Lady Enders to deal with any stampeding gentlemen, took Lord Enders as her own escort, and made for the box of an old friend of her grandmother.

Mrs. Davenant was careful to remain with the ancient dowager until the last minutes of the interval. There were several famous gossips in the audience. Thanks to Lord Brandon's attention-drawing gesture, they would be sure to seek her out.

She and Lord Enders had nearly reached the door of his box when Sally Jersey popped out of it.

"Why, my dear Lilith," the countess gushed, "Whatever have you done with your betrothed?"

"Lord Liverpool had need of him," Lilith answered tightly. "Lord and Lady Enders were kind enough to invite my niece and me to join them this night."

"Oh, yes. Rachel made me acquainted with your niece. Charming girl. Naturally, you may expect vouchers for Almack's. We dare not deny them," she said with a silvery laugh. "The gentlemen would be sure to break out in violence."

"That is exceedingly kind of you." Lilith moved to let her pass, but before the widow could step through the door, Lady Jersey's gloved hand dropped lightly upon her arm.

"Speaking of gentlemen," the countess said too sweetly, "I was not aware you were acquainted with Brandon."

"Nor was I," Lilith said with perfect composure. As soon as she spoke, she experienced once more the odd prickling in her neck.

"Not formally introduced, that is," came a low, resonant voice behind her. "May I suggest the oversight be corrected?"

Lilith turned slightly. The green eyes were lazily contemplating her shoulders — or rather, the prim few inches to be seen of them.

She threw him one frigid glance, then deliberately turned her back. Mercifully, Lord Enders was holding open the door to the opera box. As Lilith entered, she heard Sally say, "Why, Brandon, you rogue, I don't believe she wants to know you." The door closed, cutting off her ensuing tinkle of laughter.

Apprised by her husband of the confrontation, Lady Enders congratulated Lilith. "You did right," she declared. "One can only hope the others will follow your example and shun him as he deserves."

Cecily made no comment, and Lilith wondered whether the girl had heard a word. Though Cecily sat, her attention apparently fixed on the stage, a rapt expression glazed her eyes, and from time to time her glance stole across the hall.

The object of this devoted study knew nothing of it. Lord Robert Downs was, as usual, devotedly studying the countenance of his mistress.

As soon as Lord Brandon reentered the box, the mistress turned her amused attention to him.

"I wonder if I can make a guess, milord, what drove you from us the instant the curtain fell," she teased.

"There is no need to guess," he answered.

"In twelve minutes, half the audience will know. In another twelve, the other half. By the end of the performance, the Watch will be announcing it."

"Ah, he bowed so beautifully, did he not, Robin? Still, the lady will not smile. She will not even look his way."

"Which lady is that, Julian?" Lord Robert asked. He was apparently the only person in the theatre who had not observed Society's latest sensation.

"It does not signify. It is certainly not worth interrupting your conversation with your beautiful friend." The marquess dropped carelessly into his seat.

"It is the widow, *mon cher*," Elise confided. "I have the suspicion your cousin takes a fancy to Madame Davenant."

"Madame who?"

Elise touched a finger to Lord Robert's lips. The music had recommenced.

Lord Brandon joined the couple for a late supper at the Piazza. As he'd predicted, word of the widow's snub had sped through the audience — thanks no doubt to the kind offices of Silence Jersey.

"She cut you, Julian?" Robert asked, aghast. "But no one has ever done that. No one would dare. Who the devil does she think she is?"

54

"She is the Widow Davenant," said his mistress. "Half the ladies are afraid of her, and all the gentlemen. She is a paragon. Everyone in the ton is naughty sometimes, no? But they are discreet, and so everyone knows, perhaps, yet they make believe they are all virtue. But Madame *is* all virtue. She has never stepped wrong, even the little step."

"Gad, she sounds awful. I must say, Julian, when Elise pointed her out, you could have knocked me over with a feather. She's not at all in your style."

Lord Brandon slowly turned his wineglass, apparently studying its colour with great care. "Thank you for calling that to my attention, Cousin," he said. "I was ill, you know. Evidently my vision suffered. My short-sightedness has been mentioned before."

Elise shrugged. "She is very handsome, I think. Not a great beauty, but very fine. It is her air, perhaps."

Something flickered in the green eyes. It was quickly hooded, but perhaps not quickly enough, for Elise continued, "She is strong and proud. I think she has great will. It is not easy for a widow — for any woman alone — even in the Beau Monde. Or perhaps it is more difficult there. Still, one hears never a whisper of scandal about her. She presents her nieces, and always they marry well."

"You seem to know a great deal about this lady," said the marquess.

"Ah, *je sais tout*. It amuses me. The shop-girls are always so willing to repeat what they hear. Everyone wonders about Madame, because she is a mystery. She has no intimate friends. Her companion knows as little what is in the widow's heart as do the horses of the fine carriage that brought us here."

By this time, Robert had had quite enough of the widow. He had much rather hear of doings in France and wherever else Julian had been.

Obligingly the marquess turned to Talleyrand and Castlereagh and Metternich and Czar Alexander and the rest. His anecdotes were, as one would expect, wickedly amusing. If the telling bored him even more than usual and his mind wandered elsewhere more than once, one of his listeners at least did not remark it.

The following Monday, Cecily's aunt accompanied her to the dressmaker's. As usual, Lilith's in-laws' notions of a proper Season's wardrobe had been sadly inadequate. Since this was usual, she was not taken unawares. She had carefully hoarded a sum for this express purpose. She would have probably done so in any case: treating her nieces to clothes and trinkets was one of her special pleasures.

She entered the shop ... and stopped short, her pleasure abruptly extinguished.

Lounging in a chair, idly turning the pages of a fashion journal, was the Marquess of Brandon. He glanced up at their entrance, and his bored green eyes lit with amusement. Lazily he rose and made the ladies an extravagant bow.

Her lips compressed in a tight line, Lilith took her niece's arm and swept coldly past him on to the dressing-room door. At that instant, the door flew open, narrowly missing Cecily, and a woman sailed heedlessly through. Lilith stepped hastily out of the way and stumbled against her niece. The woman made no apology, but headed straight for Lord Brandon. She was the one who'd been in his box the previous evening.

"Ah, *pauvre homme*," she cried. "Were you horribly bored, waiting?"

"Unspeakably so," he answered. "That is, until the very *last*."

Lilith hustled Cecily into the dressing room.

"I do not understand," the niece said. "Is it not impolite to ignore an acquaintance?"

"He is not an acquaintance," was the low answer. "We have not been properly introduced."

"But at the inn — "

Lilith turned to the eagerly listening modiste and asked for a moment's privacy. Reluctantly, Madame Suzette exited the room.

In still lower tones, the aunt explained that it was her Christian duty to help a fellow human being in trouble. Having fulfilled her duty, she was no longer under any obligation to converse with or even acknowledge Lord Brandon. Even if she were inclined — which she certainly was not — she would never do so without a formal introduction. "A lady," she pointed out, "does not respond to every person who seeks her attention."

Elise Fourgette was not only clever, but possessed of virtually infallible instincts. Though she teased Lord Brandon about the widow as soon as they were in his carriage, Elise knew this was merely a prelude.

The marquess had come to London with a purpose. All of Robert's relatives, it seemed, had come on the same business. This time, however, her adversary was more than worthy of her mettle. Even without hearing of his reputation, Elise would have sensed immediately that Lord Brandon was a force to be reckoned with.

He spent ten minutes fencing lightly with her about Mrs. Davenant. Then the duel began in earnest, and, figuratively speaking, the sword was at Elise's throat before she had time to say, *"En garde."*

"You have some letters in your possession," he said in deceptively easy tones. "I should like to have them."

"Ah milord, that is what everyone would like, I think."

"But I am not everyone, *mademoiselle.*" His voice was soft. His green eyes were pitiless. "You may give them up to me voluntarily today — or another day, quite soon, I promise, involuntarily. You see, the matter is excessively tiresome, and I should like to have done with it as quickly as possible. I hope you are not in a dilatory frame of mind. In that case, I should be obliged to ask certain more efficient persons to see to it."

His smile was utterly devastating. Were it not for his eyes, one would think he offered her *carte blanche.*

"That would be tedious and inconvenient for both of us, I believe," he added. "They are such uncomfortable fellows to have about."

Brandon, it was said, always got what he wanted, by fair means or foul. Since he was reputed to prefer the latter, Elise had no doubt his threat was genuine. Such persons as he spoke of existed, and he would not shrink at employing them. How she hated him at this moment, this devilishly handsome, rich and powerful English lord.

"*Je comprends,*" she said tightly. Then she set her brain to work.

No more was said until they reached the cramped lodgings Robert shared with his mistress. The younger man was still out, Lord Brandon having had the foresight to dispatch his cousin on an exceedingly time-consuming errand.

The marquess accepted the glass of wine Elise offered him, and leaned back, perfectly at ease, in his chair.

"I do not have all the letters with me," she said in French. "I can give you only some half-dozen this day."

He answered flawlessly in the same language. He had rather not be overheard by prying landladies.

"I did not suppose you were so careless as to keep them all in one place. Nor do I suppose," he added lightly as he turned the goblet in his hands, "you will be so impractical as to release them all. No one knows how many there are — least of all Robert."

"I am not so reckless of my health as to deceive you, milord."

"All the same, I shall not put temptation in your way. In addition to giving me Robert's letters, you will write one of your own to him.

In it you will firmly and irrevocably, now and for all time, decline to be his wife."

Elise's dark eyes flashed. "That I will not do," she said quietly. "If you wish such a thing, you must hire assassins as well."

Lord Brandon covered a yawn. "I see you mean to be tiresome, after all. You are under some misapprehension that I cannot persuade you to write this letter. Let me assure you, dear lady, I can."

She laughed. "You will torture me, I suppose? I had not thought you so foolish. I have never told Robert how his relations bully and threaten me. He is so protective — and impetuous, you know. He would insist we be married at once."

"That is hardly to your advantage. His family will cut him off without a penny."

"We shall make do for a few months, I think. In July he is five and twenty, and no longer depends upon their charity."

"Yet you will always be outcasts. You will always be pinched for funds. His income is scarcely what a woman of your talents merits."

She smiled at him over the rim of her wineglass. "There is some compensation in wedding a nobleman. My mother is a whore, my father most likely a sailor. Mama never catered to the aristocracy, you see. How amazed she will be at my title! Perhaps she will come to live with us."

"I hope you have not built too many castles in the air, *mademoiselle*," he drawled, though it cost him something to suppress his revulsion at the prospect she painted for him. "Rest assured you will never marry my cousin. Or, in the unlikely event you do, please be quite certain the marriage will be dissolved — one way or another."

She must know she could not win, yet her features betrayed no hint of distress or alarm. In spite of himself, Lord Brandon had to admire her *sang-froid* even as he acknowledged his own uneasiness. It was, after all, preferable that Robert know nothing of his family's machinations. The young man was stubborn and, as Elise had reminded, impetuous.

"It seems we are at *point non plus*," she said after a short, tense silence. "Yet how sordid we are, to goad and threaten each other. From you I had expected better. Of all I had heard, never once was it said Lord Brandon bullied women. What sport do you find in that?"

The marquess glanced at her calculating face.

"No sport at all, I agree," he said cautiously. "The matter is so absurdly simple it is a wonder I have kept awake throughout."

"Naturally. You are more accustomed to

using guile. This requires neither wit nor daring. There is no difficulty, no challenge. I am an unworthy adversary. I cannot fight you on equal terms," she said. "I am not even your social equal."

Lord Brandon's expression softened slightly. "If you were, my dear, we should not be having this discussion."

"Thus I am left with no chance to better myself — not even to make my future secure. You will have these letters in the end, and I do not doubt you will soon drive Robert from me as well. You have not the courtesy," she added, her voice dropping, "to fight me fairly."

"You yourself admit the match is unequal. What would you have?" he asked. Though his tone was lazy, Lord Brandon was fully alert.

"A champion," she said. "I ask the right to choose a champion to fight on my behalf. Not Robert," she added quickly, before he could express his disappointment. "A woman. One who is your social equal. One strong enough to defy you, which I dare not."

"A champion, is it? You wish another woman — a lady, I take it — to wear your . . . er, favour? That bears at least the distinction of novelty. Pray elucidate." He raised the wineglass to his lips.

"Madame Davenant," she said.

63

He put the glass down.

"It is simple enough. Seduce her and I set Robin free as you and all your noble family wish. Fail, and you set me free — absolutely. You and all of them must cease to trouble me."

Lord Brandon gazed consideringly at her for a long moment. Then he laughed and said, "Elise, you are a wicked woman."

"There are many wicked women," she answered with a shrug. "But I am intelligent."

"That I readily admit. I had suspected so before. Now I am assured of it. You must know the challenge is irresistible."

"I took care to make it so. I am not blind. I have watched how you change when you see her. The ennui leaves you. You are tense, like the hound when he scents the fox. You want her. That, any woman of my" — she paused briefly — "*profession* would know. But you will not have her, I think. Not this one, my handsome, powerful lord."

"Naturally you believe so. You would not have proposed this otherwise."

She smiled. "We understand each other, then. Do you accept the challenge?"

Lord Brandon's reflections consumed approximately thirty seconds. Since he had not particularly cared in the first place what absurdity Robert committed, Robert's future and his family's distress were a minor consideration. Besides, they would be distressed only if Brandon failed, which was inconceivable.

In the second place, the marquess had fully intended to seduce Mrs. Davenant. That, after all, was why he had come to Town instead of boarding the first sailing vessel bound for the Continent. Elise's challenge only added piquancy to the pursuit, made it a bit different — yes, more exciting, perhaps — than usual.

"I accept," he said.

Lord Brandon was granted eight weeks in which to effect Mrs. Davenant's fall from virtue. This was an absurdly generous amount of time. Elise, however, had laughingly maintained she might grant him an eternity and the result would be the same. Her patent belief in the task's impossibility only heightened Lord Brandon's zest for the chase.

By the following day, one of the marquess's most ingratiating servants had made the acquaintance of certain of Mrs. Davenant's staff. Within another few days, Lord Brandon began receiving regular reports regarding the widow's comings and goings.

These reports must have been accurate, for Lord Brandon and Lord Robert Downs were to be found strolling within sight of Hookham's Circulating Library when Mrs. Davenant's carriage stopped at the door, and aunt and niece disembarked.

"I believe I must step into Hookham's for a moment," said the marquess to his cousin.

Puzzled, Lord Robert glanced towards the building in time to see the widow enter it.

"Really, Julian, you aren't going to try again, are you?" he asked incredulously. "She doesn't want to know you, and I don't see why you want to know *her.*"

The last words were spoken to air. Lord Brandon was already crossing the street. Curious, Lord Robert followed.

Since Mrs. Davenant had not seen either of the two men, she continued in an equable frame of mind. She even forbore commenting upon her niece's unfeminine tastes when that young lady went hunting for equestrian books.

Lilith took herself the other way, where the novels were. She picked up a copy of *Mansfield Park* and began to skim it, to ascertain whether this new effort by the author of *Pride and Prejudice* would be as rewarding as its predecessors.

The hour being early, the place was not crowded, and the aisle in which she stood was empty. Since she was not interrupted, she soon became engrossed in the novel.

She was halfway through the first chapter when she became disagreeably aware of being watched. She looked up.

Not five feet from her, the long, elegantly clothed form of the Marquess of Brandon lounged against the bookshelves. He played idly with his walking stick while his green eyes regarded her with amusement. Her muscles tensed.

Lilith turned to exit in the opposite direction. That way, she found, was now blocked by a set of steps. Upon it a hapless clerk stood, a stack of volumes in one hand. These he was with great deliberation returning one by one to their places. There were two more stacks of books on the steps.

Lilith steeled herself, turned once more, and marched up to the marquess. He did not move out of her way. On the contrary, he had set his walking stick across the narrow aisle.

She glanced at the walking stick, then up at him, her expression stony. He smiled. Her nerves prickled, but she had no intention of retreating. She took another step forward. He did not budge.

"Would you be kind enough to let me pass?" she asked coldly.

"It cannot be necessary. You have given me to understand I do not exist. In that case, you should not find it difficult to walk right through me."

In one carelessly graceful movement, he came away from the bookshelf and planted himself directly in her path.

Lilith was a tall woman, and he was not a heavy-set man, yet that lean, athletic form with its broad shoulders shut out everything else from her sight. She was acutely conscious of a faint scent of sandalwood.

"I do hope you will make the experiment," he went on, his voice dropping. "Surely you cannot expect a collision — though I should not object if there were."

"Your remarks are not amusing, sir. Let me pass."

"I am too tired. I am but recently — and not fully, I'm afraid — recovered from an illness. You had better scream for help. I haven't the strength."

"I see," she said. "You wish to create a scene."

"And you do not." The green eyes glittered with mischief. "The question is, which of us has more to lose?"

The goading words and his oppressive physical presence turned her hot and cold simultaneously. "I have no wish to bandy words with you," she said icily. "The aisle has two ends."

"But it is bad luck to walk under ladders. I

68

shall be obliged to warn you, very loudly, not to try it."

"You just said you hadn't the strength to raise your voice."

"Did I? My senses must have been disordered. I am struck all of a heap to find you so . . . very . . . near."

Though he had not moved, the space between them seemed to vibrate.

"You are silent," he said. "Dare I hope the feeling is mutual?"

"I will not be the butt of your crude humour, sir." With a strength born of anger and desperation, she pushed her way past him.

Her shoulder struck a muscular arm, her hip an equally hard limb. The shock of contact, brief though it was, caused Lilith to drop her book. She did not pause to retrieve it, but, palms perspiring and heart thumping, marched off in search of Cecily.

He did not follow her.

4

On the day Lord Brandon had reached Town, the Grand Duchess of Oldenburg had arrived as well. She put up at the Pulteney Hotel; or rather, was put up, for it was the Lievens who paid the two hundred ten guineas a week; or rather, was put up with, for the Czar's sister was a difficult guest, having promptly declared her own private war upon the Prince Regent.

On the same day, Czar Alexander and the King of Prussia had entered the French capital at the head of their triumphant troops. Immediately thereafter, the Czar and Talleyrand met to settle Buonaparte's fate. Within five days, the news had burst upon London, to drive the populace into a frenzy of celebration.

Nonetheless, these and other international sensations took second place one evening in early April to weightier issues: that is, the appearance — at an informal gathering of two or three hundred of the Countess Lieven's dearest friends — of the Marquess of Brandon and his cousin, Lord Robert Downs.

Lord Brandon's notoriety had not at all dimmed in the seven years of his self-imposed exile. True, he had returned from time to time, but only briefly, and rarely to good company. He had become a shadowy figure, occasionally glimpsed among the more infamous of the *demimonde*, like a dark Lucifer among a host of lesser fiends.

One might wonder then, on this particular evening, why the virtuous did not shrink from him in fear and revulsion. Instead, they crowded about his tall, athletic, black-coated figure as though he were Baal and they the idol worshippers. Perhaps virtue was a commodity in short supply in the ton, as Elise had hinted, or perhaps virtue was no match for an unimpeachable bloodline, a strikingly handsome face, a powerful masculine figure, a devastating charm, and an obscenely large income. In any case, there was scarce an individual at the gathering who did not talk either to or about the Marquess of Brandon.

Lord Robert was a lesser light. Still, he had some claim on the company's attention, for he had not been seen at a Society affair since he'd commenced one of his own with a French-born courtesan.

Even the most jaded of the countess's guests

could not resist speculating what had brought these two elusive prizes back into the Great World.

Lord Robert, at the moment, was equally perplexed.

In the blaze of thousands of candles, the glitter and flash of jewels was nearly blinding. Dashing silks and satins of every tint mingled with fragile white muslins, like a bouquet of vivid summer blooms set off by delicate sprays of baby's breath, amid the darker foliage of expertly tailored superfine and velvet. The affair, in short, was as insipid as every other.

Lord Robert had rarely been in polite company in nearly two years, yet the faces were depressingly familiar. The few new ones belonged mainly to the latest crop of misses, who were, naturally, exact replicas of the previous crop. Lord Robert had arrived very late, scarcely half an hour ago, and already he was bored nearly frantic.

He had agreed to accompany his cousin because he was curious what it was Julian said and did that drove women of every station and every shade of virtue to lose their hearts, minds, and — if they had them to lose — their morals.

What Lord Robert had observed at Hookham's only whetted his curiosity: the quiet conversation with the clerk, the glint of coins changing hands, the discreet positioning of both the steps and Julian himself. Robert had not been near enough to hear the exchange, unfortunately, or even to observe the widow's expression, until, to his very great surprise, she had thrust his cousin out of her way. Even then, her face had appeared carved from stone.

Julian, naturally, had not mentioned a word of the matter afterwards. He could be irritatingly inscrutable when he liked. Now, for instance, he conversed with Sidmouth and Eldon as though dreary politics were all he lived for.

Since there was nothing at present of interest there, Robert looked about him for an acquaintance whose conversation would not put him to sleep.

He spied two of his friends, Lord Maddock and Mr. Reginald Ventcoeur, forming part of a court around the species of china doll who appeared every Season under different names. Lord Robert sighed and made for his friends.

He was not sure afterwards how it had happened. He remembered being introduced to a pair of eyes the colour of a bright summer sky and a voice as clear and musical as the rippling of a country stream . . . and the next he knew, they were dancing.

Miss Cecily Glenwood was fresh from the

schoolroom and country-bred, as she was quick to confess.

"Now, you must keep a sharp lookout," she warned as the music commenced. "I have had ever so many lessons, but I haven't yet danced in fine company very often, let alone with a sophisticated gentleman. It would be too mortifying for me to trample on your slippers — but even more painful for you, I promise. Rodger reminds me constantly I'm no featherweight."

"Two feathers," said Robert, amused. "You can't be more. Who is Rodger?"

"My brother."

"That explains it. Only a sibling would tell such outrageous fibs."

"That sounds like the voice of experience," said Miss Glenwood.

"I'm the youngest of four. I have two elder sisters who tormented me — and still do, even though they have handier victims these days in their husbands."

"I'm fourth as well. I have a younger sister, but she can be just as provoking as the others. Are you *all* fair?"

He nodded.

"Is it not monotonous?" She coloured. "Oh, dear. I did not mean *you* were monotonous. You are not at all. At least your eyes are not blue — well, not very. They are more grey than blue."

74

Her earnest scrutiny nearly put him out of countenance, but she must have recollected herself, for in a moment her long lashes had lowered demurely over her own brilliant eyes.

"I suppose you think me dreadfully forward," she said after a moment. "Really, I am not. It is just ignorance. The hay yet sticks to my shoes, I daresay."

"Not at all, Miss Glenwood," he answered smoothly. "You appear as elegant and sophisticated as any other young lady making her debut."

She laughed. "Which is to say, not very. But you say it so convincingly I must pretend to be reassured."

"You can't possibly want reassurance," he said, smiling in return. "When I approached, I thought you'd be smothered in the crowd of gentlemen pressing about you."

"Yes, and the whole time I was terrified of blurting out The Wrong Thing. My aunt," she explained, "has warned me more than once about my alarming tendency to say precisely what is in my mind."

"Good heavens! You must never do that in Society. Not unless you mean to throw down civilisation as we know it."

"I know," she said with a sigh. "Really, I begin to think a Season wasted on me." She glanced quickly about her, then added in an undertone, "You must promise to tell no one, because they will think me ridiculous, but the truth is I am very, very bored."

"At the start of your first Season? Miss Glenwood, you are more sophisticated than you pretend."

"Not at all. I am still a child, I'm afraid. I want to go to Astley's," she confided, as though this were a heinous depravity, "and to the Tower, and Madame Tussaud's — oh, a hundred places. There is so much to see in London, but all I do is shop and dance and talk and dance and talk and shop."

She appeared so wistful that Lord Robert might have patted her on the head and promised her a sweetmeat if he had not had to mind his steps. As it was, he found himself soberly expressing sympathy and wondering what he could do to relieve the poor child's boredom.

Being occupied elsewhere, Lord Robert did not observe how his cousin closed in on his prey.

Lord Brandon remained at a distance, seemingly engaged in renewing old acquaintance. Nevertheless, there was not a moment he did not know precisely where one staid taupe gown was located.

Thus, the instant Mrs. Davenant and the Countess Lieven moved apart from their

76

neighbours to talk, Lord Brandon began making his roundabout yet speedy way across the room. Bexley, he had noted, had wandered out of the ballroom talking earnestly with Count Lieven a quarter hour before. Lady Enders was gossiping with Lady Shumway and a gawky girl with spots.

Lord Brandon was careful to come up on the widow from behind, allowing her no opportunity to withdraw gracefully. Then he greeted the countess and asked for an introduction.

Mrs. Davenant's slate-blue eyes turned to ice, but she could not, he knew, decline the honour without insulting the haughty Madame de Lieven. Given Bexley's political aspirations, this would be most unwise.

The widow did not decline. She even managed not to appear outraged, which he knew she must be. Lord Brandon pressed his advantage.

"Now that we have proper leave to know each other, I wonder if we might dance together," he said, his tones studiously polite. "Will you favour me with the waltz about to begin, Mrs. Davenant — if only to honour the delightful lady who first introduced it to Society at Almack's?"

The Countess Lieven acknowledged the compliment with a gracious nod. Mrs. Davenant's lips tightened.

"Thank you," she said stiffly, "but — "

"Ah, now we are in for a treat," said the countess. "We have never yet seen Lord Brandon waltz. I am afraid only our allies — perhaps our foes as well — have had that privilege. We shall at last see for ourselves whether he is as accomplished in this as in so much else."

The marquess raised an eyebrow.

"I referred to your skill in dancing, you teasing creature," she said with a faint smile. "But go. The music begins and my own partner approaches."

Followed by many curious eyes, Lord Brandon led his unwilling partner out. Not that Mrs. Davenant appeared unwilling. Her face was perfectly composed. He felt her tense, though, the instant his hand clasped her waist. He suspected she would have wriggled away if she might have done so with dignity. His grip was quite firm, however.

"You are displeased with me," he said. "I placed you in a difficult position. I am very sorry for it, but you left me no choice. I could hardy continue invisible forever. It is undignified."

"And to make a nuisance of yourself is not?" Her tones were cold, but the gloved hand in his was very warm.

"Once, perhaps, it might have been. But I have been a nuisance so many years now, it has become a part of my character. You may have noted that perseverance forms another part."

She did not respond.

"I believe it is accounted a virtue," he prodded.

"When properly applied," was the unencouraging reply. "Children are known to persevere in naughtiness. One wishes they applied the same industry to their lessons."

"If you were my tutor, I should listen very attentively. What would you teach me, Mrs. Davenant?" he asked, his tones softening.

"How absurd. You are long past teaching."

"No one is past teaching. Not if the lessons are pleasant ones."

"Mine should bore you to extinction. You must have heard them a hundred times in your boyhood. Given the results, I collect you had been asleep most of the time."

"Which is to say you mean to read me sermons."

"Yes, I am very dull."

"If you think so, it is you who want a lesson." He pressed her closer and drew her into a turn. In the process, his thigh brushed hers and he felt her recoil.

"You are an excellent partner," he said after a few moments' throbbing silence. "You follow my lead instinctively. I feel as though we had been waltzing together all our lives. But then, I was certain it would be so. I have remarked more than once how graceful you are, even when you are furiously storming away. It is amazing how well acquainted I have become with your back."

"In that case, there should be no need to conduct a physical examination, my lord. You will please to keep your hand in one place."

"I beg your pardon," he said. "My hands are unsteady. I seem to be nervous."

"I should say impudent, rather."

"Perhaps you're right." As though to prove it, he drew her into another perilous turn. He would have liked to keep whirling her until she grew too giddy to stand, and collapsed against him, but that was too crass. He had rather weaken her defences little by little.

A barely perceptible film of moisture was forming on her smooth white brow.

"You are breathless," he said. "Ladies *will* fasten their stays so tightly."

"I do not — " She bit her lip.

"No, I know you do not. I am acutely observant."

A faint colour singed her slender neck.

"You do not require such artificial moulding," he persisted. "Your waist is as slim and supple as a young girl's."

The colour heightened. "You please to mock me, my lord. I should not be surprised. Your manner from the first has been nothing but mockery."

"You are hopelessly confused," he said pityingly. "From the first I have admired everything about you, yet you insist upon being deaf, dumb, and blind to all my touching confessions." He glanced down at her in sudden concern. "You aren't deaf, are you? You were blind for a time, I realise, though assuredly not dumb — "

"I do not understand," she said, "how you can chatter incessantly while you waltz. Your lungs must be prodigious strong."

"When I am flirting, I have the strength of ten men. You will not flirt back, but that cannot stop me. The habit is too deeply ingrained. I find a stunning woman in my arms, and I must flirt with her."

"You have obviously confused me with some Incomparable. It is your lamentable eyesight, I daresay."

"I hope not. You have no idea the *inconvenience* I was put to in order to get you in my arms so that I should be compelled to flirt with you."

He saw the shadow of uneasiness flit across otherwise immobile features.

81

"You must not be alarmed for my health, Mrs. Davenant," he said comfortingly. "I promise to make up for the exertion by lying abed very late tomorrow."

Had Lilith suspected just how much the marquess learned about her during their one waltz, she would have been considerably more shaken than she was — and that was already too much.

She had wanted every iota of her rigid training to maintain a semblance of composure. A semblance only. Good grief — she had practically announced she did not wear stays! Not, she reflected bitterly as she sought a quiet corner of the ballroom, that there had been any need to inform him.

Before she could even begin to regain her equanimity, Lady Enders pounced upon her, canary ruffles jerking in agitation.

"Everyone is talking," Rachel said.

"It is a social event. People are obliged to converse."

"They are talking about you and Brandon. If I had been you, I should have been put completely out of countenance, with everyone staring so. To dance with the man — and of all dances, a waltz. I really do not understand, Lilith."

What she meant was that she did not approve, though Rachel had not the audacity to tell her future sister-in-law *that*.

"I am not a green girl, Rachel. I do not require the sanction of Almack's patronesses to waltz. In any event, it was one of them obliged me to. I suppose you would prefer I had offended Dorothea?"

"In your place, I should have pleaded a turned ankle."

"In that case, I should not have been able to dance with Thomas later."

"I am sure my brother would have been happy to support a necessary falsehood. A man in his position cannot wish his intended bride to be an object of speculation."

"If that is so, perhaps he might spare a moment to his intended, instead of hiding away in the library talking politics with his colleagues," Lilith snapped. "I was left to deal with an awkward situation quite on my own, and chose *not* to insult the Russian ambassador's wife."

This was so unlike her cool, immovable self that Rachel stepped back a pace. "My dear Lilith," she said placatingly, "I did not mean to question your judgement."

There was a brief pause.

"I am sure you did not," Lilith answered with something more like her customary chilly politeness. "Our friends' eagerness to make gossip of the most trivial matters distresses you, as it does me. All the same, I think we were wisest to disregard it."

Though a large circle of masculine admirers had already begun to make great demands upon Cecily's attention, she had sufficient of that article remaining to cultivate several feminine friends as well. Among these, the most agreeable was Anne Cleveson, whose mama, Lady Rockridge, happened to be Lord Robert's first cousin on his papa's side.

Lady Rockridge was a sensible, good-natured woman who presented daughters almost as continuously as Mrs. Davenant presented nieces. The two women were well-acquainted. They both respected and liked each other and had more than once traded chaperon duty. This was what Lady Rockridge was proposing on the day following Countess Lieven's informal gathering, for Cecily was invited to join a small group of young people Lord and Lady Rockridge planned to escort to Astley's.

In any other case, Lilith would have instantly agreed. This time, however, there were problems. For one, she was out of sorts, having slept poorly. For another, Lord Robert was to be one of the party, and Lilith much doubted he was suitable company for Cecily.

His connexion with Lady Rockridge was a

point in his favour. His mistress and his connexion with Lord Brandon were points against. Cecily's behaviour the night of the opera must be considered as well — though Lilith was not entirely certain in what light to consider it, because the girl had offered no indication of infatuation since.

While Lilith did not list aloud these points for and against, Lady Rockridge must have guessed some of them, because she promptly ordered Cecily and Anne to take a turn in the garden.

"My dear Lilith," she said when the girls were safely out of the way, "I know exactly what is in your mind, and of course I cannot blame you for thinking ill of him."

Lilith gave the tiniest start — so minute as to appear a flicker of shadow upon marble.

"You are too well-bred to mention it," her guest went on, "but we both know Robin has made an utter fool of himself over that French demi-rep."

"I am sure, Glenda, I should never disparage your relations."

"And I am sure you may do so all you like. You cannot abuse him — or his immediate family — any more heartily than I have myself. What a great lot of fools they are! When a spoiled child demands bon-bons, which will make him sick, does it serve to tell him, No, he must not? Indeed, it does *not* serve," said her ladyship, shaking her head vigourously. "As a child, Robin was wont to hold his breath until he turned blue in the face. At present, I believe he is doing precisely that."

"I am not certain I take your meaning," said Lilith, though a vision of the rakish Lord Robert Downs in a childish tantrum drew a hint of a smile.

"Everyone has been ranting at him to leave her. If they had simply ignored the entire matter, I'm sure he would have tired of her very soon, but every new 'No' only makes him dig in his heels the more."

"That scarcely recommends his maturity, Glenda."

"But don't you see? He is not so worldly and jaded as he likes to think. I only wish you could have heard him urging Astley's as a treat for the girls. Rather like an older brother who wants the treat for himself as well. I should like him to have it. I believe the experience will be good for him. At any rate, it is innocent entertainment for a change."

"I hope it may be," said Lilith slowly. "The question is whether it would be good for Cecily. She is inexperienced, young, and impressionable, and he is exceedingly handsome — and, as you said, worldly."

"Yes, of course, but we are going to the circus, my dear, not the Cyprians' Ball," was the brisk reply. "Rockridge and I will be there, and I daresay we may keep a handful of lively young people in order."

This Lilith could not deny. Glenda's common sense was always to be relied upon. Furthermore, for all her open warmth, Lady Rockridge was a thoroughly reliable dragon.

The following Tuesday was quickly agreed upon, Lilith being engaged to dine that evening with Lord Liverpool. The invitees were mainly of political persuasion, and Cecily had already expressed a disinclination to accompany her aunt.

"She told me she would feel like the village idiot in such company," Lilith said with a smile.

"Meaning, I take it, she expected to be bored to pieces. Well, we shall spare her that, shall we?"

5

The Tuesday evening found the eminently sophisticated man of the world, Lord Robert Downs, at Astley's. He had dextrously managed matters so that he sat next Miss Glenwood — only, he told himself, for the amusement of watching her childlike excitement. This infantile enthusiasm manifesting itself in sparkling blue eyes, half-parted moist, pink lips, and a propensity to clutch at his sleeve during moments of high suspense, he might have been accounted tolerably amused.

From time to time the lips came disconcertingly close to his ear, as Miss Glenwood was inclined to whisper eager comments on the proceedings.

"How do they do it?" she asked during a display of equestrian feats. "It takes forever to learn how to keep your seat without a saddle — but to stand — and turn — and leap in the air — I could never do that. The last time I tried to stand — "

Lord Robert's head whipped towards her. "You what?"

Captivated once more by the performance, she did not appear to hear him.

"They make it seem so easy," she said after a moment. "Yet it wants tremendous concentration."

"Miss Glenwood, did you just say you have tried to stand upon a horse?" Lord Robert asked, appalled.

"Once only. I can ride without a saddle, but no more. I shall never be an acrobat," was the modest reply.

"You do not ride saddleless," he insisted.

"But of course I do. Why, I have done it several times already in Hyde Park." She must have remarked his look of horror finally, because she hastened to explain that she had done so very early in the morning, and naturally she had her own groom from home with her, and of course she wore her brother's old clothes. One could scarcely ride bareback in a woman's riding habit, she pointed out patiently.

"Miss Glenwood — "

He got no further. Lady Rockridge's dragon eye having noted the two golden heads bent close together, she promptly ordered her husband to change places with Robert.

While the innocent Cecily was throwing Lord Robert into a dither, her aunt was experiencing her own brand of disquiet.

Sir Thomas had as usual forgotten her existence in his absorption with a political issue, but this was habitual with him. At any rate, Lilith had never expected or wished him to live in her pocket, even after their betrothal.

Tonight's issue was again the Grand Duchess Catherine's blatant hostility towards Prinny, her efforts to humiliate him at every turn, and her skill in making everyone detest her. The Czar's sister seemed to devote all her waking hours to making mischief. Since she had considerable influence over her brother, and wrote him constantly, it was feared Alexander's proposed visit to England would not be an auspicious one.

Thomas, who had any number of ideas regarding what might be done to appease the harridan, took every opportunity to express these views. He would not be averse to a diplomatic post, and this was a good way to start. Consequently, he devoted all his energy this night to business — and therefore, the most powerful men in the group.

The disquiet of the nation must, after all, take precedence over the disquiet of one woman, Lilith well knew. Her problem was not with Thomas.

The source of her uneasiness sat the length of the dinner table away. Amid the buzz of dinner conversation, one low, drawling murmur — inevitably followed by peals of feminine laughter — pierced her concentration as loudly as if there had been no other sound.

In the same way, she saw Lord Brandon without looking directly at him, because he was always there, in the periphery of her vision when she turned to respond to her dining companion. The black coat moulded to broad shoulders . . . the immaculately arranged neck-cloth in whose snowy depths an emerald winked from time to time, a counterpoint to the flickering green glance which lit here and there with equal lack of interest. Once, Lilith had felt that glance settle hard upon her, but she would not raise her eyes to acknowledge it, and the sensation soon vanished.

Her discomfort did not. He had done no more than greet her and Thomas politely at the start of the evening. At least, the words had been unexceptionable. But as they were moving past him, Lord Brandon had shifted his balance slightly, and his coat sleeve had brushed her gloved forearm. She had felt a tiny shock, and ever since, she had been unable to shake off her awareness of him, even when he stood a crowded room's length away.

Lilith ate dinner with her customary marblelike composure and could not have said later what she had put into her mouth. When she withdrew with the other ladies, she conversed in her usual coolly courteous manner and could not remember after a single word. When the gentlemen rejoined them, she talked and drank her tea and might have been talking Hindoo and drinking ditch-water for all she knew of it.

Once more the marquess spoke only a few unexceptionable words to her. Then he drifted away to a group of gentlemen in a corner, where he remained the rest of the evening. Yet he might have been breathing down her neck the whole time, so relentlessly did his presence grip her.

Thomas was among those with whom the marquess conversed. The night wore on, and Thomas showed no signs of wearing out. Instead, the conversation seemed to grow into an intense debate with Sidmouth and their host. So engrossed were the three men that they never noted the other guests taking their leave.

Rachel approached her future sister-in-law.

"Enders says they are like to keep on all night and into the morning," she said, nodding towards her brother. "Can I persuade you to leave with us? Thomas will find his own way home. Heaven knows he has done this a hundred times if he has done it once, and we shall be asleep on our feet waiting for him."

Lilith was only too willing to leave, even if it meant abandoning her betrothed.

"It is about time," said Rachel when the carriage finally arrived. "Nathan has been prodigious slow in coming."

"They are all behindhand, it seems," said Lord Brandon from somewhere behind Lilith's shoulder. "My own carriage was ordered at the same time, and even Ezra — usually a miracle of celerity — has dawdled. Perhaps they too have been debating affairs of state. Mrs. Davenant, you are losing your shawl. May I assist you?"

"No, th — "

He scooped up the end dragging on the carpet and draped it artistically upon her shoulder without touching her.

Lilith murmured polite thanks and quickly moved away, but she found him at her shoulder again as she stepped out onto the walkway.

"Perhaps you didn't require your wrap, after all," he said. "The night is unseasonably warm. You must beware growing overwarm yourself. That is an excellent way to take a chill. Shall I — Well, that is odd."

He stepped away from her towards Lord and Lady Enders, and stopped the latter as she was about to enter the carriage.

Lilith saw him whisper something to Matthew and gesture towards the coachman. At that moment, to her very great surprise, the coachman toppled sideways onto the seat.

"What the devil is wrong with the fellow?" Matthew cried.

Lord Brandon inspected the head dangling over the coach seat. "Drunk, it looks like," he said coolly.

"Drunk?" the others chorused.

"I am sorry to say the man reeks of gin." The marquess retreated a few steps from the head, and turned back to Matthew. "He will not recover for many hours, I'm afraid. May I offer my own carriage as substitute? Ezra has taken a vow of abstinence from strong spirits, and the vehicle is commodious. What good fortune," he added, with the barest flicker of a glance at Lilith. "My curricle is in pieces, or else I should have taken it and been unable to accommodate you."

After making the obligatory objections to inconveniencing his lordship and receiving the obligatory chivalrous responses, the three climbed into his carriage and were quickly on their way.

Lord and Lady Enders promptly began to quarrel regarding Nathan's future. The lady insisted he be turned off at once without a character. The lord, being more forbearing, was all for a sound scold, a signed oath of abstinence, and a second chance.

Lord Brandon pointing out the merit of both sides of the debate, it continued at full spate during the entire journey.

Lilith was too painfully conscious of a dove-grey wool-encased knee three inches from her own to formulate any opinions, let alone give voice to them. The knee was giving her a headache.

Thus it happened that Lord and Lady Enders were deposited at their front door before they knew it, and Lord Brandon's carriage had travelled merrily down the street and was turning the corner before Rachel realised what had happened.

"Good heavens!" she cried, interrupting her spouse midharangue. "He is alone with Lilith — in a closed carriage!"

It was a curious circumstance that the loss of two passengers rendered the vehicle more confined than it had been, as though the masculine presence opposite Lilith possessed the power to expand to fill all available space.

She quickly thrust this fancy aside and tried

to quell her rising anxiety. There was nothing in taking Rachel and Matthew home first, she told herself. The coachman had merely taken the shortest route, and certainly he seemed in a hurry, for they'd arrived at Enders House precipitately. Which was just as well. Lilith was eager to be home, to lay her throbbing head upon her pillow. She would travel in greater comfort and doubtless arrive more swiftly than she would have in the Enderses' coach.

She had scarcely formulated the thought when the carriage began to abate its spanking pace. Lilith glanced out the window.

"I do not believe this is the correct turning," she said. "This is South Audley Street."

"And you are alarmed. Perhaps I mean to abduct you and hold you for ransom."

She suppressed a gasp, and instantly took refuge from anxiety in anger. "You would get precious little, as you well know, my lord," she snapped. "While we are on the subject — "

"Of abduction?"

"Of money — "

"I did not know that was our topic. I hope not. It is exceedingly dull."

"I am a dull person, as I have mentioned before. My man of business tells me your representative refuses to discuss terms of repayment."

"Yes, and I wish you would stop plaguing them both, Mrs. Davenant. It hints of a disordered mind, not to mention a woeful want of consideration for poor Mr. Higginbottom."

"He is well paid to engage in such work."

"Another lamentable waste of your resources. Really, your affairs are in such a muddle it is a wonder the man hasn't hanged himself — or that you haven't been deposited in the King's Bench already. Did your previous agent not do sufficient damage? Or was his disease contagious?"

"I freely admit I ought to have kept a closer watch on him," she said frigidly, "but that is hardly to the point. The fact is, I owe you — "

"Davenant owed me. You do not."

"I will not accept your charity, my lord."

He studied the top of her head. "Now I wonder why not," he said meditatively. "It cannot be a greater blow to your pride than accepting Bexley. *That* decision carries a lifetime of consequences."

Without heeding her gasp of outrage, he went on. "Not that I blame you. Women have so few economic alternatives. Still, I cannot but wonder at your choice."

"How dare you," she said, her voice choked. "You have no right to refer to matters — to personal matters — or to speak slightingly of a worthy gentleman."

97

"I did not say Bexley was unworthy. I was referring to his hairline, which is receding at an alarming rate. I can only hope your offspring will not suffer premature baldness," he said charitably.

"I find your conversation in the worst possible taste, my lord."

"I beg your pardon. Perhaps baldness does not distress you. I have noted your preference for a coiffure designed, apparently, to pull your hair out slowly by the roots," he said, his eyes once more upon the tight coil of dark auburn braid. "I cannot look at your head without wincing in sympathy — which is a great pity, because I have very recently acquired a partiality for redheads."

Lilith decided not to dignify this with a reply. She turned her gaze to the window, and immediately discovered, with a return of alarm, that they were circling the darkest square of London.

"This is Berkeley Square," she said, forcing her voice to be steady. "Is your coachman drunk as well?"

"No, he has infallible instincts, which have apparently informed him of my wish to kiss you. Naturally, the locale must be poorly lit. I realise you are shy, Mrs. Davenant."

She had her hand on the door handle before he'd finished speaking.

"Ah, you wish to alight," he said calmly.

The coachman, to Lilith's confusion, was ordered to halt. To her further confusion the marquess assisted her in disembarking, and in the next minute, his carriage was clattering away, leaving her alone, on foot, with its owner.

He offered a bland smile, took possession of her arm, and proceeded to stroll in the most leisurely way down the street with her.

Lilith's wish to escape the carriage had been reflexive, and for perhaps two whole minutes she had actually believed she would walk home. Now, in the shadowy square, reason returned. A lady did not walk anywhere without escort, and most certainly not at night.

"You see what comes of permitting me to provoke you," he said, voicing her thoughts. "Though how you could have helped it, I cannot imagine, considering the pains I took."

"You upset me deliberately," she said, half disbelieving, half accusing.

"Yes. I hoped you would fly at me and do me some violence. But you are far too well bred for that. Your composure is extraordinary. What a dragon of a governess you must have had."

"She wasn't — " She paused and looked at him, but there was too little light. She could

99

read nothing in the arrogant profile. "Why did you wish to provoke me?"

"Because I find it disconcerting to converse with a stone monument. You do it very well, I admit. One is tempted to hold a glass to your lips to ascertain whether respiration has ceased."

She was both angry and frightened, and his remarks could not be construed as complimentary. All the same, the long-suffering note in his voice made her want to laugh.

"Stones do not scold," she said, moving on again.

"That is the trouble. Virtually the only words I can prise from you are scolding ones, yet I know you can converse quite amiably. Your suggestions to Lord Velgrace regarding the draining of his fields, for instance." He glanced at her baffled countenance. "My hearing is very acute — despite my illness."

"If you wanted my views on agriculture, you had only to ask."

"Had I? I think not. The evening cools," he went on, gazing upwards, "and the heavens make a mighty struggle to clear. I discern one courageous star striving feverishly against the London smoke."

Lilith looked up at the faint twinkle in the heavens.

"I recommend you make your wish now,

100

Mrs. Davenant, before the haze crushes it altogether. You will doubtless use the occasion to wish me to the Devil."

"I hope," she said quietly, "I have wishes more worthy of a Christian than that."

"Then what will it be? A cabinet post for Bexley? No, that is not altogether worthy, either. Too mercenary and selfish. Something for your niece, perhaps — but I will not press for details, or the wish is spoiled."

They walked on for a while in silence. The air had cooled, as he'd said, but not uncomfortably so. Lilith felt warm enough. Her shawl was cashmere, after all, and exercise was known to aid circulation. The tall figure beside her could not be a source of warmth, unless it were the warmth of security. He was trim and strong, and he moved with the grace of complete assurance. She doubted any ruffian would have the temerity to attempt Lord Brandon. With him, she was safe from others.

She wished she could feel as certain she was safe from him. She could not comprehend what he was about. Worse, she could not comprehend what *she* was about, to be ambling through the West End with an infamous libertine. But he had somehow goaded her into it, and now there was nothing she could do about it, except hope no one she knew saw her behaving so improperly.

For a moment, Lilith almost resented the impropriety. She had never before walked about Town at night. Only gentlemen might wander as they pleased. Men had, perhaps, more freedom than was good for them — did not the living proof walk beside her? Nonetheless, she had always rather envied them ... when she permitted herself such reflections. Thus, for the present moment at least, she revelled in this mild liberation.

His low, lazy tones jerked her back to Reality.

"You are exceedingly quiet," he said. "Are you tired? I am aware ladies are accustomed to traverse no distance greater than that between front door and carriage."

"I am country-bred, my lord. Walking is not new to me."

"That is a pity. I had hoped you would ask me to carry you."

"A while ago, you hoped I would fly at you. You are either a poor judge of character or in the habit of absurdly fanciful thinking."

"If you think I could not realise either of these hopes — if I truly set my mind to it — then *you* are a poor judge of character."

"You need not war — remind me you are accustomed to do precisely as you please."

"Yes, I am every bit as willful as yourself. I cannot deny that you have the greater self-restraint, but I have superior physical strength — which makes us even, you see."

"You will please refrain from placing me in the same category as yourself," she said frigidly.

"But you *are* willful, Mrs. Davenant. Your carriage alone proclaims it. That haughty lift of your chin, for instance — and one might use your spine as a scientifically exact measure of the perpendicular. It is in your voice as well, and in your terrifying eyes. I should be thoroughly cowed, of course, if I did not find the combined effect so utterly adorable."

Some long-stifled feeling fluttered within her at the last words, but she quickly suffocated it, and iced over for good measure.

"Yes, I am a great joke to you," she answered. "Do you mean to mock at me the entire way home? I ask only to be prepared. I know it is futile to hope you will stop."

"Now I have hurt your feelings," he said, all contriteness. "Upon my honour, that is never what I meant. It was a compliment, Mrs. Davenant. I was flirting with you — albeit in my own clumsy, perverse way."

"I do not wish to flirt with you, or be flirted with in any sort of way, my lord. I cannot think how I allowed myself to be goaded into this predicament. No more can I comprehend how any gentleman could stoop to provoking a lady with whom he is scarcely acquainted — one, moreover, who has done him no injury she knows of."

"Your thinking is lamentably muddled. You saved my life. That is the exact opposite of doing me an injury. Now my life is yours, you see. I am your slave *forever*."

She glanced up at him in alarm, then quickly looked away. "You most certainly are not," she responded, a bit short of breath. "I never heard such nonsense."

"Ah, you have some old-fashioned notion of slaves grovelling at the feet of their master . . . or mistress. Perhaps there are such humble beings yet in existence, but I'm afraid I can't grovel. Faulty education, no doubt. Or perhaps I can. I'm not certain. I have never tried it, but I shall, if you like. Shall I kiss the hem of your gown while I'm about it? That I should be most eager to do, inasmuch as it may afford me a view of your ank — "

"You will do no such thing!"

"No, I will not," he said, so gently that she feared his sharp ears had detected the edge of panic in her voice. "I was only teasing. I can't help it, you know. There is some fiend takes hold of my tongue at times and — "

He stopped as they turned the corner. Lilith looked up to find his lordship's carriage heading towards them.

"You are spared," he said. "Ezra has a low opinion of his betters' locomotive powers, I'm afraid, and though I had rather walk with you until dawn, I dare not disappoint him. It might result in a fever of the brain."

For the first time in many months, Lord Robert Downs did not spend the night at his love nest. Instead, he availed himself of a bed at his cousin's town house. Julian had said he might stay whenever he liked, so long as Robert did not attempt to usurp the marquess's valet or use the chandeliers for target practice.

The house was large, luxurious, and impeccably managed. The servants glided about, noiseless and efficient, magically producing whatever one needed before one had even thought of needing it.

Still, Lord Robert had not deserted his mistress this night because he missed luxury and the attention of fawning menials. He only wanted to be sure of a decent night's rest before getting up at an ungodly hour of the morning.

6

Lord Robert arose as he'd intended, at a perfectly inhuman hour, and managed to wash and dress more or less efficiently, despite his eyes' stubborn refusal to remain open during the process.

Nonetheless, they opened wide enough when he arrived at Hyde Park in time to see Miss Cecily Glenwood, attired exactly as she had described, dismount from a saddleless horse. Her groom threw him one anguished look, then turned his back and began to resaddle the beast.

As the young lady met Lord Robert's stupefied grey gaze, she coloured, as well she might.

His focus jerked from the top of her cap — from which one golden strand escaped — to stumble at the worn jacket, before colliding with the snug-fitting breeches. Heat stung his neck, and he barely skimmed the scuffed boots before returning to her rosy countenance.

"You are about early, my lord," she said brightly.

"Miss Glenwood."

"Oh, you're going to scold," she said. "As though Harris hasn't been doing it half the morning already."

Lord Robert yanked his brain back from wherever it had gone, shook it to attention, and got very little for his pains. "I — I can't scold," he said. "I hate it when people are always lecturing at me. But Miss Glenwood." He stopped dead, again at a loss.

She moved closer to stroke his mount's nose. The horse nuzzled her, and she giggled. Lord Robert dismounted.

"Miss Glenwood," he tried again.

"I suppose you are very much shocked," she said, more to the horse than to the gentleman.

"Well, you know it is not every day that one — one sees a young lady in — in, well, not in a frock, you know. It isn't the usual thing, actually, and so I suppose it is a sh — a surprise."

"You should not be surprised. I did tell you, after all."

"Yes, Miss Glenwood, and I do hope you've told nobody else."

"Oh, no. I shouldn't have told even you, because now you'll — No, you won't, because I warned you, didn't I, that I have no hope of being a fashionable young lady? Maybe I should not have told you that, either, but you are so *understanding*." The wide blue eyes opened full upon him then, a cloudless, innocent sky, and his heart gave such a thump that he started.

"Well, I do know what it is to be chafing under rules and ordered this way and that, but . . . but — Oh, really, I can't think what to say," complained the sophisticated man of the world.

"Maybe you'll think of it later." She glanced at her now-saddled mare and long-suffering groom. "You can tell me then. I had better not stay, in any case. Good morning, Lord Robert."

He watched her wave away Harris's helping hand and climb lightly into the saddle. Lord Robert should not have watched, because the rear view was even more disconcerting than the front, and the image of one small, round bottom burned into his brain as though it had been applied with a branding iron.

As Lord Robert dragged his gaze from Miss Glenwood's retreating figure, he discovered another figure advancing — if so staggering and crablike a motion could be called an advance — towards him. It was attired in a bottle-green coat and canary-yellow trousers, and its hat was balanced precariously over one ear.

"Downs!" the figure called out. "What ho, Downs!" It gave a lurch sending the hat flying, and hurled itself at Lord Robert, who stepped out of the way in time to avoid being knocked over. The figure tottered dangerously towards the horizontal, then clumsily righted itself.

"You're abroad early, Beldon," said Lord Robert.

"Jus' goin' home. But I say, d'you see that?"

"What?"

"That." Mr. Beldon flung his arm in the general direction of the vanishing figure of Cecily Glenwood. "A girl, don't you know? A girl in chap's clothes."

"You've had a long night of it, Beldon," said Lord Robert calmly as he retrieved the hat. Equally composedly, he handed it to his acquaintance. "Those were my cousin's stable lads, exercising his cattle. You had better get yourself to bed before you begin seeing pink elephants and purple tigers as well."

"Good heavens, Robin," said Lord Brandon when his cousin — after going back to bed and making a futile attempt to sleep — came in to breakfast. "You are as pale as a ghost. Was there a pea in the mattress?"

"No," said Lord Robert. "I was perfectly

109

comfortable, thank you — that is to say — well, I was not comfortable in my mind."

"I wish I could sympathise, but I am always quite comfortable in that way. I have a very well-regulated conscience. It never troubles me, and I return the favour, and so we get on famously."

"It isn't conscience — at least — no. But I can't think what to do."

"Why, nothing easier. There is the sideboard. Fill your plate, or summon someone to fill it for you. Personally, I prefer to do without my staff's assiduous attentions at breakfast. A dollop of austerity in the morning gives me a properly balanced view, I find."

Lord Robert rubbed his forehead and walked with a vacant air to the sideboard. He stood there for several minutes, staring helplessly at the array of covered dishes.

"It doesn't matter what you take, Robin. The affairs of state will continue grinding, even if you choose a rasher of bacon over a sausage."

His words proving ineffective, Lord Brandon rose, filled a plate for his cousin, and guided the young man to a seat.

"Take up your fork," said the marquess. "It is a scientifically verified mode of beginning."

"Thank you," said Robert absently, and

absently he swallowed a few mouthfuls before putting his silver down. "I am confused," he said.

"Indeed you must be. You have just emptied the saltcellar upon your bacon."

"Regarding a young lady," said Robert. "That is to say, I feel I ought to do something, but I can't for the life of me think what it is."

"Perhaps you will think of it later," said Lord Brandon, betraying not a glimmer of curiosity.

"That's what *she* said. Yet I've been churning at it for hours now, and nothing I contrive will do. No, it won't do at all," he said, shaking his head.

Lord Brandon calmly stirred his coffee. "I never pry, Robin. Still, if you wish to unburden yourself — and would not violate a trust in doing so — I shall give an excellent appearance of attending."

The younger man threw him a look of gratitude. "Yes, please, if you will — that is — well, it *is* a secret, so I must ask — "

Lord Brandon solemnly swearing himself to eternal silence, his cousin proceeded to relate the morning's experience.

"Ah, yes," said the marquess when the tale was done. "I recollect her. Miss Glenwood struck me as a young lady of uncommon energy."

"She's very high-spirited, Julian, and really she's practically a child — so how could I read her horrid sermons about propriety? But you know it won't do. Beldon saw her, and if he hadn't been utterly cast away at the time, I'd never have convinced him it — she — was one of your grooms, and the news would be all over London by now. So she must be got to stop, of course, and I suppose her ogre aunt could stop her — but then, I should be carrying tales, you know."

"No, you had better not upset her aunt." Lord Brandon might have added that Mrs. Davenant was sufficiently upset for the present, thanks to him, but he did not, for he was not, generally, a boastful man.

"Then what's to be done?"

Lord Brandon reflected for a few minutes as he sipped his coffee, while Lord Robert strove for patience.

"Well?" the young man prodded, when his short supply of that article ran out.

"Being very young and country-bred, Miss Glenwood is likely accustomed to far more freedom than she has in Town. Her family is horse-mad, I understand. Undoubtedly, she has been riding since her infancy. In that case, sedate trots along bridle paths cannot be satisfying. If she had a riding companion equally skilled and daring, and if she rode out sufficiently early with proper chaperonage, I dare-say she might have a decent gallop, even in London, without causing a stir. Perhaps that would obviate the necessity for dawn rides in breeches."

Lord Robert considered. "You think I ought to go with her, Julian?"

"Oh, any skilled horseman — or -woman — will do, I suppose," said the marquess, covering a yawn. "So long as the individual is not objectionable to the aunt. She — or her companion at least — will be a tiresome but necessary adjunct."

"Gad," said Robert. "Now I must turn the aunt up sweet, and I don't think it can be done."

"Perhaps not. That is a great deal of exertion on account of one high-spirited miss."

"But if I don't, she'll be found out, and everyone will say she is a hoyden — or worse — and really, she's a very good sort of girl. A child, actually, though — " He stopped short, flushed, and cleared his throat, then hastily rose and excused himself.

As early as was decent, Lord Robert Downs presented himself at Davenant House. He could do no more, unfortunately, than leave his card.

The family were not at home to visitors today, the butler informed him, though naturally they would look forward to seeing his lordship on the following evening.

When Lord Robert's face went blank, Cawble unbent sufficiently to say, "Miss Glenwood's comeout ball, my lord. I was given to understand you had accepted the invitation. It was sent to Lord Brandon's domicile, along with his own, inasmuch as the family had not your direction."

Lord Robert showing no signs of moving, and appearing, if possible, further at sea than ever, Cawble unbent a bit more.

"Perhaps," he invented, "the notice being so short, his lordship accepted on your behalf and neglected to mention it in the press of his numerous obligations."

Lord Robert's face cleared then. "Yes, he must have done. Yes. Quite so. Thank you. Good day."

"I do not understand," said Lilith. "How can they accept invitations I never sent?"

She, Emma, and Cecily were in what would be the supper room, revising arrangements. Following the Countess Lieven's ball, some score or more invitees had discovered they did not have previous engagements after all.

They were coming, Lilith knew, to obtain tidbits about her imagined relationship with

114

Lord Brandon. Until this morning, she had enjoyed the prospect of disappointing them, for she had not and had never intended to invite the marquess. Now the vexatious man was coming anyhow.

"Oh, my," said Emma. "It was I sent them."

Lilith looked at her. "But they were not on my list."

"No."

Cecily came to Mrs. Wellwicke's rescue. "I asked her," she said. "The other day, I asked if she had sent Lord Brandon and Lord Robert invitations yet, because Lord Robert never mentioned coming, though all the other gentlemen have — and so I thought his might have gone astray, you see. You did invite all the others I've met, so naturally I thought — " She studied her aunt's stony countenance. "You did not mean to invite him at all, Aunt?" she asked, evidently baffled.

"Oh, dear," said Emma. "I simply assumed she had discussed it with you beforehand. Meanwhile, obviously Cecily assumed I would know who might be invited and who might not. Well, this is a muddle."

Lilith's mouth tightened a bit, and her shoulders straightened a bit, and she said in her usual cool way, "Not at all." And that was the end of it.

★

The matter was ended, that is, until Lady Enders arrived to help.

She worried that the flowers would not be delivered on time, and if they were, they would be the wrong ones and the colours would clash and the lobster patties would upset Lord Enders's digestion, and the Prince Regent would come after all, which meant the windows must be kept tight shut and everyone would faint, and other like catastrophes. Then, done with "helping," she set upon the real object of her visit, the satisfaction of raging curiosity regarding Lilith's ride home the previous evening.

Rachel would not dare question her directly, Lilith knew. Regardless how she was questioned, the widow had no intention of confiding any of her troubles to anybody — and most especially not her future sister-in-law.

Still, Lilith had to endure a set of apologies: Rachel and Matthew should never have consented to being taken home first, and if that could not be helped, they should have taken Lilith with them and sent her on in a hired vehicle, if necessary, with Matthew as escort, and they would never forgive themselves, especially if Lord Brandon had been disagreeable in any way, which Rachel hoped he had not been?

When Rachel wished to pry, her idea of subtlety was to end declaratory statements on an interrogatory note.

"A libertine is by definition disagreeable to me," Lilith answered. "All the same, there is nothing to pardon in you. I am not a green girl, and I imagine one brief unchaperoned ride will not sink me beneath reproach."

"Of course, my dear. Naturally, he saw you home speedily, as he ought, and it was foolish of me to be concerned for your safety? Even Brandon must know better than to behave improperly with an affianced lady?"

"Yes, I am sure he must."

"I do hope you had not to wait up for Cecily. I recollect you were feeling poorly, and I worried you would not have sufficient rest. But I daresay she was home before you were?"

"She returned quite early, according to Mrs. Wellwicke."

Lady Enders scrutinised her face. "I fear, all the same, you did not sleep sufficiently. You seem pale, Lilith. Doubtless it is the come-out ball on your mind? Arranging a young lady's debut can be so stressful, perhaps even more so for her family than for herself?"

"Perhaps."

"Well, at least you will be spared one distressing guest. You did say Brandon was not invited. I remember distinctly, because I thought at the time it reflected so much to your credit. Many hostesses will invite some of the most unsavoury characters, merely because they are attractive and amusing — as though these men were no more than decorations."

"It appears we shall have such decoration," Lilith said, folding her hands very calmly before her. "There has been a misunderstanding, and both Lord Brandon and his cousin, Lord Robert Downs, plan to attend, I am informed."

Several stiff green ribbons jerked to attention. "A misunderstanding? You do not mean to say he had the effrontery to invite himself?"

Lilith briefly explained the situation, accompanied by her guest's expressions of disbelief and dismay.

"Indeed. Well, I am very sorry," Lady Enders said, shaking her head. "Though I see it cannot be mended now. One can only hope he will not again subject you to the sort of attentions which gave rise to so much distressing talk scarcely a week ago. One is, unfortunately, judged by the company one keeps."

"I trust you do not mean to imply I am *keeping company* with such a person," came the chilling reply.

Lady Enders spluttered and fussed and declared this was not what she meant at all. The trouble was, Lord Brandon had singled Lilith out at the Lievens' ball, had danced once with her, and left almost immediately thereafter —

"Perhaps," Lilith interrupted, "because I bored him to distraction."

"My dear, it is not I who say this, but others. You know how it is. No one has ever been able to breathe scandal about you, and lesser persons are always too eager to bring others down to their level. There are some who say he pursues you for precisely that reason — because you are so far above his touch."

"Then I must congratulate their acuteness of vision. It is far superior to my own, for I perceive no signs of being pursued and therefore need contrive no fanciful reasons. In any case, I feel we have this day expended far more breath upon the topic than it merits."

The afternoon had advanced considerably when Lord Robert's conscience finally awoke and agitatedly reminded him of his mistress. Filled with self-reproach, he sped to Henrietta Street, and within a quarter hour had thrown this same conscience into twelve fits by telling a series of bouncers.

"Drunk?" Elise repeated. She sat at her dressing table, staring at his reflection in the glass. "I cannot comprehend. You are always so moderate — in that, at least," she added with a naughty smile.

He did not observe the smile, being preoccupied with sniffing in a baffled way at the air.

"Robin?"

"What? Oh, sorry. Did that clumsy maid spill your perfume again? The room fairly reek — that is to say," he hastily corrected, "everything smells odd today, don't you know. I expect it's the aftereffects. Really, you should be thankful I kept away. I wasn't a pretty sight, according to Julian — and this morning I was cross as a bear."

"Poor boy," she said, turning slightly. She reached up to tousle his fair hair affectionately. "You had not your little Lise by to nurse you."

"Well, I didn't want to subject you. That's hardly fair, when it was my own dratted fault. But really," he went on hurriedly, "it was one of those curst dull parties, and there was no other way to amuse myself, so I made free with the wine. I should have thought. I'm so sorry I worried you. You look as though you haven't slept a wink. What a selfish beast I am!"

"But, *mon cher* . . . " She paused. Her looking glass reflected a beautiful young woman, well-rested, her skin smoothed with exotic emollients, the paint subtle, virtually invisible. She was five and twenty, yet might easily have passed this day for five years younger.

"Ah, I slept," she said after a moment. "But my dreams were bad."

In touching proof of his remorse, Lord Robert promised not to stir from his mistress's side until late the following day. He didn't want to leave her even then, he assured her, but if he appeared occasionally in Society, his relatives' ruffled feathers might be smoothed a bit. It would be pleasant, wouldn't it, to spend the next few months free of harassing visits and letters? After that, of course, the family must stop pestering him, mustn't they? Because then he and his darling Lise would truly commence their life together.

The noble self-sacrifice he proposed, along with his expressions of affection and loyalty, ought to have touched his future bride's heart. Regrettably, that was about the only way she was touched. Today there were no passionate embraces, and the few caresses he bestowed were perfunctory. Mainly Elise was showered with words — from a young man whose verbal gifts were not of the highest order.

Furthermore, Lord Robert seemed to be in the throes of very long-enduring drink after-effects, for Elise caught him more than once sniffing the air in the same vaguely disturbed way. That night, he fell asleep as soon as he climbed into bed.

Lying beside him, the wise Elise found in these and other small matters much to reflect upon. Being wise, she put them together logically enough, and was troubled all the more.

7

They were small white orchids, tinged with the exact shade of pale mauve as her gown.

With Sir Thomas's spray of white rosebuds and baby's breath had come a note, properly worded and lightly touched — but only lightly — with sentiment, as became a man of maturity and sense.

The orchids bore no card, no note, yet Lilith knew who had sent them. Perhaps the marquess thought it high irony to send such exotic flowers to a dowd. The sprays lay before her on the dressing table, where her maid had placed them a few minutes before.

Lilith now looked enquiringly up at Mary.

"I thought perhaps you'd wish to wear the orchids in your hair," the abigail said. She had served her mistress nearly fifteen years, and was therefore less easily intimidated than the rest of the staff. "I wouldn't have suggested it, but they might have been dyed to match your gown, and it seemed a shame — "

"I cannot wear these," her mistress cut in.

"Furthermore, I am not a young girl, to wear flowers in my hair."

"Well, I don't know many young girls who could wear orchids, for that matter. It would take a precious sophisticated one, I'm sure."

Mary took up one mauve-tinged blossom and set it against her mistress's ear. "I'd like to know who picked it out," she said. "Creamy white, as though it had been made from your skin. There's not another lady has your complexion, madam — as smooth and white as a flower petal. As to young girls — why, what are little rosebuds for, then?"

"Mary, Sir Thomas sent me the rosebuds. That is what I shall wear. Or, if you object to them as too young for me, I shall do very well without any flowers at all."

"*He* won't notice," Mary muttered. "He never notices anything. But the other gentleman must. That I'd swear to."

"You are very talkative this evening."

"I do beg your pardon, madam." The abigail promptly set down the orchids, took up the comb, and proceeded to plait her mistress's hair. She pulled the strands so firmly that Lilith thought her eyes would pop out of her head.

"Not quite so tight, if you please," she said, wincing. "My hair feels as though it is coming

124

out by . . . the roots. . . ." She trailed off, gazing into the mirror. After a slight pause, she added, "I feel a headache coming on, at any rate. Perhaps not . . . not so tight a coil. Perhaps —"

"You're quite right, madam. I'll pull it up behind instead, with a knot, and leave it softer at the top, shall I?"

Her employer nodded.

"Now you've mentioned it," Mary went on, though Lilith had not opened her mouth, "we might do both. One or two small orchids and two rosebuds, twined in the knot, so. Practically hidden, your hair is so thick and full. Just peeping out a bit. This way, neither gentleman can complain — or think too much of himself, either," she added with a small, self-satisfied smile.

More than a dozen bouquets had been placed upon Cecily Glenwood's altar by her admirers. Nonetheless, she had no difficulty in declining all these lesser sacrifices in favour of the greater one: a spray of pink roses delivered personally by her brother Rodger.

Overcome by some fit of fraternal obligation, he had for the night abandoned his horses and horsy friends to support poor Cecily in her hour of trial. This he did, when the ball commenced, by being rather a trial himself.

125

He announced loudly and repeatedly that he didn't know her without the odour of the stables about her. Then he proceeded to disconcert her eager beaux with malevolent stares when they dared venture near his little sister.

Luckily, Lord Robert soon took the younger man in hand, introduced him to several sporting acquaintances, and left the rustic fellow contentedly debating the merits of Tattersall's versus Aldridge's in the art of equine auctioneering.

"You are exceedingly considerate," Cecily told Lord Robert when he returned to claim his dance. "I know Rodger only means to be protective, but he does choose awkward moments, doesn't he? The way he glared when Lord Maddock asked me to dance — I'm sure his lordship was convinced he'd be murdered. But you weren't a bit afraid of Rodger, were you? Not that I can wonder at that," she said with an admiring look at his broad shoulders. "I imagine you could knock him down with one blow, if you had even half a mind to. Naturally, you must be confident when you're so fit."

"A great many of us appear fit — thanks to our tailors," her partner answered modestly, though his chest expanded and his shoulders grew even broader and straighter. "We London fellows are an idle lot, I'm afraid."

"All the same, your shoulders are not padded, nor your — " She quickly withdrew her glance from his muscular calves and went on smoothly, "At any rate, you sit your horse exceedingly well. One would think you'd been born in the saddle."

"That compliment I must return, Miss Glenwood. Though I must say — " It was his turn to change direction abruptly. "I should very much like to ride with you one day. Not at dawn," he added hastily, "but in the morning."

"I should like that, my lord."

"Then I shall persuade your aunt to accompany us. Otherwise, I'm afraid, it wouldn't be the thing, you know."

Persuasion of the aunt, Lord Robert soon decided, could wait until the morrow. At the moment, Mrs. Davenant's demeanour had all the welcoming attributes of an iceberg.

The widow was dancing with her fiancé, who gave the lie to Mary's earlier mutterings by taking note of the flowers. He told Lilith they suited her new coiffure, the effect was altogether elegant, and she was undoubtedly the handsomest woman in the room, the guest of honour notwithstanding.

"I'm not a foreign power," she answered. "There is no need to turn me up sweet, Thomas."

"I never flatter you, my dear, because I know you don't like it. But to say you are handsome is a simple statement of fact," he said judiciously. "Nor can you convince me any other lady in this room can match your elegance of manner. I know I'm a lucky man. I never wanted Alvanley's pointing it out, I promise you."

She stiffened. "What had Alvanley to say to you? I am sure he scarcely speaks two words to me."

"He is a lazy, ramshackle fellow. But he tells me to keep sharp eye, for there are some gentlemen excessively envious of my good fortune. 'While you are courting the goodwill of the Grand Duchess,' he warned me, 'others may be wooing your bride-to-be.'"

"What nonsense."

"Not at all. I have seen Brandon cast more than one glance in your direction this evening, and now I dare not leave your side. They say he has a devilish way with the ladies, not to mention most of us would give a right arm to have one half his good looks."

"Minus an arm, you should not have all your own, Thomas."

He smiled. "Well, he might keep his handsome face, I suppose — so long as I keep my handsome lady."

Lilith did not cast any glances of her own at

the marquess. Numerous other ladies had undertaken that duty for her. Besides, she had no need to study him. She had seen enough when she'd greeted him earlier, in the reception line.

His midnight-blue coat and dove-grey inexpressibles, impeccably cut, seemed knit to his powerful, lean frame. Tonight, one diamond winked in his cravat and another on his right hand. As he'd bent over her hand, she'd breathed the scent of sandalwood, and could almost feel how crisp were the black curls that glistened in the candlelight. The serpentine green eyes he'd raised briefly to hers gleamed with humour. His low voice caressed her ears, and though he uttered the merest civilities, her heart had beat a devil's tatoo in answer.

Contemptuous of superstition and magic, Lilith Davenant had never believed such a thing as fatal charm existed. Nevertheless, she could not deny the pull the marquess exerted upon her, which seemed to grow stronger each time she saw him.

With him, she was so tense she could scarcely think. Away from him, her mind churned with recollections of every word, every gesture, every expression and nuance of his too-handsome countenance. This was how thoroughly he had insinuated himself into her thoughts, after a mere handful of interactions in the three weeks since she'd found him half dead by the roadside.

Though Thomas made a creditable effort to keep by his lady, another siren call beckoned more irresistibly. In less than an hour, he was planted in a corner arguing with his Parliamentary colleagues.

Past experience told Lilith he would not be uprooted until supper, if then. Had one lady joined the group, she might have found an excuse to join as well, but few ladies would endure the somber debate above half a minute.

Cecily did not require her, being occupied with one partner after another. In the intervals between sets, the girl was speedily surrounded by young people — of both genders, Lilith was pleased to note. Her niece was lovely enough to inspire the most malicious sort of envy, yet her open, warm, unspoiled manner won feminine hearts instead of alienating them. There was no question of Cecily's success — on every count.

Since she had no need to hover by her niece, Lilith walked with apparent ease among her many guests, chatting briefly before moving on. She found she needed to move on frequently. She would no sooner begin to relax with one cluster of guests than she would hear a familiar low-pitched voice somewhere in the vicinity. Lazy, insinuating, it would rise and fall amid the buzz and laughter of other voices. Though she moved from one group to the next, his voice seemed always nearby, until she began to feel — it was absurd, she knew — like a hunted creature, never allowed to rest.

She was trying to find a partner for Lady Shumway's unfortunate granddaughter when Lilith saw Rachel try to draw Sir Thomas away from his discussion. Thomas only smiled absently and waved her away.

Lady Shumway's charge was safely deposited with a freckle-faced baronet in the nick of time, for in the next minute Rachel, all angry ruffles and ribbons, was charging at Lilith.

"It is no good telling Thomas," Lady Enders said, vexed and red-faced. "Half the company speaks of nothing else, and no wonder. I have never seen anything so brazen as the way that wicked man looks at you. When Sally Jersey finally asked what made him stare so, he only laughed — I heard him myself — and claimed he was trying to devise a name for your new coiffure."

It was only years of rigid discipline prevented Lilith from reaching up and ripping the orchids from her hair. Her grandmother's lectures rang in her ears: "A lady *never* indulges in displays of emotion, regardless how

131

great the provocation."

She did not wring her hands, as Rachel was doing, or flush with embarrassment. "There are some persons," Lilith answered coldly, "whose every word and action attracts notice. Lord Brandon is Society's latest circus animal. When the novelty of his return wears off, everyone will leave off watching and commenting."

This was uttered with such regal disdain that Rachel very nearly dropped a curtsy. "All the same, he ought have more consideration," she said, hastily recovering. "He knows he's the centre of attention, and therefore draws attention to you."

"I have never heard it remarked Lord Brandon was a considerate man. Will you excuse me, please? I believe Cawble is having trouble with one of the footmen."

Mrs. Davenant's servants were far too greatly awed by their mistress to dare experience difficulties of any sort. She had simply told a falsehood in order to escape the company. She did not hurry from the ballroom, or along the hallway, yet she was short of breath when she reached the safety of the supper room.

Everything, of course, was as it should be. Cawble had made the punch himself from his own carefully guarded receipt, a copy of which any hostess in the ton would have given a vital organ to possess. There was an excellent nonalcoholic version and a sublime spirit-laden one. The cold dishes were artistically laid out. The warm ones would be served at the last possible moment. The china and plate, the table linens, the decorations — all was in perfect order, as Lilith ought to know, having reviewed the situation some fifty times already.

She was examining every detail for the fifty-first time when a chill tickled her neck. She knew the marquess stood behind her, even before he spoke, though she had not heard him enter. Her body stiffened.

"The centre-piece wants to move a bit to the right," he said.

She turned slowly to face him. "It is precisely where it belongs."

"Unlike certain parties you could mention?" He moved a few steps closer.

"Now you have mentioned it, I would prefer you returned to the company, my lord. Your disappearance will be remarked, and I do think you have caused enough talk as it is."

"But my hostess will not talk — to me, at any rate. I wonder why that is."

Another step brought him a few inches from her, and Lilith, retreating, found herself backed up against the table.

"Now I wonder whether you mean to clamber over it," he said gravely. "You cannot be comfortable as you are."

"Will you please — "

She heard footsteps approaching. In the same instant, his hand clasped her arm, and in one smooth series of motions he'd drawn her away from the table and guided her through the opposite door into a small room adjoining.

The well-oiled door closed soundlessly behind them. Beyond it she heard two servants talking softly, then the sounds of chairs being moved. After — two or three endless minutes, the footsteps and voices faded away.

"They are quiet and efficient," said Lord Brandon as he folded his arms and lazily leaned back against the door. "Yet all servants are bound by some unwritten code to convey every tidbit they discover to every other servant with whom they are remotely acquainted. Thence the tidbit, enlarged to prodigious size, is conveyed for the delectation of their masters. Speaking of delectable, Mrs. Davenant — "

"I must insist you return to the company, my lord," she said unsteadily.

"Your new coiffure," he went on, "is a delicious concoction. Is that an orchid — no, two — nestled among the curls? I rather fancy orchids. I have a gardener who works magic in a damp, dark hothouse. Still, I have never seen the species displayed to such advantage."

"It appears they came to me by mistake. Since there was no card, it was impossible to return them. My abigail believed they looked well enough with the rosebuds."

"They suit you better than rosebuds. You are not a common rose sort of beauty, but a rare and dangerous exotic. Dangerous to my peace of mind, at any rate," he added, his voice very low. "You don't want me, but I cannot keep away, you see."

"I see that you are standing in my way. Still, there is another exit," she said, clasping her hands to stop their trembling.

His glance caught the movement, then the green eyes were piercing hers. "You are always wanting to run from me," he said. "Do I frighten you?"

"Certainly not," she answered, nearly choking on the words. "I simply do not care to be made an object of speculation. I cannot believe you are so insensitive as to be unaware of that. Yet you seem — it seems at times as though you go out of your way — as though you have some game with me. I do not know what it is or why you should wish to distress me and annoy my fiancé. We have neither of us done you any ill."

"It," he said calmly, "is attraction, and the

game is the oldest one in the world."

Her face grew very warm. "I see. You are not done mocking me."

"No, I am trying to court you."

She barely suppressed the gasp. "This offensive joke has gone far enough, my lord. Court, indeed. I, engaged to be wed — even if I were not the very last woman in England a man of your sort would be attracted to. Your idea of humour is distasteful."

He sighed. "I knew how it would be," he said, coming away from the door. "Your brain has not yet recovered from years of being tortured by those cruel coils. I shall have to provide scientific proof."

He crossed the small room. Panicked, Lilith retreated to the opposite door. Just as her shaking fingers touched the handle, his hand closed over them. His touch was an electric shock, succeeded by a wave of shocks as he gathered her into his arms and kissed her.

She had been married. She had been embraced before, and always her body had stiffened at Charles's impatient intimacies. Always she had felt awkward and inadequate. Thus, she had simply frozen, praying he would be done and her mortification ended quickly. She froze now, tense and anxious within, rigidly unresponsive without, and endured, waiting for Lord Brandon to give up.

136

Or tried to wait. Because he seemed to have no inkling he was kissing a glacier.

His mouth moved slowly over hers, lazily tasting, while his fingers idly stroked the back of her neck. Under that light, almost negligible touch, the stiff muscles warmed and relaxed, and warmth trickled down her spine. She caught her breath in surprise, and his tongue flicked over her parted lips lightly, teasingly, before his mouth closed fully over hers once more. Tingling heat washed through her then, weakening muscles, swamping will, melting everything in its path, so that she scarcely knew she was answering his kiss until it stopped.

She opened shocked eyes to a heavy-lidded green gaze. His face was still very near.

"You appear skeptical yet," he whispered. "I had better provide more evidence."

"No!"

He did not move. She could discern the faint lines at the corners of his eyes and a minute scar over his left cheekbone. His breath lightly caressed her face, and the scent of sandalwood teased her nostrils. Her heart skittered wildly.

She looked the other way, and wished frantically he would move away, because she could not. His face was so cool and assured, while her own was hot — with shame, no doubt, because he had so bewitched her that she'd very nearly brought her lips closer again . . . for more. But there was no magic and therefore could be no bewitchery, and so she made her voice cold and steady as she spoke.

"I certainly need no further proof," she said, "That you are despicable."

"I was much goaded, Mrs. Davenant. Your perfume made me desperate."

She was desperate in any event, because he still had not moved, and in the narrow space between them was a treacherous current. She had been drawn in once, all unwitting. She would not be so again.

She pushed him away and, on unsteady legs, quitted the room.

Lord Brandon discovered that the other door opened onto a hall that would take him out of the house unseen by any but a few servants. One of these, upon retrieving his lordship's hat and stick and whispering a few words, received a generous vail.

It wanted two hours until the marquess's appointment with an actress. He might have spent these at the theatre, but her onstage performance was not what entertained him. Therefore, he returned to his town house to change into less formal attire.

As he was unwrapping his neck-cloth his

glance fell upon his left shirt cuff. He frowned.

"Hillard," he called.

His valet hastened into the dressing room. "M'lud."

"Bring me a pistol."

Mr. Hillard had been with his master twenty years.

"Yes, m'lud. What sort of pistol did you have in mind? Mr. Manton has made you several."

"You cannot ask me to make such a decision at a time like this. I am a broken man. There is a thread," Lord Brandon said in sepulchral tones, "hanging from my cuff."

"M'lud, that is impossible. I beg your pardon for contradicting, but it is completely impossible."

His lordship put out his hand and pointed to the offending cuff. "What do you call that?" he asked in the same hollow voice.

Hillard stepped closer and peered at the object. "M'lud, I call it a hair. A long, reddish one," he added, his face immobile, "with a curl to it. I can't think how it got there, but it isn't a thread. Shall I remove it?"

"No, Hillard. You have suffered enough. I have grievously offended you. I hope you will come to forgive me one day, for there were extenuating circumstances. The light is dim and my eyesight is failing me. That has been pointed out to me on more than one occasion."

"I am sorry to hear it, m'lud."

"Now I have depressed your spirits. You had better step round to the butler's pantry and restore yourself with some beverage appropriate to the circumstances."

"But you meant to go out, m'lud, did you not?"

"Later. Perhaps I had better rest first."

When the valet had left, Lord Brandon carefully removed the gleaming strand from the stud on which it had caught — when he had caught her, he reflected with a small smile. Cornered and caught her, trembling, in his arms.

That had been a novel experience. He had never before embraced a frightened woman. Angry women, yes, and those who feigned shyness, and those who were eager — but never one genuinely afraid. Never before, either, had he encountered so powerful an effort to resist.

Yet she could not, and he'd known she could not. Which was no conceit in him, only statement of fact. Elise notwithstanding, he would not have pursued the widow if he had not believed there was an attraction from the start.

His instincts never failed him in such cases.

Even so, he had toyed with her first, to be certain, and all his artful teasing since had had one clear object: to make her inescapably aware of him.

Lord Brandon's smile twisted slightly. He had teased himself as well. That could not be denied. Wooing her he'd known would require patience. Nevertheless, though he was not an impatient man, tonight . . .

He drew the strand of hair out between his fingers.

For that endless time when she'd refused to succumb — when she stood, rigid as a marble column in his arms — he had wanted to shake her. The silken alabaster skin, the rich mass of curling hair, the surprisingly lush perfume wafting languorously to his nostrils . . . yes, the haughty countenance as well, and the strong, lithe body recoiling from his own. It had been, for a moment, maddening. But only for a moment, because she had weakened at last.

"At last," he murmured. "What was it then, madam?" he asked the fragile trophy of his night's work.

Then, he answered silently, he had tasted a young girl's kiss, tentative and inexperienced. Though she had been married six years and widowed five, one might have believed it was a virgin prisoned in his arms. All the same, her response had moved him. Even now, reflecting upon it made him . . . uneasy.

He glanced at the fresh linen, coat, waistcoat, and pantaloons Hillard had set out for him. It was time to dress. Brandon never kept his paramours waiting.

He could not repress a sigh. He had done it all a thousand times before. He had known them all, drab to duchess, and they were all, apart from details of packaging, the same. There was no challenge in the pursuit — no pursuit required, actually. No need for guile, as Elise had said. No danger and certainly no consequences of failure.

Small wonder the widow excited him.

"Thank heaven *that's* done," said Cecily when the door had closed behind the last of their guests.

"My dear, I hope you don't mean your comeout ball was an ordeal," said Emma. "You seemed to be enjoying yourself well enough."

"Oh, I did," Cecily said with a quick glance at her aunt. "How could I help it, when Aunt Lilith made all so splendid — so perfect?"

The widow was staring at a centre-piece one of the footmen was carrying out of the supper room. She did not respond.

"Aunt Lilith?" Cecily moved to her aunt's

side and took her hand.

Lilith looked at her blankly.

"Thank you so much, Aunt. It was the most beautiful party, and I cannot think when I've had a better time — away from my mare, that is," she added with a grin. "I was only relieved I managed to survive the evening without committing any outrageous *faux-pas*."

"Oh, Cecily." To the girl's astonishment, her aunt threw her arms around her and hugged her — almost desperately, it seemed.

Then, just as abruptly, she drew away. "You are a great success," she said with her usual composure. "Equally important, you have deserved it. I am very proud of you, my dear."

"Well, I'm glad to hear it, Aunt. I shall have to tell you every compliment I received, naturally, and every silly thing the gentlemen contrived to say, and draw up a lengthy list of the men in London who'd do better for a dancing master. But not tonight — or this morning, rather. It's nearly dawn, isn't it? You must be exhausted, because the hostess has the most laborious job of all. Indeed, my aunt had better go to bed right away, don't you think, Emma?"

Emma bent a troubled glance upon the widow. "You have one of your headaches," she said. "Why don't you go up, as Cecily ad-

143

vises? I shall make you a nice herbal tea, shall I?"

"Thank you, but I am only a bit weary. This has been altogether a long day . . . and evening . . . and . . . " Lilith turned back to her niece. "Of course I shall want to hear every detail of your triumph," she said with a forced smile. "But we will all do better for some sleep."

As soon as she had attained the safety of her dressing room, Lilith tore the flowers and pins from her head, took up her brush, and savagely attacked her hair. Tears had started to her eyes when she heard her abigail's light footstep. "Go to bed, Mary. I told you not to wait up."

The brush was taken from her hand. "But it's as well I did, isn't it? You being run off your feet, and your head probably ringing from all the noise. I'm sure this was twice the crowd we had for Miss Georgiana. And, naturally, twice the number of biddies needing to be attended to. I could hear them squawking all the way downstairs, pesky old hens," Mary grumbled, all the while plying the dark auburn tresses with slow, soothing strokes. "And here I am, bad as any of them, jabbering at you when you must be tired to death of talk."

144

Lilith was more than tired to death. Her guests had pricked and stung her at every turn, in chorus to the pricking and stinging of her own conscience.

Every female in the company, it seemed, had remarked her brief disappearance and felt compelled to point out the odd coincidence of Lord Brandon's vanishing at the same time.

Their hostess had her answer ready, the same answer for them all. Had Lord Brandon left? She had not noticed, yet she was scarcely surprised. A young girl's comeout must seem to him a very tame affair. One could not be amazed at his leaving to seek livelier entertainment.

Thus she had endured, and told herself she had endured worse — her marriage, for instance. Still, she prayed for great news from abroad to distract the Beau Monde from its obsessive attention to herself. Such news would not be forthcoming this evening, but tomorrow, perhaps. Tomorrow, perhaps, Lord Brandon's odd whims would be forgotten . . . by others, at least.

8

Unfortunately for Mrs. Davenant, rumours of Buonaparte's attempted suicide the previous day could not possibly reach London in time to distract her gossip-hungry acquaintances. The afternoon following the comeout saw her drawing room packed with visitors, not all of them Cecily's dancing partners.

Lady Enders did her best, making a great piece of work of minor matters, such as Hobhouse's obstinate determination to procure passports to Paris for himself and Lord Byron, despite the Government's equally firm resolve not to issue any. She even went so far as to describe in tedious detail the illuminations at Carlton House celebrating the triumph of the Bourbons, though everyone had seen them and raved sufficiently days before.

Neither illuminations, Louis XVIII, nor even the capricious Lord Byron could be half so sensational a subject as the lavish bouquet of lilies that arrived just as Lady Jersey did, and five minutes before Lord Robert Downs made his appearance.

"I have never heard such a fuss about a lot of posies," he whispered to Cecily when he had elbowed several other fellows out of the way and had her, for the moment, to himself.

"I know. You'd think Napoleon himself had been delivered. But Lady Jersey recognised your cousin's servant, it seems, and so she must peep at the card, and then declare it is Lord Brandon's hand, for she'd know it anywhere, and then she must tease my poor aunt to read the note to the company."

Robert looked at the flowers, which had been exiled to the darkest corner of the room in a futile attempt to subdue curiosity. Then he looked at Cecily. "*Julian* sent them?" he asked. "What did the note say?"

"Good heavens, you don't suppose Aunt Lilith actually read it out, do you? She never even looked at it, but crumpled it up and thrust it into her pocket." Cecily grinned. "Lady Jersey is ever so vexed. She's bursting to know what it said. If she dared, I imagine she'd wrestle my aunt to the floor to get it from her. But even she is a little afraid of Aunt Lilith — though she hasn't left off teasing altogether."

Lord Robert certainly would not have had the audacity to tease Mrs. Davenant. She had never looked more glacierlike than now, her

147

face frozen in politeness, her chin high, her gaze at its most imperiously icy. He would as soon take a dip in the northernmost depths of the North Sea.

"I suppose," he said, "this is not the best time to ask permission to ride with you."

"Actually, it's the perfect time," said Cecily. "Just don't mention flowers or your cousin. Since you'll be the only one to refrain from those topics, she'll be touched by your delicacy."

His expression must have been very doubtful, because Cecily added, "Shall I ask her, then — or would that be excessively forward of me?"

If the widow's own eighteen-year-old niece was not intimidated at the prospect, then a man of the world certainly could not be.

When Mrs. Davenant had seen off a frustrated Lady Jersey, Lord Robert approached his hostess.

"Riding?" she echoed blankly, as though he had been speaking Egyptian.

He was not sure after exactly what he'd said to that frosty figure, though it must have been some garbled paraphrasing of Julian's comments the other day. Whatever it was, it worked — or else the widow was too much preoccupied with other matters to interrogate him closely, for she gave her consent rather abstractedly, and agreed to accompany the two young people the following morning.

"Well, my dear," said Sir Thomas after the remaining visitors had left, "What is this I hear about a rival?"

"What is it you hear?" his betrothed responded stiffly.

"I met up with Sally Jersey — not long after she'd left here, I take it, and she tells me Brandon is sending you love notes and lilies."

He stood by the table that bore the infamous bouquet. His hands folded behind, he appeared to be weighing the flowers as Parliamentary evidence.

"I have been hearing a great deal of Brandon lately," he went on. "In fact, in the last twenty-four hours, I have heard his name linked with yours more often than my own. I know better than to credit every piece of idle gossip I hear, and I know better of your character than to credit what has been hinted to me. All the same, I do not take my treasure for granted." He turned to her. "Have I any reason to speak to him regarding the matter?"

Lilith removed the crumpled note from her pocket and handed it to him. "Judge for yourself," she said frostily. "I have not read it. I have no wish to read it." Her chin was high.

He scanned the note quickly, then threw

her a puzzled glance. "He thanks you, according to this, for your 'exceedingly wise counsel.' He says your advice was invaluable. What advice was that, my dear?"

"Drains."

"I beg your pardon?"

"Drainage. Of his fields. It is . . . it is one of my hobbyhorses, you know."

Sir Thomas chuckled. "Poor Sally. All a-fever to know of midnight assignations and stolen kisses, and we can offer her nothing but agriculture. How I wish you had read her the note."

"I had no desire to read it, as I said. In any case, whatever was written, she would have put some base construction upon it — and certainly it is none of her affair."

"No, my dear, and none of mine, I am sure. I am done with farming, thank heavens. All the same, I wish Brandon would take himself off to tend those fields of his. Even innocent, he is a troublesome fellow to have about, I think."

Lilith watched the two young people tear off at a frightening pace, Cecily's groom trailing doggedy behind them. Cecily was a country-woman, happiest in the saddle and — judging by her speed — galloping neck or nothing. Fortunately, her companion was a match for her.

As Glenda had said, there was an eager boy under the veneer of jaded sophistication. Lilith had not observed Lord Robert very closely before. She'd had too many distractions — or one too great a one. But en route to the meadow, she had found much to meet with her approval. He was not sly or insinuating. He was good-natured, and behaved towards Cecily as though she were his sister.

Equally important, Cecily was her usual level-headed self. The elegant gentleman did not seem to throw her into any sort of confusion. He might have been her brother.

Such fraternal behaviour scarcely promised a match, yet so long as Cecily's heart was not affected, one could not object to the friendship.

All the same, one could not help wishing the Season done already, with Cecily wed or soon to be. Lilith had never been overly fond of Town, though she made the best of it for her nieces' sakes. At present . . . oh, London seemed a den of fiends. One, certainly, plagued her mind and heart.

The hoofbeats seemed to come in response to the thought. She glanced over her shoulder at what might have been an apparition, for in the shadowed path man and beast appeared one. As she recognised the rider, her heart began to thud ominously. In a moment, Lord

Brandon was beside her, his restless dark stallion pawing impatiently at the ground, agitating her mare.

"She is like her mistress," he said, subduing his mount. "She wants to bolt — though we mean them no harm, do we, Abbadon?"

The beast snorted, and Lilith's mare backed away.

"We have only come for our scold," he went on. "I trust you've had sufficient time to compose a thundering one."

"That would be a waste of intellect and energy. You are beyond sermons. You are beyond any civilised rules of behaviour."

"I object to having my life ordered by prigs, if that is what you mean by civilised rules. It was but a kiss, after all."

She winced.

"I shall never be sorry I did it," he added, his smile as unrepentant as his words, "though you threaten me with all the fire and brimstone of all eternity. You, on the other hand, *are* sorry, and therefore obliged to take it out on me. Well, do your worst. I shall gaze at your lips the whole time and not comprehend a syllable."

A breeze ruffled the boughs above them. The shifting beams of sunlight played over the clear planes of his face and softened it, gentled even the mocking smile and insolent green gaze. Or perhaps it was the low, beckoning sound of his voice that weakened something within her. Her own glance lingered on his mouth longer than it ought, and then upon his eyes, and within her grew a yearning that shamed and enraged her as soon as she recognised it.

"I *am* sorry," she said tightly. "To you it is nothing — a whim to amuse yourself. It is no joke to me, my lord. It does not amuse me that I have betrayed my affianced husband, dishonoured myself, earned the censure of my peers — oh, yes, and earned your contempt as well."

"Good heavens, one would think you had committed patricide. It was not even adultery — though I'm hardly the man to discourage you from *that*."

Lilith tried to hold her temper, but it was already ripping loose. She was sick at heart at the sin she'd committed, while to him it was nothing. *She* was nothing — her feelings were a joke to him.

"No, you would not," she said. "You delight in wrecking marriages. A betrothal must be a mere bagatelle."

"Not at all. *Your* betrothal is an atrocity. A woman of your spirit — to be shackled to that stale speechmaker. No wonder you are so short-tempered."

"Your opinion is of no consequence, my lord. Whatever you think of him, Sir Thomas is my own choice. I will not permit you to sully my reputation and make a laughingstock of him. I will not permit you to taint my existence any longer. You have already killed one husband," she went on in low, furious tones. "Was that not sufficient? Must you make a shambles of my life once again?"

There was a heartbeat's pause. The teasing light went out of his eyes, and his voice was cold as he answered, "As I recollect, madam, your first was consumptive."

"Consumptive, yes — though I know it was his so-called friends hastened him to an early grave. If you can call it friendship to encourage a sick man to exhausting follies — drinking, gambling, dissipating — when he should have rested. Perhaps you call it friendship to lead such a man to the stewpots of a filthy city, when he needed to breathe fresh air." She blinked back angry tears. "He might have had a few more precious years — even one — were it not for *friends* such as you. But with you it is always an endless pursuit of pleasure. You have no care for anyone but yourself. Now you have a whim to amuse yourself at my expense. You shall not," she said, her voice choked. "I despise you and all you stand for."

It seemed as though every sound had been stifled about them, so potent was the silence when she finished. Even his restless mount stood still as a statue.

"I am not omnipotent," he answered at last. "My mere presence is not sufficient to befoul your lily-white reputation and cuckold your fiancé. As to your late husband, I doubt even the Almighty Himself had the power to sway Davenant from his chosen courses. He was a wastrel and debauchee long before I met him. If marriage to a wealthy, eager-to-please, generous-hearted girl was not enough for him, then his case was hopeless."

The pain wrenched her so suddenly that the tears spilled over before she could recall them. She turned her head, though she knew he'd seen her weakness.

"I beg your pardon," she heard him say more gently. "My presence distresses you. It will do so no longer."

Then he was gone.

"Idiot!" Lord Brandon muttered as he rode away. "Clumsy idiot!"

Abbadon uttered a derisive snort.

"You needn't rub it in," his master grumbled. "It was clumsy, yes — and craven — to stoop to defend myself. Still, I was much goaded. You must admit that, at least."

155

The unsympathetic animal tossed its head.

"Ah, you had your mind — or some part — fixed on the mare. You were not attending. You did not hear her contempt. You could not read the loathing in her eyes. Until, that is, your crude bully of a master reduced her to tears. That is a fine way to win a mistress, don't you think? Damn."

Abbadon pricked up his ears at the oath.

"Away, then, you devil," Brandon growled, nudging the impatient animal's flanks with his heels. The horse surged into a gallop, and man and beast thundered recklessly along the bridle path. Had anyone observed their headlong fury, that witness must have been convinced it was the devil and his familiar, plunging to the fiery place.

While the furious ride eventually pacified his horse, it did little for Lord Brandon except make him hot and dirty. A bath and change of clothes improved his appearance but not his temper.

Later, he stood in his dressing room, glaring at his reflection in the glass. He was not, he thought, vain — or not excessively so — yet he could not understand how a rational woman could look upon him with such utter revulsion. His crisply curling hair had not turned white suddenly. It was as black and thick as ever. His face was not yet mottled with age and dissipation. His green eyes were clear, his posture straight. He had not turned into a troll overnight.

His appearance was not the trouble.

Lilith Davenant hated him for what he was, and what she believed he had done, and though he had done a great many things deserving of her prim displeasure, he had not done what she accused him of. Yet it was not the injustice that had angered him — and perhaps the feeling wasn't precisely anger. Maddened for a moment, yes . . .

He turned away from the mirror.

There was no denying. Her slate-blue eyes had turned to ice, and she had raised her stubborn chin and opened her mouth, and — while the accusation was unjust, or only partly just — her words had pricked him. Very well, *wounded* him. He was not one to shy away from facts, however lowering they might be.

To be wounded by a woman was a novelty — not an agreeable one, certainly. Still, it was a fact: Lilith Davenant had stabbed him, and he was still smarting.

As he formulated the thought, he smiled wryly. He must remember to congratulate Elise on her choice of champion. Meanwhile, he had better set his mind to repairing the damage. Nearly a fortnight had passed since he had made his wager — and all he had to show for it was one absurdly chaste kiss!

Elise had not attended Eton, Harrow, Winchester, or any other ancient educational institution. All the same, she could count. Since the night he'd spent at his cousin's, Robert had made love to her exactly once, with a conspicuous want of enthusiasm. Once in nine days. Last night, again, he had not come home.

Being wise, Elise had immediately sensed a woman in the case. Being well-informed, she had not required the entire nine days to ascertain who the woman was. Being practical, she turned her intelligence to determining the simplest, most direct way of eliminating her rival. Accordingly, she paid a visit to her dressmaker, and a bribe to Madame Suzette's assistant.

On the Sabbath, Mrs. Davenant took herself to church. She prayed for forgiveness and strength. She came away feeling unshriven and weaker than before. She'd found no comfort in the minister's words, though he, accustomed to preach to the nobility, wisely forbore mentioning such vulgarities as hellfire and eternal damnation.

Lilith had looked up at him and seen herself, standing all those years ago before another minister: The shy girl, barely seventeen, who'd wondered at the powers that had given her as husband so golden and godlike a creature.

The young bridegroom at her side must have wondered as well, for he'd got the worst of the bargain. Even now, at eight and twenty, Lilith was no beauty. As a bride, she'd been a carrot-haired, freckle-faced, skinny adolescent, inwardly awkward and unsure. Outwardly, she had been poised, of course, cool and perfectly mannered, because manners, poise, and self-control had been drummed into her from the day her grandparents had taken in the orphaned child of their only son.

They had not, however, taught her how to make her husband love her. That, perhaps, was too much to ask. His family had wanted the match because their youngest son was too expensive to keep any longer. Her grandparents, their own title spanking new, had wanted the connexion with ancient nobility.

Love in such a case was not to be expected — even if there had been anything remotely lovable or attractive about her. Yet she had wished. She had wished at least that Charles Davenant would teach her how to please him. She could never express such a wish aloud, though.

Thus his rare visits to her bed were impatient and hurried, and his distaste only made the intimacy the more humiliating. When he was done, he left her hating her own body because it could never please him. Charles's gawky child bride could not compete with his London beauties. She could not even inspire affection. She bored and embarrassed him, and even drunk — as he inevitably was — he could not wait to be gone from her.

Lilith had not wept for her husband in years. Even at his death, her tears had been for the waste of the man he might have been. So young, strong, handsome . . . to dwindle to a frail shadow, weak, fretful, and afraid. She had wept as well because he'd left her no golden children to whom she might give the love he'd never sought or wanted.

Now she wept silently in the church after the others had gone, because Charles's friend had pierced the cold tomb of her heart, and revived the pain so long sealed within.

9

Early Monday morning, the much-harassed Mr. Higginbottom met with both Lord Brandon's man of business and the marquess himself. Two hours later, Mr. Higginbottom was able to inform Mrs. Davenant that terms had been arranged at last, and to remind her, with gloomy satisfaction, that she would now be obliged to practice the strictest possible economy.

The greatest of her expenses having been incurred already, Lilith had few qualms about her ability to last the Season. Shortly after, she would be wed, and money would no longer be an issue. All she would lose was her independence. She persuaded herself she'd already more of that article than most ladies.

For five years she had been free to manage her own affairs, without having to accommodate a husband's whims. She had not to chase him down when major decisions were required. She had done it all herself, without interference — and in the end she had made a bad job of it, had she not?

Furthermore, there must be some gratification in having at last won this particular war of wills with Lord Brandon.

To Mr. Higginbottom she expressed her satisfaction. Inwardly Lilith felt as though she were now a bill marked "Paid," filed away and forgotten, and her victory was tinged with regret she despised herself for feeling.

By early afternoon, this matter took second place to a more urgent one.

Lilith was in her sitting room with Emma and Cecily, the two older women plying their needles while Cecily read aloud from *The Corsair*. That was when the box arrived from the dressmaker for Cecily.

"I declare I'd forgotten completely about the walking dresses," the girl said as she untied the string. "No wonder. I'm sure I have dozens already, though I never seem to *walk* anywhere lately. It is always — Oh, my."

She giggled as she pushed away the tissue paper. "Not a walking dress, I don't think."

Emma, sitting by her, turned pink. Lilith promptly rose from her chair to investigate.

Even the widow's marble features became tinged with colour as Cecily withdrew from the box two intriguing garments.

They were negligees. One was a maidenly pink. That was its sole connexion with maidenhood. It was of gossamer silk, its plunging neckline caught with cherry-coloured ribbons. The other was a froth of black lace, equally transparent.

"Not walking dresses, to be sure," said Cecily with a smile as she held the black one against her and modeled it for her two stunned companions.

Lilith, who had stood numb with shock, hastily recovered. She snatched the two garments from her niece and threw them back into the box.

"Obviously there has been a mistake," she said.

"I should say," Cecily answered, grinning over the note she held in her hand. "I cannot be anybody's 'Dearest Lise,' and who, I wonder, is my 'adoring Robin'?" She giggled again. "I have never seen such naughty nightrails."

"I should hope not," said her aunt. "This box will be returned immediately, and I shall certainly have something to say to Madame regarding her carelessness. The idea — to send such — such wicked things to this house."

"Of course it was a mistake," Emma soothed. "There must have been another package, and another lady has Cecily's frocks, I daresay."

"A *lady*, indeed," Lilith said half to herself.

163

"That *her* lewd belongings should pollute this house, and *he* — " She broke off, recollecting her niece.

Cecily, however, was still studying the note. "But of course," she said. "It's Lord Robert's *chere amie*, is it not? Anne told me her name was Elise, and that she's French, and the family's in an uproar because he's been living with her for years and years."

Lilith tore the note from her hand.

"Anne should have told you no such thing. Ladies know nothing of — of these matters."

"Well, they pretend they don't, but they must be blind and deaf to be unaware, I should think. It's not as though he hides her away. Why, he was with her that night at the opera. I recall distinctly. She was very lovely and elegant. Frenchwomen are so stylish, are they not?"

"I most certainly did not regard her," the aunt answered quellingly.

Unquelled, Cecily continued, "I was much amazed. I'd always thought trollops looked like the tavern maid at Squeebles. Molly's rather stout, but I daresay she's the best the gentlemen can find in the vicinity when they're of a mind for that sort of thing."

"Cecily — "

"I wonder if Lord Roberts's friend is witty and clever," the girl said meditatively. "They

164

say that's why Harriette Wilson is so popular. Certainly she's no great beauty. Still, she has a very generous figure, so perhaps it's not all conversation. When the horses are bred, you know, the stallions — "

"Cecily!"

"Well, they do go directly to it," the girl said, turning her innocent blue gaze to her aunt.

Mrs. Wellwicke covered her twitching mouth.

"It looks rather uncomfortable for the mares," the niece added. "No wonder the gentlemen must pay — "

"Cecily, pray hold your tongue," Lilith snapped. "It is bad enough these disagreeable objects are among us. Worse still that they should elicit such unladylike, immodest speculations. You see how depravity taints whatever is near it. I shall have a servant return this package immediately. Furthermore, as of this moment you are to have nothing to do with Lord Robert Downs. He is obviously not a fit person for an innocent girl to know."

She marched from the room, bearing the box well in front of her as though it were a chamber pot.

Cecily chased after her. "But Aunt, you can't mean it," she said. "It isn't his fault."

"We shall not discuss this before the entire household."

Cecily followed her aunt in silence down the stairs and into the study. She waited patiently while Lilith wrote a short note, sanded and sealed it, summoned a servant, and dispatched box and note to the modiste.

When they were alone, the girl tried again. "Dear Aunt, you know it isn't Lord Robert's fault the package was misdirected. It hardly seems fair to blame him — to cut him — because of an innocent mistake."

"Innocent?" Lilith echoed coldly. "Innocence does not purchase such immodest costumes for — for such persons. Innocence is not acquainted with such persons. And so you shall not be."

"Well, what on earth else is a gentleman to do? He must get his pleasure somewhere. That's how men are. I think it's far more sensible to keep a mistress than to take his chances in the streets and alleys."

"Gracious heavens, child, I cannot believe what I am hearing. Where on earth did you learn of these — these matters?"

"From Rodger." Cecily shrugged. "Though living in the country in a horse-breeding family isn't likely to keep me in ignorance, is it? Though I've never understood why I should be. How is a girl to protect herself when she doesn't know what to protect herself from?"

"She leaves her protection to her elders,"

her aunt said in awful tones. "Which is precisely the case at present. You will have nothing further to do with that man."

Further argument, as Cecily later informed her maid, was obviously futile.

"Still, I tried," she said with a sigh. "But I'm afraid Aunt Lilith is a bit irrational on the subject. It isn't logical at all. I'm sure half the gentlemen I know do far worse than Lord Robert does. Why, he's been with the same woman two whole years, Anne says. Other men are not so faithful to their wives."

"Mebbe when you've been a wife, you'll think different, miss."

"But I'm not a wife now, am I? At any rate, I certainly can't cut him without explanation. That would be monstrous rude, as well as unfair."

Accordingly, Cecily found her writing materials and immediately composed a note to the ill-used young man. When she attempted to hand the note to her maid, Susan demurred.

"Your aunt won't like it," the abigail said.

"Then obviously she'd better not know about it, had she?"

"But Miss Cecily — "

"Don't be tiresome, Susan. You know perfectly well how to get this note to him. You and Hobbs have passed along other pieces of news easily enough to his cousin."

The maid's mouth dropped open.

"I suppose you mean to marry one day, and wish to set something aside. I know Papa does not pay you very generously, so really, I can't blame you, can I?"

The maid stammered and protested, but her mistress only looking reproachful, Susan ended by muttering that Miss Cecily had always been a deal too *quick*.

"Well, I shall not pry into your private affairs," Cecily said magnanimously. "Everyone says Lord Brandon is irresistible, and of course he is dark and devilish-looking, so I collect you couldn't help yourself. Still, if you're not very discreet, my aunt will find out what you've been about, and I daresay she won't be best pleased."

She thrust the note into her mortified abigail's hand. "So you'd better be discreet, hadn't you?"

The note reached Lord Robert some hours later, when he and his cousin had returned to dress for the evening. Dressing being a wearying business, they had elected to fortify themselves first in the library with a glass of Madeira.

The note was presented on a silver salver.

Lord Robert took it, stared at it a moment, then opened it.

168

The butler glanced enquiringly at Lord Brandon, who shook his head and gestured the servant away.

Betraying not a smidgeon of interest, the marquess poured the wine and handed a glass to his cousin. The young man absently took it while he perused the note a second time. Finally he looked up.

"I have been cut off," Robert said in disbelief. "I am banned, banished, and outlawed." He handed the sheet of paper to his cousin. "Did you ever hear the like?"

The older man quickly skimmed the round schoolgirl script. "I have never *seen* the like," he answered. "She has not mis-spelt a single word. Moreover, she states the case so plainly and simply, it might be a receipt for a poultice. Most extraordinary."

"I told you she was level-headed. I only wish her aunt were. You'd think I'd tried to ravish the girl."

"You did not order up lingerie for Elise?"

"How should I know? We're always at the dressmaker's or the milliner's or somebody's. That is to say, of course I must have — but what's that to do with anything?"

Lord Brandon dropped gracefully into a chair. "It has everything to do with everything, Robin. Miss Glenwood is fresh from the schoolroom. She is not supposed to know of mistresses and their intimate attire. Now the girl is no longer ignorant, and, unluckily for you, Mrs. Davenant knows precisely where to pin the blame. This is what comes of excessive letter-writing."

"It's completely irrational. I'm banned because some fool servant delivered the wrong package to the wrong house. Banned — and I'm not even *courting* her niece, drat it. Does she mean to investigate the private affairs of every fellow who talks to the girl? Ventcoeur isn't banned, and he spends half his nights in the Covent Garden alleys. Even that loose fish, Beldon, who has the bailiff camped on his doorstep — "

"Their indiscretions have not been waved under Mrs. Davenant's nose as yours has been by this unfortunate accident. An accident of fate, Robin. Drink your wine and put the matter from your mind. We shall dine with Scrope Davies tonight and bury our disappointments in wine and laughter. He is a very amusing fellow, an intimate of Byron's. Perhaps the poet will join us. I understand he's decided not to accompany Hobhouse to Paris after all."

"He's a moody, pretentious bore," was the sulky answer.

"I admit he has not Miss Glenwood's immense blue eyes and guinea-gold curls, and being some years older and lame as well, he cannot be as lively — "

"It's nothing to do with her looks, Julian. It's the — the principle of the thing, dash it! Here I've been dutifully going about in company to pacify the family. I meet one girl who doesn't bore me out of my wits. At last there's someone sensible to talk to, so the evening isn't an endless punishment — and now I'm not to talk to her, not to go near her. I feel like a damned leper. Confound her aunt. Mrs. Drummond-Burrell isn't half such a prude."

Robert stomped to the tray and refilled his glass. "It's all the more astonishing to me now how you ever got such a stiff-necked prig to even speak to you — let alone dance with you."

"Perhaps I took advantage of a fit of temporary insanity," said the marquess. He rose. "I believe I shall dress now. You, of course, may amuse yourself as you wish. Freers will bring you another bottle when you have done soaking up that one. I expect he'll also provide a litter to carry you to bed when you have completed your liquid meditations."

Lord Robert had not meant to drink himself unconscious. Still, he was exceedingly put out, and in the course of execrating Mrs. Davenant at length, grew thirsty. Since he continued grumbling to himself for hours, he had frequent need to soothe his parched throat, with the result his cousin had predicted.

The young man awoke very late the following day and, suffering the usual consequences, was more out of sorts than ever. He spent that night in a fit of the sullens with his mistress.

Elise's forbearance only compounded Lord Robert's unhappy state, for she added a generous dollop of guilt to the already indigestible compound of indignation and frustration. Consequently, Robert spent the greater part of the following week in his cousin's company.

The constant companionship of a young man behaving like a petulant little boy must eventually irritate even the most serene of natures. Otherwise, Lord Brandon would have been his normal unruffled self. Certainly he could not be chafing yet over the mere pinprick of one lady's displeasure.

Lord Brandon had known he'd be unwise to seek the widow out immediately. He'd told himself she wanted time. She was not a stupid woman. Given time to reflect, she must surely come to see the injustice of her accusations. Being the soul of rectitude, she must therefore repent of them.

He was confident of this. The waiting was tiresome only because Robert was tiresome.

This, clearly, was the sole reason Lord Brandon rounded upon his cousin on the seventh night of Lord Robert's banishment, as they were leaving Watier's.

"What the devil is the matter with you?" the marquess snapped as they reached the street. You've been growling and sulking without cease for a week. I do wish you'd entertain your mistress with your megrims. She's paid to endure you. I merely have the misfortune to be related to you."

"Why should I talk when there's nothing to say? Everyone says the same things and makes the same jokes over and over. Why can't a man hold his tongue if he wants? He might as well, when he's a damned *leper*. An outcast. A — a — "

"A bloody bore is more like it. I see we are about to play once again the monotonous tune of your persecution."

"She danced twice tonight with Ventcoeur," muttered his unheeding cousin. "And twice with Maddock. And once with that lout, Beldon. And once with Melbrook. And she went in to supper with — "

"You've already been through the catalogue with me three times this night. Confound you, Robert. You might try to understand the aunt's position."

"She's a stiff-necked old cow. Aargh."

This last remark was occasioned by Lord Brandon's taking his cousin roughly by the neck-cloth and lifting him several inches off the ground.

As he put the young man down again and released the mangled cravat, the marquess said in low, dangerous tones, "Mind your manners, boy."

He was answered by a series of croaks as Lord Robert strove to recover from near strangulation. When he'd regained his wind, he apologised.

"That sounds more like reason," said Lord Brandon. "A reasonable man would understand that Mrs. Davenant was obliged to take the steps she did. A reasonable man would also clearly perceive her to be neither ancient nor in any way bovine. That her posture is stiff may be blamed upon the board strapped to her spine at a tender age. Your mama was once so accoutred. Ask her if you don't believe me."

Subdued, Robert withheld further comments until they were at the marquess's town house.

Never one to hold a grudge, Lord Brandon invited his cousin into the library for a brandy.

"I suppose," said Robert after sipping quietly for a time, "I have been rather disagreeable."

"I will not debate that."

"Still, you must admit the situation is provoking, fair or not."

"The situation is provoking," said Lord Brandon, gazing at the amber liquid in his glass, "though probably fair enough."

"Gad, I wish I had your cleverness. If it were you in my place, you'd have her talked round in no time."

"Would I? I wonder."

"What would you do in my place, Julian?"

"Whatever it is, I suppose I had better do it," came the bored reply. "Since you are not philosophical by nature, you'll go on worrying the thing forever. Even as a child, a word of denial would send you into fits for hours. Now you are a man, you have graduated to weeks."

"You mean you'll talk to her aunt?" Robert eagerly asked, disregarding the aspersions on his maturity.

"I shall try. But be warned, my impetuous cousin. I am not at present in Mrs. Davenant's good graces myself. My interference may do you more ill than good."

10

Though it was a nearly two-hour journey to Redley Park, no one who received an invitation thought of declining. The elderly Earl of Redley and his young countess were reclusive, rarely seen in Town. Once a year, however, they invited half the Beau Monde to a lavish entertainment on their sprawling estate.

There, champagne flowed like a mighty river, delicacies of every kind beckoned from the great table under its ornate canopy, while jugglers, magicians, and fortune-tellers practised their amusing arts. The atmosphere was that of a street fair, but untainted by the vulgar rabble that usually mobbed such events. For those of higher sensibilities, a string quartet performed in a shady arbor of the vast garden. Perhaps most delightful of all, the half who had been invited enjoyed the sweet prospect of lording it over the half who were not.

The house itself was a small, rather shabby relic of Tudor times, to which little except basic maintenance had been done in centuries. The Earls of Redley preferred to devote their energies and incomes to improving upon Nature.

For the previous earl, Lancelot "Capability" Brown had built gently rolling slopes where before had lain a generally flat expanse of meadow and woodland. A lake, replete with swans, now glistened where once had been a narrow stream and minuscule duck pond. Even the village had been relocated another mile distant, because the present Lord Redley's mama had complained of its cluttering the landscape.

Redley Park, in short, was a kingdom unto itself. It was also an excellent place in which to become lost, as amorous couples knew. Twisted, mazelike paths and shady, private nooks abounded, and so long as the heavens did not loose a downpour, one could always declare an urgent need to find shelter from the sun's fierce rays.

Following a luncheon best described as wretched excess, one after another lady made such complaints of the heat and glaring sun to Lord Brandon. He sympathised, he spoke charmingly, and then — to the bafflement of each lady in turn — he vanished.

It happened that, just as he eluded these others, one lady eluded him. Certainly, he always knew where to find her. The trouble was, she had constantly someone clinging to her like a leech — her companion, her fiancé, her future sister-in-law — and she and the leech of the moment would be found amid a group. One bodyguard Lord Brandon might detach her from; a host of them was too much even for his ingenuity.

He waited with mounting impatience until his opportunity arrived at last. His gaze lit upon Miss Glenwood just as she was slipping away from a crowd of young people watching a juggler. He glanced at Mrs. Davenant. She, excellent chaperon she was, had her eye upon her niece.

Lord Brandon promptly made for the niece.

He'd scarcely uttered two sentences before the aunt was upon them.

"Ah, Mrs. Davenant," he said. "I was about to recommend Miss Glenwood not allow herself to become separated from her friends. Redley Park is a veritable maze of paths and byways, and on her own, she might be lost for weeks."

"I know," said Miss Glenwood. "That's why I was looking for Anne. I can't think where she's got to."

Though she appeared not at all flustered, Lord Brandon was certain the girl was lying. The particular lie, however, was a gift from

Heaven. He decided he approved of Miss Glenwood.

"Your aunt and I shall find her, Miss Glenwood, never fear," said he. "You may watch the juggler with an easy mind."

The girl left, and he turned to Mrs. Davenant.

"Perhaps I was presumptuous," he said. "Perhaps you would prefer I sought Miss Cleveson on my own?"

"Thank you, my lord, but I'm sure Sir Thomas will be happy to assist me," she said stiffly.

"He is well-acquainted with Redley Park, I take it? If not, I must accompany you both, or we shall have three lost sheep instead of one."

He saw her glance towards Bexley. The baronet, true to form, had promptly got himself entangled with Clancarty.

She turned back to Lord Brandon, her cheeks tinged a faint pink. "He has never visited here before today, my lord, and — "

"And at present he is occupied with more momentous matters."

They soon spied Anne Cleveson, for she had hauled her brother only far enough from the others to quarrel without being overheard. From what Lilith caught of the debate — she and Brandon were several yards from

179

the two — Freddie had hurt Lady Shumway's granddaughter's feelings, and Anne, in her own way, had decided to call him out.

"Shall we leave them to their squabble, Mrs. Davenant?" said the marquess, moving towards an alternate path. "Miss Cleveson has the right of it, and he wants his ears blistered, I think."

Lilith was surprised, though perhaps she shouldn't be. The marquess was not, she knew to her shame, entirely without compassion.

"Indeed he does," she said. "Miss Twillworthy can't help her spots — not when her foolish grandmother overindulges her in sweets and keeps her trapped in that oppressive, musty house all the day. The girl scarcely ever goes out, but at night, like a little mole."

While she spoke, Lilith debated what to do. To go with him was asking for trouble. On the other hand, she had something to say that could not be said before others. The matter on her conscience proving powerful enough to squeeze out other anxieties, she walked on with him.

She had kept clear of Lord Brandon all the past week. Now they were alone, she knew she could no longer — and should not — shrink from the apology she owed him. Had he appeared as coldly hostile as he had that morning in the park, her task would have been easier. She might simply make her speech and, her duty done, exit quickly.

His amiability made her far more uncomfortable. Either he was a remarkably forbearing man or too careless and unfeeling to be affected by — to even recollect — the harsh, unjust accusations she'd flung at him.

It didn't matter what he was, she chided herself. She had made a grievous error and must apologise. She swallowed, lifted her chin, and spoke.

"My Lord, a few minutes ago you referred to — to ears being blistered. I believe — I know — that is — some days ago, we had words."

He stopped and looked at her. "We did. Mrs. Davenant, I do humbly beg your pardon for that. I was a beast. I was just this moment trying to compose my apology. Yet what expressions of regret could excuse me? I am still appalled by my behaviour. I never knew I had a temper, but I must have, because I lost it. And for what? Because you spoke some unpleasant truths."

"Unpleasant, yes, but the truth — "

"Oh, it was that."

"It was not," she blurted out guiltily. "It was not the truth you hastened my husband's death. He did that himself. It was not the truth you destroyed my marriage. It was wreck from the start. There was no repairing it, no matter how I — "

She hesitated, but that was foolish, when he knew already. His words the other day — as though he had known her intimately all those years ago, or had somehow looked into her heart. A generous heart, he had said. He must be generous, certainly, to forgive her and regret his own remarks.

"No matter how I tried," she said softly. Though tears pricked her eyes, there was relief, she found, in saying it aloud, finally, after all these years, and so she went on. "If I had been older and wiser, perhaps I would have seen the futility." Willing back the tears, she mustered up a smile. "Or perhaps not. I am supposedly older and wiser now, yet I needed you to point out my mistake."

"You are far more generous than I deserve. No more on this topic, I beg, or I shall commence sobbing uncontrollably."

A small titter escaped her, and she had to admire how deftly he'd drawn her back from perilous emotional waters.

He threw her an admiring glance. "What a remarkable girl you are," he said.

"Hardly a girl," she answered as she resumed walking.

"You are eight and twenty. I am seven years your senior. What do your calculations

182

make me, I wonder? Shall I order a Bath chair at once?"

Her smile broadened at the image. "Now, there's an intriguing picture. My Lord Brandon — a pair of spectacles upon his nose, a horn at his ear, shawls wound round him — being trundled about in a Bath chair."

"A fitting end. I know that's what you're thinking. You can't deny it."

"I should not presume to say what would be fitting in your case. Recollect I have but recently been tumbled from my throne of judgement."

"Then you must be in need of support."

He offered his arm and she, reluctant to spoil their truce, took it.

"If you continue in a penitential frame of mind," he said, "I had better hasten to take advantage. I have a case to plead with you. Not my own," he added before her newfound ease in his company could dwindle. "You may assume your wig once more, My Lady Judge. Take out your black cap if you will — though I hope you will not have occasion to don it."

"A cardinal offence, is it? Not murder, I hope."

"Not precisely, though a life is at stake, in a manner of speaking. A man's life or in the interests of accuracy — a fool's. My cousin, Robin."

His handsome face was serious now, or appeared so. Lilith thought she had better not study it too closely.

"I do not see how any judgement of mine could in any way affect Lord Robert's life," she said carefully. "If you refer, as I assume you do, to this business with Cecily — "

"I do, and I beg you to reconsider. I do not believe you acted wrongly. I have told him so myself, repeatedly, but he refuses to listen. In consequence, I've had to endure a week of his incessant complaints and gripes and sulks and sullens. If you will not take pity on him, I wish you would take pity on me. Another day of it and I shall shoot him."

His face was still grave, but his aggrieved tones made her grin. "I am to be responsible for your cousin's murder and your own hanging, my lord? Is that not excessive?"

"You would not say so if he were moping and grumbling the livelong day in *your* house, or if you had the hauling of his morose carcass about."

"You cannot be hinting he is serious about Cecily. He cannot have serious intentions towards two women simultaneously. I need not, I hope, remind you of the moral character of one of these women."

"Miss Glenwood is the only human being who has managed to draw Robert from the *demimonde.* I cannot say what his feelings are. I know only that since he met her, he has neglected his mistress. He has taken up quarters in my house — he who would scarcely leave his paramour's side for an hour, is gone from her days at a time."

"Yet he continues to send her gifts."

"When passion dwindles, one often finds presents easier to give than time and attention. In any event, the less time he devotes to his mistress and the more among his social equals, the better his chances of finding a more suitable object in the family's eyes, at least."

"I do not prevent his enjoying good society," she said.

"Miss Glenwood's is the only society that interests him at present. Banished from her, he is bored and fretful. Worse, with each passing day, the risk increases he'll return to his mistress." He paused briefly, as though to allow implications to sink in. "I'm convinced Robert means your niece no harm. Still, I shall promise to keep a close watch on him, if you will be so compassionate as to end his exile."

She did not answer immediately, though she knew what her reply must be. She who had accused Brandon of leading her husband astray could not refuse to help lead another man aright.

"You are an eloquent solicitor, my lord," she said at last. "I seem to be hoist by my own petard."

"Not at all. I counted on your generous heart." His gaze was warm.

Lilith looked away. "The heart that concerns me is Cecily's. If I discern any signs of infatuation — unreturned, that is — "

"Then I shall knock the lad unconscious and drop him onto the first vessel bound for New South Wales."

"I do not demand so extreme a remedy. Paris will do," she said magnanimously. "Or Rome. With the end of hostilities, I expect half the Beau Monde will be flocking abroad."

"With the hostilities ended, the Continent is not so interesting to me," he said, a shade of meaning in his voice. Then, more briskly, he went on, "At any rate, Redley and his ancestors have transported half the Continent here. What works of art they could not buy or steal outright, I understand, they copied. There was once and I expect may still be an excellent reproduction of Bernini's 'Apollo and Daphne' round the next turning. Will you permit me to expound upon its aesthetic qualities?"

The path, shaded by enormous rhododendrons, opened into a large clearing, in the centre of which the statue stood. The shrubbery all around was tall and dense. A narrow opening through the leaves indicated yet another path, leading heaven knew where. The foliage was too thick to permit more than a glimpse of the way beyond. The place was quiet, except for the occasional ruffling of leaves in the light breeze.

"I was mistaken," said Lord Brandon as they approached the sculpture. "This, as I recall, is the work of Lord Redley's artistic great-grandfather. He called it 'The Abduction of Helen.' The pose obviously owes something to Bernini's 'Pluto and Persephone' — though I never considered the two ladies' cases quite the same. I prefer to believe Helen went with Paris of her own free will."

He had already treated Lilith to several amusing theories regarding the expected Bernini. He was surprisingly well-read. Lilith wondered wryly when he'd found time for books. She had known he could be charming, but she'd expected a more shallow, social charm. She had not expected to find his conversation quite so . . . stimulating.

She smiled up at his sun-dappled face. "You think Helen willingly abandoned the throne of Sparta? Were Greek women so impractical, then?"

"I have decided she was very young, in an alien land, the husband chosen for her an old, insensitive lout. Paris appeared, and the two young beauties were instantly smitten. They tried to be discreet, but their affair was betrayed to Menelaus. Helen fled with her lover to escape a horrible death."

Lilith laughed. "Leave it to you to devise extenuating circumstances."

"I can't help it. I am a hopeless romantic." There was a pause — two heartbeats, maybe more.

Then, in lower tones, he went on. "I can guess, at least, what the Trojan must have felt when he met Sparta's queen. In my vision she is tall, proud, and spirited, with eyes like Poseidon's storms and hair tinged with Hephaistos' fire."

Lilith's smile faded, along with her quiet pleasure in his company.

He was no longer looking at the statue, she knew, though she dared not meet his gaze. She must not listen, she told herself. He was too perceptive, too clever, and honeyed speeches came too easily to him. With forced calm, she disengaged her arm from his and walked to the entwined marble figures.

"Have you seen the Bernini?" she asked, keeping her voice light. "Is this very like, do you think?"

"I'm afraid at the moment I can't think." He moved up behind her. "I should not have brought you here. I should never be alone with you. Every good resolution I've made is smashed to pieces."

His breath was warm on her neck.

"My lord — "

"Lilith." It was a whisper, and his lips touched her neck, light as a whisper, yet the touch seared her.

He is the Devil, she told herself. It is all practised wickedness. But his lips had touched her neck again, and the hand gently clasping her arm burned too. A dangerous yearning incandesced within her. He turned her unresisting, betraying body towards him.

"I meant to be good," he said softly, sadly, it seemed, as his face lowered to hers. "I cannot."

"No — "

His mouth silenced her and her lips answered his kiss, just as her body answered the light pressure of his hands urging her closer. Light, yes, and gentle, yes, but she was helpless against the current drawing her to him. There was too much tenderness in its beckoning. She, who had never known tenderness of any kind, who had never heard sweet words of longing, could not resist what he offered, but hungered only for more.

She knew nothing of moments passing, nothing of the world about her. There was one world only, in his arms, a world that smouldered, then glowed, then crackled into flame against a growing darkness. There she was lost, utterly.

Lord Robert, emerging from the other path, immediately turned and pushed Cecily back.

"That wasn't at all necessary," she reproached when they were out of range. "You can't think I would burst upon my aunt without warning. I hope I'm not such a clodpole."

"Your eyes are a deal too sharp, Miss Glenwood," he complained. "We'd better go back — or I shall be in your aunt's black books *forever.*"

"We can't leave them like this."

"We most certainly can. They're adults. It's none of our business."

"What if someone else comes? My aunt will be ruined."

Lord Robert forbore rejoining that Mrs. Davenant was as good as ruined already, if that passionate embrace was any indication. "I am not going to stand guard until they're done," he said. Then, as he recollected what getting done would inevitably entail, he added primly, "And you certainly will not."

"Don't be silly. We must simply give them a moment to recover themselves. Lord Robert," she said, so loudly that he winced, "you must go away. You should not have followed me. My aunt will be most displeased."

"Miss Glenwood — "

"Louder," she whispered. "Don't be such a slow-top. Argue with me — or plead — or something — but so they can hear you."

The feminine voice pierced Lord Brandon's consciousness like a gunshot, though it took another moment for the message to be relayed elsewhere. Then, cursing inwardly, he reluctantly raised his lips from the widow's right earlobe. Her eyes fluttered open.

"Someone is coming," he said, his voice thick.

Instantly, Lilith jerked away from him, leaving chill emptiness where her warm, supple body had just been. Forgetting other voices, he reached out instinctively to draw her back, but she had moved apart. With trembling hands, she was trying to smooth her frock and her hair simultaneously.

He heard Robert then, complaining loudly. Lord Brandon bestowed another silent though heartfelt malediction upon his cousin. "I shall *kill* him," he muttered. "Was ever a man so cursed in his relations?"

He looked to her again, and felt a stab within. She was still flushed and utterly discomposed. Unlike many of her noble sisters, she was unaccustomed to coolly erasing evidence of an indiscretion. Her eyes appealed to him for help.

He moved to her, quickly smoothed a few curls from her face, and twitched the waist of her dowdy grey frock aright.

"It's only the children," he said. "Appear enraptured with the sculpture."

The children came into view minutes later, stopped abruptly as they caught sight of their elders, and showed every evidence of surprise and confusion.

Cecily hastened to her aunt. "Please do not be angry, Aunt. We came upon each other quite by accident. I was just telling Lord Robert that I am not to speak to him, because I might say that at least, mightn't I?"

"Mrs. Davenant, I do apologise," said Lord Robert. "It's all my fault — "

"Certainly," Lord Brandon interjected. "It is always your fault. Here I have been trying to explain the misunderstanding, and this lady has not only kindly heard me out, but graciously allowed you a second chance. Now you blunder in like the confounded, clumsy idiot I have just been telling her you are not," he finished with some heat.

The widow found her voice, though he detected a slight quaver as she spoke.

"We shall not compound one misunderstanding with another. Naturally, your meeting with Cecily was an accident." Her gaze fell upon Cecily. "I know my niece would never deliberately disobey me. Therefore I cannot entertain for a moment the notion she arranged, behind my back, to meet with you."

"Oh, never," said Lord Robert chivalrously.

He reddened, though, and the marquess had no doubt why.

"Lord Brandon tells me you are the . . . the victim of a hoax," the widow went on.

Brandon gazed at her in surprise. That was inventive of her. A hoax would serve admirably.

"Did he? Yes, well, I am — was — that is to say — "

"Then we shall consider the matter closed, Lord Robert. Though I should advise you in future to choose friends with less distasteful notions of humour. I will not have my niece suffer further shocks to her sensibilities."

"No ma'am. You're quite right. Thank you, ma'am. You're exceedingly kind. Really, I — "

"As to you, Cecily," Mrs. Davenant said, disregarding Lord Robert's protestations, "I thought you had already been advised against wandering off by yourself."

As she spoke, she put her arm protectively

193

about her niece's shoulders and took the girl away, so that Lord Brandon heard nothing of the ensuing lecture.

He heard as little of his cousin's expressions of gratitude and wonder, although Robert walked beside him. They had taken the other path. While it was a more circuitous route to the party proper, Lord Brandon was in no hurry to be back. His rage with his cousin had subsided, yet the marquess was not quite as easy within as he appeared without.

He was still irritated, which was foolish, when naturally matters could not have proceeded to any satisfactory conclusion. He'd no intention of ravishing Lilith Davenant in broad day in somebody's garden. The problem was, he'd no intention of allowing matters to go even as far as they had done.

He knew by now that her conjugal experiences with Charles had not been happy ones. That was why she was so skittish. Accordingly, Brandon had taken care not to lead her too far too soon.

The trouble was, he'd found himself drawn too far, from pleasure . . . to hunger, and long after she'd broken from him, the feeling remained, like an ache. It lingered yet, not so strong as at first, but uncomfortable nonetheless. It should not have existed at all. Lovemaking was an art, not the mere release of some base animal need.

Impatience, he reassured himself. He'd never had to woo so long or face so many obstacles. What aroused him was the difficulty and challenge of this pursuit. The seduction of Lilith Davenant was proving a more exhilarating and novel experience than he could have predicted. Since it *was* novel, one must expect the occasional aberration.

These reflections eased his mind considerably, and he began at last to respond to his chattering cousin. Occupied in devising ironic sallies to Lord Robert's effusions, the marquess neglected to explain satisfactorily to himself the other, altogether different twinge he experienced from time to time, at the recollection of one pleading pair of smoky blue eyes.

11

Members of the company who'd noticed Lilith's departure with Lord Brandon held their collective breath while counting the minutes until her return. They would have all been asphyxiated if Lady Fevis hadn't decided to have her fortune told.

The Future was no sooner revealed than the heretofore sweet and gentle Lady Fevis burst from the gypsy's tent, flew at her husband, and began thumping his head with her parasol. When the weapon was wrenched away by her mama, and her husband dragged away to safety, the enraged wife fell back momentarily. She collected herself, then made another mad rush — this time at Lady Violet Porter, whose hazel eyes Lady Fevis showed every inclination to tear from their sockets.

Mr. Porter tried to pull Lady Fevis away from his wife. Lady Fevis's brother, Mr. Reginald Ventcoeur, ordered him to remove his filthy hands. Mr. Porter made an uncomplimentary observation. Mr. Ventcoeur rushed forward, spun Mr. Porter round, and knocked him down. Mr. Porter jumped up and rushed at Mr. Ventcoeur and brought *him* down. The two young men commenced to savagely pummelling each other.

Lady Violet screamed. Lady Fevis fainted. Friends rushed forward to help. Two gentlemen, trying to separate the foes, knocked their own heads together. Instantly, they gave up pacifism and began flailing at each other. One of Mr. Ventcoeur's friends was heard to make a remark regarding "horns." Two of Mr. Porter's friends immediately fell upon him.

In short order, thanks to the enlivening effects of large quantities of champagne, nearly all the younger gentlemen had thrown themselves into the battle. Of their elders, the greater part busily made wagers, while an unheeded minority called for order.

It was during the melee that Cecily slipped off to her forbidden rendezvous with Lord Robert. He, having retired to a distance to await her, was unaware of the excitement until it was well over.

In fact, the battle itself lasted scarcely five minutes. The confusion it engendered, however, continued long after. Though the ladies of the company had been led away to safety, a score felt duty bound to fall into swoons or strong hysterics. Between tending to these and the male wounded, considerable time and effort was expended in restoring tranquillity to Redley Park.

Thus, except for those directly concerned, not one person of the several hundred realised Mrs. Davenant had been gone with Lord Brandon nearly an hour. She rejoined her battle-weary fellows to find her reputation safe. Of her virtue, Lilith was not so certain.

The first time Lord Brandon had kissed her, at Cecily's comeout, he'd taken Lilith by surprise. Though this scarcely made it right, it was an excuse of sorts. Unfortunately, such a frail excuse works but once. What she'd done this time didn't bear thinking of.

Had her schooling in deportment been less mercilessly thorough, Lilith could never have faced her fiancé. As it was, the strain soon told in the usual way, with a headache. Fortunately, she never needed to plead illness. Thomas was eager to be gone from a party that had turned into a thoroughly barbaric spectacle.

Though Lilith said little during the ride home, her silence went unremarked. Cecily was too busy trying to extricate details about the contretemps from tight-lipped Sir Thomas. He refused to discuss the cause, except to speak vaguely of silly misunderstandings and a lot of ill-mannered youths drinking more than was good for them.

On the subject of manners, he grew more talkative. Striking one another with fists and rolling upon the ground like a lot of Cockney ruffians was not Sir Thomas's idea of gentlemanly behaviour.

One of the combatants had been thrown against a servant who carried a tray of champagne glasses. The tray, sent spinning into the air, had struck the back of Sir Thomas's head. He was lucky, he told the ladies, not to have been cut to shreds by broken glass. It was the sort of episode one might expect in a gin shop — not at a great society affair.

"Young men nowadays," he intoned, "have no notion of self-restraint. I can only blame this obnoxious fad for boxing. In my day, the gentry set the example. They did not imitate their inferiors. But what can one expect of fellows who consider it the height of fashion to adopt the costume and manners — or lack thereof — of common coachmen?"

"Well, I'm sure it was very disagreeable for you," said Cecily. "All the same, I do think fists preferable to pistols and swords. I'm glad duelling is illegal. It may be more elegant, but it's also far more deadly. I do wish I knew what had started it," she added with a sigh. "I should like to have something exciting to write Rodger."

Lilith was not altogether surprised to see Lord Brandon at Almack's the following night, though the assembly hall's staid exclusivity, unappetizing refreshments, and inept orchestra could scarcely appeal to a man of his cosmopolitan tastes. He *would* come, of course, because he was the last person on earth she wished to see. She had but to glimpse his gleaming black hair and broad shoulders, and every mortifying detail of the previous afternoon came back to flog her conscience.

When he approached, her heart raced. But the marquess stopped only long enough to exchange a few civilities with her and Thomas.

Brandon danced with several ladies, including two of the patronesses and, to Lilith's astonishment, Lady Enders, who blushed and giggled throughout. He also danced twice with a very pale Lady Fevis. The second was a waltz, during which the lady's colour and spirits revived remarkably. Lord Fevis's colour was observed to heighten about the same time. When the next set commenced, he gratified the company by stalking up to his wife to announce it was time to go *home*.

Eventually, Lilith realised she was studying Lord Brandon's movements more intently than was seemly. Her gaze went immediately in search of her niece.

Lilith's eye lit upon Cecily just as Lord Robert was taking the girl's hand. The widow did a rapid calculation and began to move even more rapidly across the hall. Before she could reach them, she saw Lord Brandon approach, say something to Robert, then lead Cecily out.

The marquess brought Cecily back to her aunt at the dance's end.

"You needn't scold her," he said. "I've just rung a peal over them both. Robert apparently experiences difficulties with higher mathematics."

"I'm so sorry, Aunt," said Cecily. "I had my mind on something Anne said and forgot completely I wasn't to dance with any gentleman more than twice."

"There are some matters one has not the luxury of forgetting," Lilith said repressively. "In future, Cecily — "

She was interrupted by the arrival of Mr. Ventcoeur, who, sporting a swollen upper lip and bruised jaw, had come to claim his dance.

When the younger man had swept Cecily to safety, Lord Brandon turned to Lilith. "Will you do me the honour, Mrs. Davenant?"

"No, thank you." She managed a polite smile for the benefit of any interested onlookers.

"I knew you would refuse. I kept away so I would not be tempted to ask. It's no good, you know. There's no substitute for dancing with you — a matter *I* have not the luxury of forgetting." He turned his gaze to the dancers.

Though she wished he would go away, Lilith was obliged to acknowledge the service he'd performed.

"Thank you for rescuing Cecily from her mistake," she said, her eyes, too, upon the dance floor.

"I promised to keep watch on Robert. At any rate, it was the least I could do. Miss Glenwood's timely appearance stopped me in the midst of a greater error yesterday. I should have had more care for your reputation, regardless the heat of the moment," he added gently. "I was abominably selfish and thoughtless."

Her chin went up. "My reputation is not in your keeping, my lord," she answered. "You will please refrain from making me out to be a helpless victim of your irresistible charm. I resent your implying I do not know right from wrong. I am not a backward child." With another polite smile, she left him.

The next morning, Lilith chaperoned Lord Robert and Cecily on yet another attempt to break their own and the horses' necks simultaneously.

The black stallion and its master arrived moments after the young pair had dashed across the meadow.

"Is this not devotion?" his lordship asked. "To arise at such an hour, merely to speak with you?"

"I wish," she said tautly, "Lord Robert did not make a habit of revealing his plans to everybody."

"He had no need to tell me. I had but to observe his retiring betimes and hear him at daybreak clomping down the stairs. Not that I wouldn't have stretched him on a rack for the information, had that been necessary. You cannot tease me with provocative statements, madam, and expect to be left in peace."

She stared blindly ahead, trying to recall exactly what she'd said the night before, when the marquess had so infuriated her.

"You set me down for taking the blame all to myself for our . . . indiscretion," he reminded. "Now I'm on pins and needles to know whether or not you've concluded it was entirely your fault. Was it you led *me* astray, Mrs. Davenant?"

Her face grew warm. "You know that is not what I meant."

"What did you mean, then?"

"I wish you would not affect stupidity. It is another insult to my intelligence."

"I want to know exactly what you meant," he said stubbornly. "Your remarks might be construed in several ways. Shall I conclude you came with me knowingly and willingly? I should very much like to believe that."

"Though I'm engaged to be married, my lord? I know you have little regard for such commonplaces as vows — but have you so much contempt for me as to believe I deliberately — Why do I ask?" Lilith said bitterly. "I've earned your contempt. You were selfish and thoughtless, you said. Does that excuse *me?*" she asked, pressing her hand to her thumping heart. "I'm no cypher. I have a mind — and a will — and morals — or so I thought. But now I scarce know what to think myself."

He dismounted, threw the reins over a bush, and approached her. "Come down," he said, holding up his hands.

"No."

"Don't make me pull you from the saddle, Lilith."

His hands grasped her waist, and she, seeing no alternative, cooperated. She caught her breath as her body brushed his in the process, but in an instant she was on solid ground and he'd let go of her waist to take her hand instead. Even through the leather glove, she felt

204

pulse beating against pulse.

"More than once," he said, "you've spoken of my contempt for you. As if that weren't bad enough, you persist in claiming you've earned it. Because of a few kisses, a few caresses? Be sensible, Lilith. If my disdain is so easily earned, what must I think" — he paused and smiled — "well, of the other women, you know."

She would not be weakened by that slow, affectionate smile. "I've never believed you could have a high opinion of women," she said. "If you had, you wouldn't make a habit of using and discarding them."

"Such habits reflect the frailty of my own character. Therefore, I should be the object of contempt."

"It's always the women despised in these cases for their weakness."

"That's what Society says, and Society is composed merely of human beings, as fallible as ourselves."

"It's hardly necessary for Society to point out my error. No one need remind me I've been false to my betrothed — twice — or that I ought — " She stopped herself.

Too late.

"I see," he said. "You're in torments because conscience tells you to break off your engagement, while self-preservation warns you'd better not."

"I have no intention of sacrificing my entire future because of a few foolish moments," she answered frigidly, drawing her hand away. That sounded mercenary, she knew. Very well, then. Let him think her so. She had rather that than his pity.

He was silent a moment, studying her flushed face.

"Odd," he said. "I persist in seeing your betrothal as the sacrifice. Why did you accept him, Lilith?"

"I know you have a low opinion of Thomas. Try to understand that others may not share it."

"I'm trying to understand *you*," he answered gently. "Your conscience demands you pay a debt you don't owe me. The same conscience insists you marry a man you believe you've played false. The one I may ascribe to pride. The other? The better I know you, the more difficult it is to explain satisfactorily."

She turned a bit away from him. "You don't know me."

"Not well, perhaps. I know what all the world does — that you're a model of breeding and deportment. But I know also that you're astonishingly well-informed. Also, you have an eye for the ridiculous and thus a proper appreciation of my wit." He paused, then added

206

more somberly, "And I know you're in pain. I can't be the cause of all your trouble. You were suffering before you met me."

He touched her shoulder lightly, to turn her back to him again. "You don't want me for a lover . . . and I suppose I must accept that."

"Yes, I wish you would."

"May I be a friend, then?"

"A friend?" she echoed, incredulous.

"Yes. To tell your troubles to. Why should you not, when I know so many already? By now you must be aware I don't repeat all I know."

"I know you can be inscrutable when it pleases you."

"Also sympathetic. However, we must draw the line at your crying upon my shoulder or into my neck-cloth. No matter how great the emotion, there is no excuse for wrinkling fabric. Not to mention the proximity of . . . well, we won't mention it." All the same, his eye fell upon her somber riding hat.

She remembered how, a few days before, his fingers had lovingly stroked her hair. Though at the moment she wanted solace, she was wary of that species of comforting.

"I don't think we can be friends," she said. "Not, at least, the confiding sort."

He seemed to be studying her face still,

though he answered lightly enough. "Very well. Let us be the gossiping sort, then. What do you make of Lady Fevis's extraordinary behaviour?"

Lady Fevis's rout was that evening.

Routs are intended to be crushes. Always there must be more people than square feet to accommodate them. This one was a suffocation.

Cecily had elected to go with Anne Cleveson and her mama to a small card party. Cecily, her aunt reflected as yet another person trod upon her toes, had better sense than to go to a gathering the sole purpose of which was to make everybody hot, tired, bruised, and — since refreshments were rarely provided — hungry and thirsty as well.

Lilith stood next her betrothed. He was reviewing with Lord Gaines the Grand Duchess's latest machinations on behalf of Princess Caroline. The two men had been talking nearly half an hour, and Thomas was just getting his steam up.

Lilith was very weary with standing in one place listening to the same opinions she'd heard two dozen times before. The air was stale and heavy with clashing perfumes. She would have liked to step away, to try to find a cooler, less crowded spot, if such was to be found. Around her on all sides was an impenetrable mass of bodies — some, she noted, in grievous want of soap and water.

She interrupted Thomas to remind him they hadn't yet greeted their hostess.

"Yes, my dear," he said. "Certainly. In a moment." Then he turned back to Lord Gaines.

Lilith gazed about her in despair. She was looking longingly down at the staircase they'd scaled with such difficulty when her gaze fell upon a head of crisply curling hair, black as midnight. Lord Brandon looked up at that moment. The boredom left his green eyes, and he smiled.

It had taken Lilith and Thomas twenty minutes to move from the first landing to the first floor. Lord Brandon covered the distance in one tenth the time. In another minute, he was at her side.

"Mrs. Davenant looks ready to faint, Bexley," said the marquess. "Shall I hew a path for her to an open window?"

"Oh, yes — That is . . . are you ill, my dear? Only too happy, of course, if my lord Gaines would — "

Lord Brandon assured the baronet there was no need to interrupt government business. "I must seek out our hostess in any case," he said. "I daresay she's chosen an

209

airier position for herself."

The preoccupied Thomas managed a nod before plunging back into his debate.

They found Lady Fevis by a window embrasure at the far end of the corridor.

She appeared very embarrassed, and very young, as they came upon her. "I did not mean to hide from the company," she explained, "but I needed a breath of air, and this is the only place where any is to be found."

"If you will share it with Mrs. Davenant, she will be much obliged," said Lord Brandon.

"Oh, of course. I do beg your pardon, Mrs. Davenant. I know these affairs are supposed to be shocking squeezes, but this is altogether unbearable — and all because I was — "

At which point, she swooned.

Brandon caught her, lifted her easily in his arms, and carried her to the nearest room. Lilith meanwhile got the attention of a servant and, adjuring him to complete discretion — lest the entire crowd bear down upon his mistress at once — ordered water and *sal volatile*.

Lady Fevis came to before the remedies arrived, but Lilith made her sip the water and lie still while Lord Brandon went in search of her husband.

They returned a few minutes later. Lord

Fevis rushed to his wife, fell to his knees before her, clasped her hands, and cried, "My poor darling! Oh, such an idiot I've been. The woman was nothing to me, I promise, nothing. Oh, but Clarissa, my dearest, why did you not tell me?"

The marquess was already escorting Lilith from the room. He closed the door upon the reunited couple.

"She ought to have told him, you know," he said as he led her back to the secluded embrasure. "A man has a right to know he's going to be a papa."

"How did *you* know?" Lilith asked, astonished. "She could not have told you such a thing when you danced with her."

"When I danced with her? When was that?"

Lilith looked up at him. His green eyes glittered wickedly.

"I had no idea my actions were under such close scrutiny," he said. "I must exercise more caution in future."

"You are a coxcomb," she said.

"If I were, I should not have been surprised at your knowledge of my dance partners. Yet I'm altogether amazed . . . and flattered. This is a far cry from invisibility."

She returned his gaze, her face expressionless. "When I cross the street," she said, "I look up to make certain no vehicles are bearing recklessly down upon me. I also look down, to make sure no noisome object lies in my path. I have found it necessary in recent weeks to observe similar precautions at social events."

He laughed. "A reckless vehicle is apt enough — but the other? I am put in my place, just goddess. Your hair curls naturally, doesn't it?"

"Yes," she said, uncomfortable to find the talk redirected so speedily to her person.

"I thought so. You've never had to suffer the indignities of curl papers or scorching tongs."

"Not those, no."

"But others? What were they? Steel corsets when you were but a babe?"

"We will not speak of such garments, if you please," she said in her best *grande dame* manner. "I meant applications of lemon juice, three times a day, day after day, week in and week out."

"Ah, *freckles*," he said. "Ghastly things."

"Well, they were."

"Don't be silly. I'm sure you were adorable with your freckles."

"I was not remotely adorable. I was too tall and too skinny, and my hair was too red, and I had forty-seven freckles upon my nose alone."

"Then I wonder they never stood you in a field to frighten away the birds. You might have made yourself useful," he said in tones of reproof. "Still, it is a relief to know you, too, had a misspent youth."

She bit her lip, but the vision of a gawky, adolescent Lilith standing haplessly in a field of newly seeded corn was too much for her, and what began as a titter swelled into laughter.

"Mrs. Davenant," he said sternly, "a misspent youth is nothing to be giggling about."

"A scarecrow," she said, still smiling. "Isn't it odd that I'm one now? Flapping my arms to frighten off any wicked gentlemen birds from my nieces."

"Protecting the tender young crop."

"Yes."

"Someone must, I suppose."

"Yes." Her smile faded. The mischief was gone from his eyes, and compassion had taken its place.

"That is why," he said almost inaudibly.

She pretended not to hear, though she knew what he meant and what she had, unwittingly, revealed to his too-keen perceptions.

"Thomas will be wondering what's become of me," she said coolly enough, though her voice sounded shrill to her ears.

Lord Brandon returned Mrs. Davenant to her intended, then, more perturbed than he'd ever expected to be, left the Fevis house.

He'd known about the nieces and their Seasons with their widowed aunt. He hadn't suspected she financed these ventures single-handedly, though now he recollected that there had been some oblique reference to the matter in his conversation with Higginbottom.

He should have realised. If Mrs. Davenant was too proud to let him cancel Charles's debt, she must be too proud to accept Bexley merely for her own financial security. She must have more compelling reasons for so ludicrous a match.

Still, this information changed nothing, Lord Brandon reminded himself. He'd never intended to break up her engagement. There was no reason Bexley should not marry her . . . after. No reason she should not continue presenting nieces until she had daughters of her own to bring out. A dozen daughters if she liked. A dozen fiery-haired, tall, passionate creatures like their mama.

He frowned. Or bland, tiresome, priggish, prating creatures like Bexley.

Gad, what did it matter? She would dote upon them even if they all looked like Lady Shumway's unfortunate granddaughter.

"You will *not*," he told himself firmly as he headed for the Cocoa Tree, "contemplate the *getting* of these grotesqueries."

12

"The blue silk?" Sally said, aghast. "But Mrs. Davenant don't wear blue. Brown, grey — "

"If you know what Suzette makes for her, then you must know as well why she doesn't give Suzette her custom any more," said Madame Germaine as she nudged her assistant towards the rack in the sewing room.

"That was because Suzette sent some tart's negligees, and Mrs. Davenant is very prim and proper," Sally answered stubbornly. "She'll take a fit if you show her the blue, mark my words."

"Seeing you're so wise, I wonder you don't open your own shop."

Thus silencing her assistant, Madame Germaine drew out the slate-blue gown she'd made for Lady Diana Stockmore before her ladyship had discovered she was increasing. "They're nearly a size," she went on thoughtfully. "We can do the alterations in a minute."

Sally groaned. "But, missus, we're over our ears as it is."

216

"The others can wait. Everyone knows Mrs. Davenant pays her bills as soon as she gets them."

"Oh, no," said Mrs. Davenant when the slate-blue silk was displayed. "Nothing for me. My niece only."

"And Sally's measuring her at this moment, isn't she? Such a lovely girl Miss Glenwood is. I'm sure anything we put on her will do us credit. Still, it takes time to measure properly. There's no careless haste in *my* shop, Mrs. Davenant."

"I shall be content to look at your pattern books," said Lilith, though her glance lingered upon the tempting silk.

"Madam," said the modiste. "I scorn flattery. I will *not* say this gown was made for you. It was made for another lady. But just once I'd like to see it on a proper figure before I have to cut it to pieces for some dab of a creature and trick it out with ruffles to make it look *dainty*." She spoke disparagingly, though she had a score of petite customers whom she happily garbed.

"I suppose we giantesses are few and far between," said Lilith wryly.

"Giantess, indeed. And you so slender and well-proportioned — and with such posture." She led Lilith to the dressing room. "I'll assist you myself," she said as though she were bestowing the Order of the Bath.

The slate-blue silk appeared at Lady Gaines's ball that evening.

"I was sure my eyes were playing tricks on me," said Lord Robert, glancing past Cecily towards a corner of the room. "I couldn't believe that woman was your aunt, even when I heard her speak."

"You did stare, rather," said Cecily.

"Everyone's staring — not that you can see her for the crowd about her. Why, she looks ten years younger. What a difference a frock makes!"

"And to think we have your naughty friends to thank for it," said Cecily. "If they hadn't played their joke, Aunt Lilith wouldn't have changed dressmakers. Madame Germaine must have a gift for managing her customers. She managed my aunt beautifully. Still, I'll take some credit, because I did persuade Aunt Lilith to let Mary cut her hair a bit."

"Well, I never thought I'd say so, Miss Glenwood, but your aunt is a stunner. No wonder Julian — " Scarcely missing a beat, he went on, "Is that a new scent? You remind me of a garden after a spring shower."

"Damp and mouldy, you mean. What a pleasant compliment."

218

"That isn't what I meant at all. Clean and sweet and fresh."

"I'm glad you think so. Your cologne is much more agreeable than Mr. Ventcoeur's, so I'm sure your judgement must be sound."

Lord Brandon stood by the French doors leading onto the terrace. The doors were open now. Prinny having come and gone, the company might at last inhale fresh air. The marquess might have stood nearer Lilith Davenant half the night without calling undue attention to himself, since there was a respectable crowd of gentlemen about her. He'd tried that already, and didn't like it.

Unlike the others, Lord Brandon had not needed to see Mrs. Davenant costumed in a becoming gown to know she was desirable. Nonetheless, he could not have guessed the impact such a gown would have upon him.

At first, it was her hair he'd noticed. The tightly braided coils had disappeared the night of her niece's comeout. Even so, the widow's style remained far too severe for a young woman of eight and twenty. Tonight, however, gleaming auburn curls danced wantonly about her face. The rest was caught up loosely behind, so that she looked tumbled, as though she'd just risen from her pillows.

Then he'd bent over her hand, and a

creamy, silken expanse of bosom swam into his vision in swelling curves. He'd caught his breath . . . and remained breathless as his gaze slid discreetly over the smoky blue fabric that gleamed softly against alabaster skin and clung lovingly to her long-legged, supple figure. A wave of hot impatience had washed over him then, and he told himself he'd waited long enough.

Yet the marquess waited now, standing idly by the terrace doors, his habitual expression of lazy boredom masking the discontent within.

He'd grown wary of this restiveness. More than once it had led him to rush his fences, which had meant time wasted repairing the damage. He knew himself better now. He must not seek her out when he was chafing. If she wouldn't come to him, he'd let it go this evening and entertain himself elsewhere. All the same, knowing he wanted no elsewhere, no other, he *willed* her to come to him.

An hour passed while he watched his friends gravitate to her. In that time he saw a dozen expressions cross her face. They were unreadable to others, perhaps — the faintest trails of expression crossing her cool countenance.

All the same, Lord Brandon comprehended her confusion and surprise, and every phase leading her gradually to understand that the gentlemen suddenly found her very attractive. He read the widow's feelings as easily as if they'd been writ out in bold letters above her head. Then, as he perceived the faint flush of pleasure and slow, beguiling curve of her mouth, he found himself smiling as well. Whatever else he'd wanted of her, it was not her unhappiness. Her own kin first, then Davenant, had given her enough of that. Yet it never ceased to amaze the marquess that so desirable a woman should have so low an opinion of herself.

Before the hour elapsed, Brandon watched her stand up with her betrothed and be taken from him in the next set by Lord Worcester, who relinquished her in the next to Brummell.

It was Brummell brought her to the marquess when the dance had ended. This was to settle a dispute.

"Mrs. Davenant insists it is *not* milk baths," the Beau announced, "but the consumption of vegetables and exercise in the open air accounts for her flawless complexion. Bexley will not tell me whether this is cruel teasing, for he is blasting Hamilton about some tiresome political triviality. You are better acquainted with this lady than I, Brandon. Is this irony or fact?"

"I certainly have no notion of her bathing habits," his lordship said wickedly.

A rosy tint glowed upon the widow's high cheekbones.

"I beg your pardon, Mrs. Davenant," said the Beau. "This was my fault. An injudicious choice of phrasing." He returned to Brandon. "I only wished to ascertain whether you had ever seen Mrs. Davenant eat vegetables."

"Indeed I have. Moreover, I am informed by reliable witnesses that she rides, several times a week, in the early-morning air."

Brummell's face fell. "I have an open mind," he said bravely. "I shall take a turn about the terrace. But *vegetables*. Good heavens!" He sauntered through the French doors.

"Does he never eat vegetables?" Lilith asked.

"He claims he once ate a pea. You're very beautiful tonight, Mrs. Davenant."

Slowly, her mouth curled into a delicious smile.

"Thank you," she said. "I've been terrified into it, you know."

"Have you indeed?" he asked, intrigued, charmed. "I've never heard of anybody's being terrified into beauty."

"Then obviously you're not acquainted with Madame Germaine. I've never been so scolded and threatened — not since I was in the nursery, I'm sure."

"Good grief! What had this dread female to say?"

"You are not to repeat it," said Lilith, lowering her voice.

He bent his head to listen and caught a whiff of jasmine.

"She said Cecily's beaux will wonder whether she'll take after me."

"But you're not her mama. You're not even a blood relation."

"Her mama wears nothing but ancient riding habits, which is worse, I daresay, and I'm on the spot to be taken as model."

"You did not tell this upstart shopkeeper you've already riveted several nieces successfully?"

"I did," said Lilith, her blue eyes dancing with an amusement as enchanting as it was rare. "In my best set-down manner. She only shook her head pityingly and sighed and answered, 'But only think how much better the dear creatures *might* have done.'"

"If you will excuse me," said Lord Brandon. "I believe I must depart now — to set fire to her shop."

"You don't approve my transformation, then, despite the compliment."

"No, I do not. All these weeks I've feasted upon your beauty in solitary dignity. Now I must dine with a mob," he complained. "I shall be forced to listen to Brummell rhapsodise about your complexion. I must endure

Byron's odes to your eyes and Davies' puns upon your lips. No doubt there will be violent quarrels whether your hair is Bordeaux or sienna, copper-tinted or russet, and one numskull will call another out on the issue." He paused. "Now, there's a thought," he said. "Perhaps they'll all kill one another."

"So long as a duke or two remains standing to marry Cecily, I can't object," she said. "Madame Germaine won't be satisfied with any lesser rank, I'm afraid."

"I wonder, if you dance with a marquess, whether that will send one peltering after Miss Glenwood. Then, seeing the marquess give chase, perhaps a duke will join the pursuit. All of which is to say I wish you'd dance this waltz with me."

There was a heartbeat's pause, enough to send a shiver of anger through him, but she consented, and the only vestige of rage remaining was with himself, for being so shaken at the prospect of refusal.

His hand clasped her waist — and encountered something altogether unexpected. "I shall burn down her shop," he muttered, *"and* throttle her with my own neck-cloth."

"What on earth — " Her eyes must have caught the mischief in his, because she became flustered. "You will not — "

"Stays," he said grimly. "That wretched female has persuaded you to crush your rib cage in one of those fiendish instruments of torture."

"My lord you have an annoying habit of referring to exceedingly intimate matters," she said with a touch of asperity.

"I am appalled to find you have acquired an even more distressing habit."

"I had to wear it," she said, vexed. "The gown was indecent otherwise. Oh, stop looking at me in that aggravating manner. Why did I ever agree to dance with you?"

"An attack of conscience. You haven't danced with me in an age. I daresay you finally decided I'd been punished long enough."

"I was not punishing you."

"It felt exactly like punishment."

Her face became shuttered, and he cursed himself silently. "You needn't poker up," he said. "It's simply that you've found me in bad temper."

After a moment, she asked what had put him out of temper.

"Who knows?" he said. "Talk to me and make me forget. Quiet my mind with some tranquil image. Tell me of your place in Derbyshire."

"It isn't very interesting," she said. "In Derbyshire, I'm a farmer."

"Very well. I shall give up Athena for the

moment and transform you in my mind to Demeter. Tell me of sheep and cows and corn and — oh, above all, tell me of *drainage.*"

He watched her face soften and her eyes light up with enthusiasm as she described the vast, ill-maintained estate her grandparents had given her as a wedding gift, and of the years spent making it productive again. She could not suppress her pride in her accomplishment. Not that she should, he thought. She deserved a great deal of credit. She'd educated herself about modern agricultural methods, single-handedly set about persuading her tenants from their old-fashioned ways, and managed the whole herself.

She'd had time enough on her hands, hadn't she? No social life until after her husband died. No children, except those she adopted temporarily for some three or four months of the year.

The estate, his lordship knew from conversations with Higginbottom, was at present let to a retired military officer, who would very likely make a purchase offer at the summer's end. That, Brandon realised as he studied her animated countenance, would probably break her heart.

The waltz ended and Mrs. Davenant went on talking, like an eager girl. He continued to ask questions, and she answered happily, even after he led her back to Bexley.

This would do no harm in Bexley's view — if he were paying attention, which was not altogether certain. Still, the spirited discussion of agriculture must silence the gossips, at least temporarily. Moreover, it was not a topic to excite her new admirers. Those who owned property preferred to leave the business of maintaining it to others. They knew less of modern agriculture than their sheep did.

Fortunately, the marquess knew something — more than something, actually. Thus he enjoyed the added pleasure of watching surprise, then growing respect, brighten her beautiful eyes.

The following day, Mrs. Davenant met in her study with her butler.

"Certainly, madam," said Cawble when she'd done explaining. "It can be managed discreetly. I shall send Jacob with the centrepiece, the two larger candelabra, the great coffee-urn, and the other items you suggested. They will not be required, unless you plan a large entertainment in the near future."

"I am sure we shall redeem them long before I plan such an affair," said his mistress.

"Yes, madam. This is a regrettable necessity, yet one cannot plan for every emergency, I am sure."

All the same, the loyal butler could not help reflecting disapprovingly upon his employer's man of business. Mrs. Davenant should not be placed in the mortifying position of pawning her silver, simply because men who were supposed to sign pieces of paper chose to dawdle over the matter. They had no business dawdling, Cawble reflected indignantly. They had little enough to do. That a lady of her means should not be able to put her hands upon ready money the instant she required it was an affront to the British Constitution.

Shortly thereafter, Mrs. Davenant reappeared at the dressmaker's. Instead of her niece, she brought a footman, who carried several large packages. Mrs. Davenant explained she'd lost some weight. Perhaps Madame would be so kind as to make a few alterations?

Madame contemplated the dismal colours, then her client, then shook her head sadly. "I never speak ill of a colleague," she said, "but sometimes I do *not* understand what they're thinking of."

"These were made precisely as I ordered," was the defensive answer.

"Yes, madam, and the question I ask is 'Why?' Meaning no offence, because I'd never question your taste. But this taupe . . . " She took up the offending garment and pursed her lips. "Enough fabric here for two gowns. Such a *waste*." She shook her head again. "It wouldn't trouble me if you had flaws to conceal, but with *your* figure . . . well, I can't understand why the gown had to be made like an overcoat."

So saying, and without appearing to hear any of her customer's stammering negatives or observe the crimson repeatedly suffusing the lady's face, Madame proceeded to measure and pin and snip and slash.

What she proposed might be an outrage to her client's sensibilities, but the client was no match for the evangelical fervour that possessed Madame Germaine. It was in vain to protest that one felt half naked, when one's dressmaker only cried, "Precisely!" and flourished her scissors like a sword.

13

Mrs. Davenant's altered garments began making their appearance the following week.

Tonight, at Almack's, she was dressed in the same taupe gown she'd worn to the Countess Lieven's party. Well, not quite the same. At least a yard of fabric was gone from the skirt, causing it to hug her hips as it had never done before. Madame had insisted "only an inch" was taken from the bodice. This was the grossest of understatements.

Though such renovated costumes did not trigger quite the sensation the blue silk had, they continued to win admiring glances, and not a little flattery. Even Cecily's beaux seemed less intimidated. Sir Matthew Melbrook had begged a dance of the heretofore terrifying dragon aunt, and Mr. Ventcoeur, Lilith was told, had startled his friends by boldly asserting that Mrs. Davenant had a sense of *humour*.

Lilith bit her lip. She'd heard that from Lord Brandon.

Determined, apparently, to be the gossiping sort of friend, he'd begun sharing with her every *on dit* that came to his ears. What he didn't hear, he invented, leaving her laughing helplessly at outrageous stories of Lady Shumway's passionate affairs with a series of fictitious Cossacks, or the ancient Lord Hubbing's adventures at Vauxhall, or any of a host of other imaginative atrocities.

Yet, ever since Lady Gaines's ball, he'd become the confiding sort of friend as well, because he had a knack for getting past Lilith's guard. Once launched upon the topic of Derbyshire, she was easily led to more personal subjects: her grandparents, her childhood, the young parents she scarcely remembered, her nurse, her governess, her studies. Somehow, too, she'd revealed something of her own girlish dreams and hopes, even as she thought she spoke of Cecily and Georgiana and the rest.

But a few weeks ago, uttering one sentence to him had been an effort, because his presence disturbed her so. Of late, the struggle was to keep from telling him every thought and feeling.

It was a struggle now to keep her eye on Cecily, dancing with Mr. Ventcoeur, rather than on the tall, dark form that moved so gracefully through Almack's throng.

Lilith never knew when she'd find Brandon

at her side. She knew only that he always came, and they would dance once and talk a great deal. Strangely enough, no one else seemed to regard this new camaraderie.

Perhaps the Great World was preoccupied, as Thomas was, with Louis XVIII's arrival in France and its consequences. More likely, Society wasn't remotely interested in so dull a matter as mere friendship between a man and a woman.

After all, Lord Brandon's compliments were light and civil, no more. He scarcely flirted with her lately, though other gentlemen did.

This quieted Lilith's conscience somewhat, but not altogether. She had no defence against his amiability, no excuse for shunning him, yet she wished she had.

She could no longer deny she'd been drawn to him from the start, attracted in spite of herself by his compelling physical beauty and charm. Now the pull was stronger. She'd discovered kindness, sense, compassion, intelligence — oh, and too many common interests.

Or so it seemed. She frowned.

"Your brows are knit," came a low voice behind her. "Brummell will be cross with you for wrinkling the flawless surface of your complexion." The marquess moved to her side, brushing her arm in the process.

"I can live with his disapproval," Lilith answered coolly enough. "Until a week ago, the only notice I got was a singularly pained expression whenever he happened to glance my way."

"Which only shows he's not so discerning as he appears. Why do you linger in this dismal corner? Are you hiding from your beaux? Or waiting for one? If so, he's unforgivably dilatory. I'd better take his place and teach him a lesson."

Lilith caught the edge of impatience in his voice. Wondering at it, she threw him a puzzled glance. He stood with his usual careless grace, but the tension in that stance was not usual. He seemed . . . angry?

"What is it?" he asked. "Have you discovered a crease in my lapel?"

"If I had, I should never dare tell you, for fear your valet would be found murdered in the morning. You seem a trifle out of sorts this evening, my lord," she said frankly.

Surprise flickered in his green eyes, only to be hooded in the next instant. "Hardly. I've been dead bored, as usual — until now, of course."

"You were with Thomas. If he bores you so much, I wonder you bother to speak with him at all."

"I'm obliged to appear as friendly with the gentleman as I am with his fiancée. If I'm not, my motives become suspect, and the fiancée suffers for it. Society punishes the victim, while the alleged criminal goes scot-free. A curious kind of justice, is it not?"

"Society is hardly a court of law," she answered uneasily. "One might well be blamed for not avoiding dangerous company."

"You think so? Why shouldn't my alleged victim decide for herself whether I'm a menace? You believe we must none of us think for ourselves, but always adhere to the general opinion?"

More disquieted still, she glanced away. "I used to wonder how Eve could have been so foolish as to listen to the serpent. But whenever you and I debate morality, I can only conclude he must have had your gift for turning right and wrong inside out, plain black and white to shades of grey."

"It isn't morality we discuss, but the appearance of it. My wish to enjoy your company is a crime for which you'll be punished, unless I dress it up as a general wish to enjoy every damn fool's company as well."

"Sir Thomas is not a fool," Lilith reproved, as she must. "Because he isn't as witty and entertaining as you, you find him boring. All the same, he doesn't want intelligence."

"He wants something in his upper story — or in his heart — to neglect you so shamefully.

234

If you were my affianced bride, I'd exploit the privilege. I'd talk with you the whole day and dance with you all the night."

She made herself smile and pretend he'd spoken lightly, though the intensity burning in his eyes told her otherwise.

"That is mere theory. When you get a fiancée, we shall discover whether or not you live in her pocket."

"I don't speak of imaginary females. It's your company I want, your voice I want to hear," he said, his tones dropping lower. "It infuriates me — he can have all I want so easily, incurring no one's displeasure, and he doesn't care. I meanwhile must make do with five minutes snatched here, ten stolen there. I must amiably accept every interruption, all the while anxious lest your reputation be sullied by my contaminating presence. God knows," he went on with suppressed fury, "I don't dare touch you."

Thus he shattered all the fragile tranquillity she'd achieved in the last few days.

She'd wanted his company too. She'd needed to look at him, hear his voice, find him near. No wonder her conscience would not be quieted. Under the veneer of friendship, her shameful longing had only grown. Why else should he make her heart ache when he spoke so?

"You will not disparage Sir Thomas to me," Lilith made herself say. "Our relationship is our own affair."

"What of *ours*, Lilith?" he demanded. "Is this all there is for us? Are we to share nothing but what can be found in a few minutes, with all the world watching and listening?"

She remembered where she was then, and made herself glance easily about her. Lady Jersey was smiling at her. Lilith smiled back, before turning again to the marquess.

"Perhaps," she said, "we'd better not share even that." And with the same civil smile pinned to her face, she walked away.

"How kind of you to take so much trouble for me," Miss Glenwood told Lord Robert as he swept her into the waltz. "I was sure it would be months before the patronesses let me waltz."

"It wasn't any trouble at all," he said. "Why shouldn't they let you? They've all had plenty of time to approve your behaviour, the tiresome prudes."

"Still, I was much amazed when the Countess Lieven presented you."

"Because she's so haughty? Or did you think I wasn't a respectable enough partner?"

"Good heavens, why should I think that? If you weren't respectable, they wouldn't let

236

you in, would they? But you're right. I shouldn't have been amazed at your gallantry. You always know what to say and do to put a girl at her ease. I never feel clumsy when I dance with you."

He smiled. "You're never the least awkward, Miss Glenwood, and you waltz exceedingly well. Not at all like a beginner. You've been practising in secret."

She did not appear to hear the compliment. Her attention had fallen upon something — or someone — past his shoulder. Lord Robert experienced a twinge of irritation. "What is it?" he asked. "Has someone fallen into a fit?"

Her gaze came back to him. It was troubled. "I rather think someone has," she said softly. "Only look at Lord Brandon."

Robert drew her into a turn in order to observe his cousin. The marquess's countenance was black as a thundercloud.

"He looks like murder," said Robert, taken aback. "He's a devil of a temper, you know. Usually he doesn't show it — not in public, I mean. What's set him off, I wonder."

"I think he's quarreled with my aunt," said Cecily. She sighed. "Oh, dear, how tiresome of them."

"Quarreled with — Well, it's none of our business, of course."

"Of course it is. He can't go on glaring at

her all night. People will notice."

"I wouldn't have noticed if you hadn't called my attention."

"That's because you're not a prying busybody. But Lady Enders is, and half a dozen other ladies as well. Now everyone will begin buzzing again. I'm sure I'm not the only one saw how they were arguing. And then my aunt marched off in that horrid outraged Empress of the World way of hers, and he hasn't taken his eyes off her since. Lord Robert, you must do something."

"I?"

"You must make him stop."

"I? Make Julian stop?" he said, aghast. "What do you expect me to do, drag him from the premises?"

Miss Glenwood's small gloved hand squeezed his, and her enormous eyes opened wider yet. "I know you can think of something," she said confidently. "You're so clever. Probably you'll find some tactful way to let him know he's wearing his heart on his sleeve — though of course you'd never say anything so silly as *that*."

Although the pressure of her hand sent a surge of strength through him, it was not quite enough to conquer all Lord Robert's sense of self-preservation.

"Egad, I should hope not, Miss Glenwood.

Not if I mean to keep all my teeth in my head," he said, feeling beleaguered as her gaze grew reproachful. "I shouldn't say so, but Julian's hideously touchy about any references to your aunt. When he's in a good humour, he only delivers a set-down, but when he's moody he . . . well, he doesn't know his own strength."

"Then you must be sure to step out of the way quickly, mustn't you?" the pitiless girl responded.

The waltz ended far too soon, in Lord Robert's opinion. He dutifully returned Miss Glenwood to her aunt and saw the girl promptly swallowed up in a crowd of admirers. Then, reluctantly, he made for his cousin's gloomy figure. Julian's gaze was not welcoming.

"I've had enough of Almack's," said Lord Robert. "I think I'll be going now."

"I am not your nurse. Do what you like."

"Still, a man can't always do what he likes, you know. Most of the time, he can't even show what he's thinking, which is even harder . . . well, for me at least . . . "

"Robert, I hope you're not about to honour me with boyish confidences. I'm not in a humour for confidences."

Not open to hints, either, apparently. Nothing for it, then, but to state the facts . . . and step quickly out of the way.

"You've been staring daggers at her for half an hour now," Lord Robert said, moving back a pace. "If even I noticed, don't you think half the world is going to?"

Instantly, the familiar mask of boredom was back in place.

"If this is half the world," said Lord Brandon languidly, "we're best advised to seek out the other half tonight, I think."

Lilith was badly shaken, yet she chatted with her normal composure and danced with her betrothed without stumbling. Tonight of all nights, Thomas danced with her several times, as though Lord Brandon's vexation had somehow communicated itself to his rival.

Not a rival, Lilith hastily amended. She'd already made her choice — not that there had been or could be any choice. It was a husband she needed, not a lover.

Thus she behaved as she always did, and when Thomas had taken her and Cecily home, Lilith invited him, as she often did, to stop for a glass of wine.

Brandon thought her betrothed took her for granted. This wasn't just. To Thomas, socializing was business, and she'd never expected or wished him to neglect his chosen business on her account. During these quiet times at the end of an evening, Thomas would share with her his thoughts and wishes, reporting on what he'd said and learned. He even solicited her opinion from time to time.

He did not take her for granted, she argued with the sardonic masculine voice in her head. He simply chose an appropriate time and place for private conversation.

Tonight he was occupied with Norway, and vexed at the prospect of a blockade of that nation, for it was Sir Thomas's firm belief that Norway was the King of Denmark's problem, as Earl Grey maintained.

Lilith did not remind her fiancé that Lord Liverpool had already taken measures towards a blockade. For one, Thomas was already troubled by his mentor's actions. For another, she had no wish to prolong the monologue. She had rather hear of the Corn Laws or even the Catholic Question. The technicalities of peace treaties made her head spin.

Her confusion must have shown, because Thomas stopped mid-speech to give her a rueful smile. "Ah, the matter shall be debated all the coming week, and a word or two on my part would have sufficed. Yet every issue these days seems to go against me," he said, shaking his head. "I am concerned that sufficient precautions have not been taken regarding Buonaparte's move to Elba. I wish I might have spoken to Castlereagh myself. If only I had been on the spot as Hobhouse was, to carry those dispatches."

"One day you'll have a direct voice in such matters," Lilith said loyally. "I'm certain of it. I wish for your sake you had it now, Thomas."

"Well, I cannot altogether regret it. Had I gone with the dispatches, I must be away from you, and that I should be sorry for."

He set his empty wineglass upon the tray and stepped towards her. "It seems to me you become more elegant every day, my dear. Is that a new frock?"

"You've seen it before."

"It appears different somehow. *You* have appeared different."

"A few alterations." She made herself smile. "A great man ought not be shackled to a dowd."

He took her hand. "I have never approved of slavishness to every fashion, as you know. Yet you wear the change with dignity, and it becomes you."

"You hadn't mentioned it before. I thought perhaps you disapproved this . . . this frivolousness."

"You are never frivolous, my dear. We two are past frivolity, I hope. Still, I am not so aged a fellow as to be unmoved by grace and elegance, though I do not shower you with flattery every minute."

He brought the hand he held to his lips. The kiss he placed there was a lingering one, as was the glance that fell upon her bodice. Thus, Lilith was not altogether taken aback when her heretofore decorous suitor enfolded her in his arms.

Nonetheless, she stiffened when his mouth touched hers. The warm, moist kiss did nothing to warm her inwardly. On the contrary, her muscles grew more icily rigid, and within was the familiar rush of anxiety . . . and distaste. In seconds, it seemed, he grew more heated, while she grew frantic to break free. She endured it as long as she could, which was not very long, though it seemed an eternity. Then she made a slight struggle, and he released her.

He appeared not at all happy about it. A few strands of hair stuck damply to his forehead, and his brown eyes were clouded.

"My dear, we are betrothed," he said, a shade of irritation in his voice, "and you are not a green girl."

"We're not yet wed," she said, flushing at her hypocrisy. Even as she was trying to contrive a better excuse, Thomas was collecting himself.

"We are not — yet," he said stiffly. "All the

243

same, it is not improper to embrace the woman one has solemnly pledged to wed."

"That is so, and I do not mean to be missish, Thomas. Yet I cannot be comfortable — that is, do recollect it has been many years since . . . since I was a wife."

He seemed to understand then, because he apologised for his haste. Still, the edge of vexation in his voice warned this was not the end of the matter.

Lilith could not blame him. Neither, however, could she bear his touch — not now, not so soon. She'd endure it once they were wed, as she was obliged, but not before. She hadn't misled him, she told herself. She'd never pretended passion, never even mentioned love. She'd never been given to displays even of affection . . . with one appalling exception.

"Modesty, naturally, is always becoming in a lady," he was saying in his considering, Parliamentary tones. "You are quite right. We are not yet wed — though I assure you I had no intention of anticipating our conjugal vows. In all fairness, I must admit I have not been loverlike. I suppose I have shocked you this night. Let us hope you will not be shocked in future when your husband-to-be wishes to embrace you. I have been preoccupied of late. Nevertheless, I trust you understand our life together will not be entirely taken up with matters of state."

Lilith nodded and forced a smile.

"Believe me, my dear, I look forward to the peace and intimacy of domestic life," he went on sonorously, "and to the growth of mutual affection which provides man his greatest happiness. Mutual affection and, of course, such tokens of that esteem as Providence sees fit to bless us with."

He had no need to say more. Lilith understood him well enough. For all his decorousness, he was a man, with a man's needs. This man also wanted children.

He left soon after. She bid him a polite farewell, then returned to the library to pour herself another glass of wine.

Wine perhaps would deaden the vile clamour in her brain.

What of us, Lilith? Angry, pleading. Against that voice, which made her heart pound even now, the tones of her intended husband, judicious, yet annoyed. Disappointed, impatient — as he had a right to be.

Perhaps it was wrong to marry Thomas. Perhaps he wanted more than she could give, and she'd make him unhappy.

No, of course she wouldn't. She'd chosen for herself this time. No one had coerced her. She'd known exactly what she was choosing and why, and she'd make the best of it.

Thomas would never know a devil possessed her heart.

The devil was not abroad this night. He watched the play at Watier's for an hour or so and drank a glass or so, and was in his own bed by two o'clock in the morning. At three o'clock, Lord Brandon woke from a disagreeable dream and found himself in process of throttling the pillow — not, as he'd thought, Sir Thomas Bexley.

"By God, woman," he muttered as he jammed the pillow back into place, "you shall pay for this, and dearly. To keep a man from his proper repose — "

He fell back upon the pillow, his green eyes wide, staring at the canopy above. "Believe me, I'll return the favour, Lilith Davenant. Before the week is out, I vow."

Having vowed so, Lord Brandon ought to have been easy in his mind, but his gaze remained fixed upon the canopy.

He hadn't meant to speak as he had. It was a tactical error to press her when he'd only begun to win her trust. He'd promised himself he'd keep away from her this night, to make her wonder . . . and worry. But he'd watched her move, so proud and graceful, through the crowd, talking with her friends. He'd observed the other men as well. He was aware how their eyes lingered upon her imperious face, and dwelt longer still upon her slim, supple form. He'd recognised the instinctive masculine drive to conquer and possess. He'd not very much enjoyed seeing his own feelings reflected in a dozen other men's faces.

Unbearably restless, he'd gone to her. Then the words, wholly unprepared, had spilled from him, and once begun, he couldn't stop himself. Some fiend indeed must have taken hold of his tongue. It could not have been his own heart produced that lovesick speech.

Well, he'd never been a saint. Why should he have the patience of one?

Frustration, then. Nothing to be alarmed about. As to the speech itself — there was no harm in *seeming* lovesick.

She'd left him, true, with a rebuff. Nonetheless, she'd not heard him unmoved. He'd read her inner struggle — a painful one — in her eyes. Even as he raged at her, he'd known she was weakening. Which made him rage all the more within. She wanted what he wanted. Why not yield and be happy? Why should not two adults find pleasure in each other's arms? And why must those troubled eyes haunt him? No, he corrected, that was only his frustration with her.

It would end soon. The serpent in the garden, she'd called him, unwittingly revealing that she, like Eve, was tempted. Would she fall? She must.

All the same, for all his confidence, Lord Brandon's eyes did not close again that night.

14

On the following day at breakfast, Lord Brandon made a remark regarding what Hell hath no fury like. Though several more specific comments were needed, Lord Robert eventually recollected the long-suffering Elise.

Before noon, Robert was with his mistress. He brought her a bouquet, a box of chocolates, and an exquisite midnight-blue silk shawl.

Elise gazed at these sadly and told him he was too extravagant.

"Not at all," he said, neglecting to add that Julian had provided the money. "I should shower you with diamonds, you've been so patient and understanding."

"Yes, but I must be. I know you make the sacrifice for me. I never see you now, but for a few hours at a time. Every night you must go about with your friends and be so bored and lonely — and all for me," said Elise, smiling bravely.

"Yes, hideously bored. But I do bear it for

your sake — for ours, I mean."

She took up the shawl and draped it over her shoulders. "So beautiful Robin. How lovely it will be with my gown — the wine-coloured one, you remember?"

Lord Robert nodded enthusiastically, just as though he did remember, which he didn't. His mind was taken up lately with pastel muslins.

"Of course you remember. It is your favourite," she said, stroking the shawl. "You are so good to me. I think tonight you must have some reward for all your sacrifices. Why do we not go to the theatre? I shall wear the gown and this beautiful gift."

Panic shot through Lord Robert. Miss Glenwood would attend the theatre this evening, and he'd promised to be there. She was a remarkably open-minded girl. Her aunt, unfortunately, was not. To be seen tonight with Elise was to invite permanent exile.

"I can't," he said, thinking rapidly. "Promised to dine at Holland House, don't you know? Julian begged off at the last minute, and Lady Holland pounced on me so quick I couldn't think." This was not actually a lie, Robert told himself. Lady Holland had invited him.

Elise sighed. "Well, it is unfortunate, but I know you cannot be rude to the lady. Still, it is wearying to remain always at home."

"Perhaps you could visit some of your friends," Robert suggested. "I think Julian mentioned Bella Martin was having one of her soirees tonight. You like Bella."

"No, there will be too many gentlemen, and it is so tedious always to be saying no, no. They do not understand I am not the Elise I was. My heart is not free now." Her smile was tender, but the sparks in her dark eyes made Robert nervous.

"I think I shall go all the same," she went on. "I shall take my maid. It is better that way. The play will distract me, and I shall not feel sorry for myself."

His heart sank. If she couldn't be got to change her mind, it must be Holland House for him after all. Ahead, instead of Miss Glenwood's lively company, lay a stuffy, stupid evening — not to mention being forced to jump up and down a dozen times, because Lady Holland was inclined to revise seating arrangements straight through dinner.

Although Robert did not leave his love nest for several hours, nothing he said or did could sway his mistress. As he made his lachrymose way down the street, he wondered why he hadn't noticed before how obstinate Elise was. Furthermore, something must be done about her taste in perfume. A man ought to be able to breathe in his own lodgings.

The marquess arrived at the theatre earlier than was his custom and headed immediately for the Enders box. He found Lady Enders, Bexley, Cecily, and Mrs. Wellwicke, but no Lilith. Assuming she must have stepped out with Lord Enders, Brandon lingered. Consequently, he had to endure Bexley's opinions of the King of Denmark at numbing length. He listened, the time passed, and neither Enders nor the widow appeared.

Finally, minutes before the curtain was due to rise, Bexley paused to catch his breath, and Cecily spoke up.

"Was there a great crowd in the corridor as you arrived, my lord?" she asked. "Lord Enders very kindly offered to fetch me a glass of lemonade, though I would have been happy to wait until the interval. I do hope he won't miss the opening scene on my account."

"In such a service, Miss Glenwood, any gentleman would gladly forgo the entire drama," Brandon said gallantly. "Still, if I spy him, I shall convey your anxiety."

"There is no need for alarm," Lady Enders told the girl sharply. "Enders will be along any minute."

"Yes, how silly of me. I am just uneasy in general, I daresay, on account of my poor aunt. Perhaps I should have stayed home with her after all. It isn't good for her to be all alone, whatever she says."

Lord Brandon shot the girl a glance, but she had turned her attention to the stage.

Moments later, having expressed appropriate sentiments regarding Mrs. Davenant's ill health and feigned fascination with Bexley's imbecilic explanations for her headaches, Lord Brandon was striding rapidly down the corridor. So intent was he upon his plans that he did not observe Elise's approach until it was too late.

"A moment, milord," she said, taking hold of his arm.

He was about to shake her off, but a glance at her face stopped him. Her dark eyes glittered an angry warning.

Fortunately, the corridor was empty. Leading her to one side, so that he could keep watch on the stairs for late arrivals, he politely asked how he might serve her.

"You might serve by keeping to our agreement," she snapped. "It was simple enough. But you play another game as well, I think."

"There is only one game I am aware of, *mademoiselle.*"

"I am not blind, milord. Little passes in your Great World that does not reach me. I comprehend what you have done. Our bargain, you find, is not so simple as you thought, so you arrange to win another way. You keep Robert from me, and use as bait that pretty child with her golden curls and so-blue eyes."

"I see you have been spending too much time alone, brooding," said his lordship. "Otherwise you would not have persuaded yourself that a mere girl — pretty or no — gives you any reason for alarm, or that I have any need to hedge my bets."

"Do you not? How long is it now? Nearly five weeks, I think."

"You were so generous as to give me eight. I see no reason for haste."

"But reason for other precautions, no? Is this your honour? I trusted your word as a gentleman. Why did you tease me with a bargain you never meant to keep?"

"I fully intend to keep it," he said, controlling his swelling anger. "Do you call me a liar, *mademoiselle?*"

Though he'd kept his voice level, the tart must have sensed she was treading on thin ice. "I only wish to be assured," she said in lighter tones. "Can you blame me? To win our wager, you need only seduce Madame Davenant. Why do I see Robert kept from me meanwhile? That was no part of it."

"I have done nothing to keep him from you," he said as patiently as he could. "If you believe he's playing you false, you must deal with that between yourselves. Now, if you will excuse me, I must be going."

For all her assurances to Cecily, Lady Enders was not at all easy in her mind about Matthew's tardiness.

It was Matthew who'd hastened to Lady Violet Porter's assistance during the battle at Redley Park, and Rachel had not at all approved the assiduousness of his attentions.

Forced to relinquish Lord Fevis to his wife, Lady Violet was free to pursue other game. This evening, Lady Enders had perceived the smile the woman threw Matthew when she arrived. Consequently, Rachel little doubted it was Lady Violet her husband was reconnoitering, not lemonade.

This was why, as the curtain was rising, Lady Enders left her box and stepped into the corridor.

Thus she saw Lord Brandon lead the demirep round the corner by the staircase. Judging by the woman's tones, she was in a temper.

Rachel told herself she had no interest in their discussion. This was a public corridor, and she had as much right as anyone to walk there. She needed to drop a hint to Mr. Porter, didn't she? And wasn't his box that way?

Just before the corner, however, she stopped

dead. The tart's words rang perfectly clear now. Perfectly, monstrously clear.

Lady Enders did not wait to learn more. Trembling with shock and indignation, she turned and hurried back.

Lilith, who had every sort of trouble but the headache she'd claimed, was bent over her desk, reviewing accounts, when she heard the tap at her study door. Expecting Cawble with the tea she'd ordered, she didn't bother to look up when she bade him enter.

"Is this a new cure for the headache?" a low, familiar voice asked.

She jumped from her chair, knocking over a stack of papers. "How did you get in?" she gasped.

"Bribed the footman. Your butler was otherwise occupied, thank heaven. He is lamentably incorruptible."

This evening, a deep-blue coat made Lord Brandon's hair glint blue-black. His linen was blinding white, nearly as dazzling as the diamond that shot sparks from the folds of his neck-cloth.

His tall, broad-shouldered figure made the small, cluttered room seem a narrow cell. Lilith herself felt like a peasant. She wore an old grey muslin day dress whose right sleeve bore a spattering of ink stains. It was her working costume.

Stunned at his entrance and embarrassed by both the room's and her own appearance, she could only watch helplessly as he gathered up the papers. To her dismay, he did not return them to the desk, but commenced perusing them.

"These are scarcely two days old," he said reproachfully. "It is bad ton to pay one's creditors before one has been dunned twenty-five times at least. I must warn you against the practice. The upper orders are obliged to set proper examples for their inferiors."

"I see no merit in driving to bankruptcy tradespeople who serve me in good faith," she said. "Nor do I see how this is any business of yours. You will please to give them back — and leave this house." She put out a shaking hand for the papers.

He turned away from her and continued to thumb through the stack. "Ye gods," he said. "This is only the past month's? Thank heavens I leave all that to my secretary. I should never have time for anything else. Why don't you leave it to Bexley? What's the point of marrying a rich man if you don't let him pay your creditors?"

"I have no intention of presenting my betrothed with a pile of debts. May I also repeat, this is none of your concern. Nor have you any right to invade my privacy — particularly at this unseemly hour."

He did not even look up as he answered. "I know you're angry with me, my pet, but I wish you wouldn't make stuffy speeches. It spoils my concentration and — Aha!" He spun round, holding aloft the pawnbroker's ticket. "What is this? Have you played too deep at piquet, wicked girl?"

Heat tingled in her cheeks. "Even the most well-regulated households at times have need of ready cash."

"Ah, yes. An unplanned expense. What was it? That ghastly corset? Or perhaps a provocative negligee — black lace, I hope — for your wedding night?"

It was scarcely a cry, more a painful catch of her breath, but he heard it, for he dropped the papers on the desk and moved to her. Placing his hands on her shoulders, he asked gently, "What is it?"

"Let go of me. It is no great matter. The blue silk . . . some alterations . . . Madame — well, she did it all practically overnight. I wished to pay at once, in thanks for her trouble."

"So you pawned your silver? Higginbottom didn't tell me matters had reached such a pass."

"I will have something at the end of the

month. I have enough now — or nearly — but I'd rather keep it in reserve. Cecily may need stockings or ribbons — or her fan may break, or some catastrophe."

If he did not take his hands away soon, she would be stuttering. As it was, she had to stare hard at the diamond stick pin to maintain any composure.

He released her. "I see." He stepped back to the desk, picked up the stack of papers, and thrust them into his coat. "This is utterly absurd," he said. "You should not be tormenting yourself with creditors. Why should you not have new gowns if you want them? Why should you not have whatever takes your fancy? What have you done to deserve penury?"

"I am not tormented. I don't want any new gowns. And I most certainly will not permit you to pay my debts. If I would not permit my betrothed — "

"Don't preach at me, Lilith. It's bad enough I must see you shackle yourself to that staid Parliamentarian. I will not watch you pinch and scrape in the meantime."

There was again the barely contained anger she'd heard the night before.

"Don't," she said. "Don't speak this way."

He moved to her again. "What does it matter what I say? Who's to hear it? Is it so villainous that I don't wish to see you suffer?

Come, my love," he said, lightly touching her cheek. "I have so few real amusements. This is amusing, truly it is. To keep a woman for my rival will be a novelty. I've never attempted such a thing before, you know, and we are told love makes men do the oddest things."

The distance between them had closed to mere inches. He was so near he must hear her heart pounding. There were many sensible things to say, any number of proper speeches, all of them dismissals.

All she could say was, "Don't."

"Lilith."

Slowly, she raised her head. In his green eyes burned the same compelling ardour she'd tried to ignore last evening.

"I love you," he whispered. "Is there to be no happiness for us?"

"My lord, I beg you — "

"Julian. Not your lord, but yours."

He raised her trembling hand to his lips, then turned it over and kissed the palm.

Lilith had battled with her treacherous self all night, and believed she'd conquered at last. She'd thought Reason and Right had won. Her will must be stronger than her need. More potent even than physical desire, that need encompassed the happiness he spoke of. He'd given her joy she'd never before dreamt of, just as the guilty misery he'd brought her was beyond even her long experience of pain. Into her life as well he'd driven passion, which she'd never known at all until he'd touched her.

But her will had conquered all this madness, she reminded herself as his lips pressed her wrist and her limbs grew weak. She pulled her hand away.

At that moment came a soft tap at the door. Lilith retreated from the marquess.

The door opened, and Cawble entered with the tea tray. Apparently unmoved by the presence of a gentleman in his mistress's private study, the butler calmly set the tray upon a table by the small, well-worn settee.

Lord Brandon bit his lip and strode to the fireplace.

The butler had brought but one teacup. Politely, he enquired whether madam required another.

"No," she said. "His lordship is leaving."

His lordship threw her a reproachful look.

"Leaving shortly," she added weakly.

Cawble exited.

"You *are* leaving," she said more firmly when the door had closed. "You will return those papers to me, my lord. I am not at the workhouse door yet, and even if I were, I should not accept your *carte blanche*. That is what you mean, though you put it so prettily. I am not a fool, though at times I seem to behave like one. Still, having no experience with men of your ilk I cannot be as well-armed as I could wish."

A shadow crossed his features, leaving his eyes dark and uneasy. "You can't believe that," he said. "After all this time, you can't believe my feelings aren't genuine. You must believe I love you."

Too tender. Too sincere. It was a dangerously beguiling voice, uttering those melting words.

"I can scarcely believe you have so little conscience as to give your desire for mere pleasure the name *love*," she said. "Mere pleasure, or the sport of ruining me — I don't know which. I shall never understand you," she added wearily, unhappily. "But if there is any pity in your heart, I beg you to leave me in peace."

He hesitated, his face stiffening. Perhaps, at last, she'd touched whatever he had of a conscience. She waited, praying he'd go quickly, because the sorrow in his countenance was weakening her with every passing second.

He moved at last, but not to the door, and by the time his arms folded round her, all her resolve was crumbling.

"I can't leave you," he breathed against her

hair. "Don't talk to me of pleasure, when I haven't known a moment's peace since I've met you. Oh, yes, this is fine sport — to scheme and wait, just for a word or two — to want to touch you, hold you, care for you — and know all the while that what I want can only hurt you. You drive me mad, Lilith. What am I to do?"

All the same, he knew what to do. His fingers raked her hair and drew her head back, and his mouth was claiming hers before she could answer. Then it was her body answered, as it always did.

His mouth was hungry and seeking this time, and the hands tearing the pins from her hair moved urgently, impatiently, until the whole heavy mass fell loose upon her back.

She knew heat, and the wild rhythms of her quickening senses. The scent of sandalwood . . . the throb of muscles tensing under her fingertips . . . cool, crisp curls brushing her face and throat . . . a trail of kisses like sparks leaping into flames. Strong hands moulded her to the lean, powerful length of him in a hungry meeting that burned up all her will and left Reason in ashes. He was the Devil, consuming her, body and soul. She could not withstand him. She only craved.

Her hands moved to his neck, to pull his teasing, tormenting mouth harder against her own. In the growing turbulence, she never knew how they came to the settee. In his arms, where she had to be, she was lost to all the world. Only his world existed: his mouth and hands, caressing, inflaming . . . his heart, pounding its fury against hers . . . and his voice, low, and ragged with longing as fierce as her own.

Somewhere, miles away in the storm, a bell tolled.

Julian was about to tear off his neck-cloth when he heard the sound again. A chime. Coming from somewhere. A hall . . . in a house.

His hand paused at the knot of his cravat. *Her* house. He groaned as reality thumped down upon him. A house, filled with servants — and a niece and companion likely to return any minute. What time was it?

He had not counted the chimes, and he could not reach for his pocket watch, because a lady was in the way.

Her eyes, dark with passion, opened, and a shaft of pain shot through him. Gad, those eyes. Oh, and that mouth, swollen now, ripe and so inviting. He bent and kissed her lingeringly, then groaned again, because it must stop. Now. *Now,* he commanded himself as her hand crept to his hair.

He took the hand away and kissed it. "My love," he said hoarsely. "I must go."

She blinked once, twice, uncomprehendingly. Then the world must have come back to her as well, for the colour rose in her cheeks even as the smoky passion ebbed from her eyes . . . and left them troubled.

That, he thought, would not do. He kissed her again, then wished he hadn't, because there could be no surcease for him this night, and holding her in his arms with no hope of consummation was only torment. He'd been tormented enough, all this long while. Was it an hour, two? Or only minutes?

He couldn't think, not with her warm body pressed against him. But the body began to struggle, and a hand was pushing at his chest.

He drew back slightly.

"You said you were going," she said, panting. "Then *go*."

He looked at her. Her hair was a riotous tumble of gleaming, fire-tinted curls. At her throat, a mere three of the long parade of tiny buttons were undone. That had been accomplished with so much difficulty, he thought a lifetime needed to undo the rest.

"You might at least contrive to appear sorry," he complained as he helped her sit upright. "Obviously, you have no notion the agonies I suffer at having to stop."

The teasing note was in his voice only, not in his heart. He should never have been so incautious. What might have happened had he not chanced to hear the clock chime?

"You would have had no difficulties if you hadn't begun." She pushed her heavy hair back from her face.

"Don't say that, Lilith," he said quickly, appalled at the ominous glistening in her eyes. "Don't make me feel like a criminal for loving you." He took both her hands in his. "Look at me," he commanded softly.

The smoky blue gaze swept his face.

"I can never hurt you," he said. "I only wanted to hold you for a little while. No, that isn't true. You know I want more — but I can be content with what you're willing to give." He smiled wryly. "If not, I should have ravished you by now."

"Indeed. In my own house, filled with servants — in my study, no less. And my niece. Good heavens! What time is it?" She jerked her hands free and jumped up so quickly she nearly knocked him off the settee.

He recovered his balance and drew her back down beside him. "Not so late," he said. "But I shall not go without a promise."

"No promises. Oh, Julian, please leave, do." She tried to pull her hand free again, but his grip was firm this time.

"In a moment. But I must see you again — and not in a crowd of Argus-eyed friends. Drive with me tomorrow."

"Oh, certainly. In Hyde Park, I expect, at five o'clock."

"There's no reason we may not take a turn in the park. My new curricle is ready. Surely you can ride in an open vehicle, with my tiger to lend us countenance?"

"No."

"My love," he coaxed. "Only a short drive. Can I not have you to myself now and then?"

"You've had me to yourself half the night — and see what comes of it. Oh, heaven help me, what is to be done with you?" Her searching scrutiny of his countenance made him uncomfortable. "You've the Devil's own tongue, and all his arts, I'm sure. You're like the bad angel, whispering in my ear — and I always *listen.*"

All of which was to say she'd consented. His heart should have soared, because she'd listen, too, when he coaxed her to a small but luxuriously appointed house in Kensington that had been awaiting her some time now.

Lord Brandon's heart did not quite soar, though he wanted her more than ever, if that were possible. He could not recollect when any woman had so stirred him with mere kisses, or when the lightest caresses had ever aroused such maddening desire. It had been enough, certainly, to make him forget where he was — aye, and who he was, if it came to that.

He was happy, and relieved, naturally, because his trials would soon be over. Still, her words troubled him. Though he'd used all his arts upon her, he did wish she wouldn't remind him.

As soon as Julian had gone, Lilith ran up to her bedchamber. Having firmly declined Mary's services, Lilith doggedly prepared herself for bed, though she was in such a tumult she could scarcely see straight.

She was not, as she'd reminded her would-be lover, a fool. Besotted though she was, she possessed sense enough to understand tomorrow's ride would be no mere turn about the park. He would not be content to sit beside her, talking about draining fields or breeding cattle. Nor, she admitted to her shame, would she.

She had sufficient sense as well to comprehend that "love" was Julian's euphemism for physical pleasure. Why he should want Lilith Davenant she would never understand. That hardly mattered any more. She wanted him, craved his company, longed for the sound of his teasing voice, yes, and ached for his touch.

He was, just as everyone had claimed, irresistible. Thus, yet another infatuated woman would succumb to him.

She sat at the dressing table and brushed out her tangled hair. He'd pulled out every single pin in seconds, it seemed. Tonight he was not the teasing, lazy lover she'd first known. This night, passion had come in a thundering fury. He might have ravished her easily enough in that tempest.

Yet a sweet tempest it was, sending joy surging through her . . . and that was why.

She put down the brush and began to braid her hair, the steady motion a counterpoint to the quivering ache within.

She'd never known such furious joy. She never would with any other. She would have it once, with him. She would not deny him, though she knew he'd leave her soon after. That was his nature. All the same, she would not deny him, because she would not deny herself. She must have his passionate lovemaking once — though she be damned for it. She must have that . . . because she would go on loving him all the rest of her life.

15

Rachel's first instinct was to tell her brother what she'd overheard. In any case, had he bothered to glance at her shocked face when she entered the box he would have questioned her immediately. Luckily, the box was dark, and he was too busy explaining the moral of the play to Cecily.

Thus the first wave of outrage passed, leaving more sensible second thoughts in its wake: if Thomas learned of the wager, he'd have to challenge Brandon to a duel, and the marquess would kill him. Even if Thomas survived the duel, his career would never survive the scandal.

Consequently, Rachel kept her news to herself, and took out her frustration on her husband when he appeared some ten minutes later.

At eleven o'clock the next morning, Lady Enders was closeted with Lilith in the latter's sitting room.

Though her husband was an active MP, Rachel was scarcely a politic woman, and her terse revelations fell plain as bludgeon blows. All the same, except for a momentary loss of colour and the rigid set of her features, Lilith appeared to digest the news with her usual impassivity.

"A wager," she repeated expressionlessly when Rachel had done ranting about perfidious males and the punishment they'd suffer if ever *she* had a hand in the nation's management.

"Yes — as though a defenseless woman were a pack of cards or a set of dice. Oh, I knew he was a villain, but this is beyond mere villainy. It is beyond anything! How can a man appear so pleasing, with his heart so black and vile inside him? 'Whited sepulchres,' " Rachel quoted, " 'Which indeed appear beautiful outward.' And so he did, my dear. Even I was taken in, so amusing he was, and such an agreeable smile. I should have known better. The leopard doesn't change his spots. I shall never forgive myself."

"For what?" Lilith asked coldly. "It is merely a wager — a foolish one, since he cannot but lose, and I'm sure it's nothing to him to lose a few thousand pounds. Or a horse. Or whatever the . . . the stake was."

"But to wager on such a thing — a lady's honour — "

"I have my honour still, Rachel. Or perhaps you had doubts?"

There was a flurry of ruffles, and Lady Enders's face turned puce to match them. "Good heavens! How can you say such a thing? The thought never crossed my mind. I should never have mentioned the matter, I am sure, but that you . . . well . . . " She hesitated.

Lilith lifted her chin. "Yes?"

"My dear, it is only that you have been quite friendly with him of late."

Lilith made no answer, and Lady Enders plunged on. "I thought it my duty to let you know what sort of *friendship* he had in mind. Knowing of this matter, naturally you will not wish to continue the acquaintance? We do not know how many others are part of this infamous speculation, or in what manner he is to demonstrate — that is — "

"I understand what it is, Rachel. You need not be anxious. I hope I know how to conduct myself in these — or in any — circumstances."

Lord Brandon arrived, as he'd promised, promptly at a quarter to four o'clock.

He'd scarcely contained his impatience the whole long day, though he found enough to do in ordering up champagne and every sort of delicacy, in seeing the small house in Kensington filled with flowers, in checking the gowns hung in the wardrobe and the lingerie tucked with sachets into drawers. Today, for a few precious, uninterrupted hours, Lilith Davenant would be entirely his, at last.

And at last he was shown into the drawing room. He was not surprised to find her alone. He was surprised to discover she was not dressed to go out. She wore a plain brown frock, and her hair was braided tight about her head. Deep shadows ringed her eyes. As he moved eagerly across the room to her, he saw as well that she'd been weeping. A chill of anxiety ran through him.

"My love," he said, holding out his hands.

She retreated a step. Her white face set into taut lines and her posture stiffened.

"You will not touch me," she said. "You will not say another word. I meet you this once only to tell you our acquaintance is at an end. Henceforth, I do not know you."

The chill clawed at his heart now. "Lilith."

She turned and pulled the bell-rope. "Cawble will show you out. Good day, my lord."

"Lilith! What is this?" He reached for her hands, but she moved back another step and folded them tightly before her.

"This is how you lose a wager, my lord," she said.

He felt the blood rushing to his face.

"Good God," he breathed. "You must . . . "

273

The door opened, and Cawble appeared. "Madam?"

"His lordship is leaving, Cawble."

Lord Brandon left quietly enough.

Dismissed.

In a few cold sentences.

So cold, so certain, they'd crushed argument before it could begin, or when he might have begun, came the death-blow. He'd not mistaken the words: "This is how you lose a wager."

Numb, he climbed into his curricle. He stared blankly at the house a moment, then set the horses in motion.

He'd driven on blindly, he knew not how far — a street, a turning, another street — when Sims, his tiger, spoke up.

"My lord, it's that Hobbs. He wants you to stop."

Only then did Lord Brandon take note of the figure running after the curricle, shouting something. The marquess drew the horses to a standstill, threw the ribbons to Sims, and jumped down.

"Beggin' your pardon, my lord, but Susan told me I was to stop you no matter what."

"So you have," said his lordship. "I am at your disposal."

"She told me to tell you Lady Enders was

by this morning. Her and my mistress was locked up private most of an hour, and when the missus come out she was — she was — What was it?"

Lord Brandon waited.

"In a taking, I think. What did Susan say? Up in the boughs. That was what Miss Glenwood told her. Up in the boughs like no one ever seen before." He looked up at Lord Brandon's still, hard countenance. "I 'spect she was warning you, my lord, or trying to. But I was down in the kitchen and no way to step out before you come. But Susan said I was to tell you anyhow."

Lord Brandon gazed blankly about him. Lady Enders. That was how Lilith had found out. Lady Enders must have overheard . . . last night. His fault. He'd been so impatient to get away, he'd scarcely watched the stairs, let alone the corridor. Anyone might have overheard.

He dropped a few pieces of silver into Hobbs's hand, thanked him, climbed back into the curricle, and headed for the village of Kensington.

When they reached the house, the marquess sent Sims and the curricle away. Neither would be required this evening. He'd already dispatched the other servants, because strangers would have made Lilith uncomfortable.

275

Julian entered the small, tastefully furnished room where a cold meal had been laid out. The door to the adjoining bedchamber was partly open. He closed it.

He pulled a bottle of champagne from the silver ice bucket, opened it, and filled one crystal goblet.

Lilies had been cut into the crystal. Lilies bloomed everywhere, in one form or another — upon the wall coverings and draperies and carpets. There were orchids, as well, because he'd once compared her beauty to orchids, and because she'd worn them in her hair — his gift. The first of many gifts, he'd thought. He would shower his imperious mistress with tributes.

He took his wineglass and walked to the window, where he stood a long while. Evening was hours away, yet black night seemed to be falling already. The heavy clouds had darkened, and rain tapped steadily upon the windowpanes.

She might have been with him now. They might have stood together, watching the rain draw hurried, swirling patterns upon the glass.

He would have appeared to watch the rain, but his glance would steal to her face, to study her proud profile. He would not have heard the pattering beat against the windowpanes, only her quiet, cool voice, its cadences rich and smooth, even when animated, when she talked of Derbyshire and her land. Or wistful, as she sometimes was, caught by some bitter-sweet memory.

He would have made her laugh, perhaps. But he would not have been quite content until he had taken all the pins from her hair. He would not have been altogether easy until she was in his arms. Then he would sweep her into the storm with him, because hers was a passionate spirit, demanding and willful as his own. Not to be broken or bent. Still, he might have possessed it. Even now, all that was Lilith Davenant might have been his.

This is how you lose a wager.

He turned and hurled his wineglass across the room. It struck the mantel and shattered into sparkling shards.

Lost — aye, lost *her* — and all his own doing.

What had he told Elise? Something about the challenge being irresistible, wasn't it? A challenge merely. The tart had known him better than he knew himself. She'd comprehended quickly enough the extent of his overweening vanity.

That was it. Vanity and one thoughtless moment — and his was a lifetime of such moments — had cost him this one woman he wanted above all others. Wanted, he discovered now, as some blade seemed to twist in his chest, more than anything else in this world.

A few minutes after Mrs. Davenant had left her niece's room, Susan appeared to dress the girl for the evening. She found Miss Glenwood curled up in a chair, her chin resting on her hand and her brow puckered. She looked up at the maid's entrance.

"Oh, Susan, how I wish you and Hobbs had been quicker — though I much doubt it would have helped. It is worse than I thought."

"I was as quick as I could be, Miss Cecily," said the maid. "But Hobbs couldn't get away in time, and if the missus was to get wind — "

"She's got wind of something, and I wish I knew what it was. It must have been dreadful, because she is so miserable, and terribly, terribly confused. Why, she just now said she'd been *neglecting* me. Have you ever heard the like? And such a long lecture about my gentlemen friends. She said it all so kindly and sadly, I didn't have the heart to remind her I already knew all *that*."

"All what, miss?"

Cecily stood up and walked to the wardrobe. "I should like to wear the pink muslin, but tonight we'd better do without the lace."

"Do without? Your aunt'll have my head.

You know how she feels about young girls showing their bosoms."

"Yes, and I should not wish to upset her, so I must be late going down, and you must be certain to arrange my wrap very carefully."

The widow's party was unusually late arriving at Lady Violet Porter's rout.

Lord Robert, who'd been elbowed, backed into, and trod on this last hour, was beginning to wonder how he could have been so mad as to come. He had no one to talk to, and he couldn't breathe. He'd have done better to spend the evening pacifying his mistress. Julian had warned that an emotional woman like Elise might so far forget herself as to create scenes at the most inconvenient times.

Then Lord Robert spied Miss Glenwood proceeding slowly up the stairs, her aunt on one side, Sir Thomas on the other. Miss Glenwood met his glance and smiled. Lord Robert promptly began shoving his way through the crowd. He reached the top of the stairs just as the trio did, greeted the widow and the baronet politely, greeted Cecily — took a second look at Cecily — then hastily excused himself.

He was about to plunge back the way he'd come, when he happened to glance back. He saw Mr. Ventcoeur bend over Miss Glenwood's small hand. In the next moment, that hand was tucked into Mr. Ventcoeur's arm.

Lord Robert left the rout.

Indecent was what it was.

What on earth could her aunt have been thinking of, to allow the girl to go about half naked, so that every lout in London could ogle her? And of all the louts to give her arm to, that crude imbecile, Ventcoeur.

Well, if the aunt didn't know better, Lord Robert Downs certainly did. He would give Miss Glenwood a serious talking-to. Tomorrow.

Tomorrow came and went and there was no talking-to, because Lord Robert found no opportunity. The one country dance Miss Glenwood allotted him was hardly conducive to serious conversation. She was winded at the end of it — as was all too evident in the rapid rise and fall of —

At any rate, by the time they'd both caught their breath, her next partner had stepped in to claim her.

The following night was exactly the same.

Consequently, early Monday afternoon, Lord Robert borrowed his cousin's curricle without permission, called at the house, and invited Miss Glenwood to drive with him.

She was very quiet until they reached the park gates. Then she sighed and said she had something to tell him.

"Yes, well, I have something to tell *you* Miss Glenwood," he answered. Before he could lose his courage, he plunged into the sermon he'd rehearsed.

She listened very attentively, then looked at him in a puzzled way. "I don't understand," she said. "When Papa wants to sell a mare, he doesn't cover the poor animal with blankets, but displays her to best advantage. I'm on the market, you know."

"On the what?" he cried.

"To be married. That's why I'm in London, isn't it? That's why all the girls come. And I don't at all understand what's so immodest. Lady Rockridge is quite strict, yet Anne's frocks are much more daring than mine, and no one's shocked. Even my aunt had to admit *that*, though she blushed the whole time. But poor Aunt is so confused."

Lord Robert made no answer. Miss Glenwood was a level-headed girl, and it was quite true about Anne's frocks — indeed, about most of the gowns to be seen in any Season. All the same, it seemed very wrong for Miss Glenwood to go about in such revealing costumes. She was a child, still. Well, not exactly, but —

There burst into his mind at this moment a vision of a feminine form in breeches, and he grew dizzy.

"It's because they've quarrelled, you know," Cecily continued. "I know it was something dreadful because I heard Aunt Lilith tell Cawble that Lord Brandon was not to be admitted to the house. And your cousin must be just as angry, because he keeps away."

Lord Robert shook himself to attention. His cousin he could talk about articulately.

"Miss Glenwood, I must tell you, Julian would never keep away from anything on account of a woman."

"He was not at Lady Violet's rout Friday, or at Lady Shumway's Saturday, or Lady Greenaway's last night."

"Saturday was Kean's first appearance as Othello," Robert argued. "Naturally, Julian would go."

"For weeks and weeks he's always appeared wherever my aunt is. Yet ever since they quarrelled, we haven't seen him. I expect he's just as miserable as she is, and they're both too proud and stubborn to admit it."

"In that case, they're better off apart, don't you think?"

"How can you say such a thing?" Her blue eyes flashed a reproach. "You know they must marry. Fortunately," she added reassuringly, "I have a plan."

He was so startled he nearly dropped the reins.

282

"Marry? Each other? Your aunt is *engaged* already."

"Well, she can't marry that tiresome, preaching man, can she?"

"Miss Glenwood — "

"You're confusing the horses, Lord Robert. Do call the one on the left to order before he takes us into that tree."

Lord Robert drew the carriage to a halt.

"Miss Glenwood — "

"You needn't be anxious. It's a very good plan, and really, quite simple."

At this moment, an enormous grey cloud swallowed up the sun. The heavens darkened, and Lord Robert felt a chill at the base of his skull. "Drat," he said. "It's going to rain."

Miss Glenwood glanced up. "Not for hours," she said.

Sure enough, the cloud moved on and the sun shone brightly again. Nonetheless, Lord Robert felt as though the cloud had settled within him. "Miss Glenwood," he said gently, "You really oughtn't be contriving any plans. It's none of our affair, and even if it were, it wouldn't do any good, because Julian's a hardened bachelor. If they've had a row, maybe it's for the best."

Miss Glenwood appeared to consider. "Perhaps you're right," she said after a moment. "It must be the strain telling on me.

Aunt won't let me stir a step without her any more. I assumed that was because she didn't know what else to do with herself. And, naturally, when I heard all that long lecture about you, I was bound to think she must be a bit irrational. How could she imagine I didn't know all that already?"

The cloud within seemed to grow heavier and darker then.

"About me?" Lord Robert said uneasily. "I hope she wasn't repeating a lot of idle gossip."

"Not at all. But such obvious facts, I'd be utterly feather-brained not to be aware of them. Really, there was no need to tell me you couldn't possibly be a serious suitor. Even if you weren't desperately in love with that beautiful Frenchwoman, what on earth would you want with an ignorant country girl? Certainly I'm not grand enough for you, and naturally your family must object. I couldn't blame them, could I? After all, my portion would hardly keep you in neck-cloths."

The sophisticated man of the world blushed hotly, which must have vexed him, because he grew altogether unreasonably irate at the perfectly reasonable way in which Miss Glenwood had just discounted him.

He did not see, he told her, why there was any need for her aunt to warn her against him. Had he behaved improperly? He hadn't even attempted to kiss her — though he had no doubt Ventcoeur had, such an unprincipled, crude character he was. Her aunt didn't warn Miss Glenwood against any other fellows, though Lord Robert had seen them all ogling and gawking in the most *obscene* way. As to portions, he had far less need of a huge dowry than Beldon had.

"I may be a younger son," he raged, "but I'm certainly not so pinched for funds that I have to dodge the bailiff. I'm very shocked, Miss Glenwood, indeed I am, that you'd for a minute think I'd ever marry for money, or be looking out for some duke's spoiled, stuck-up daughter just to please my stiff-necked family."

"Of course not," she answered calmly. "That would be so silly, when you practically have a wife already — and very beautiful she is, too. Also clever, I expect, or you'd be excessively bored, being so very clever yourself."

"Miss Glenwood," he said, acutely uncomfortable, "this is not a proper subject to discuss."

"Very well. What would you rather talk about?"

While he was desperately seeking a topic, his cousin's spirited cattle began snorting and prancing with impatience. Experienced horsewoman that she was, Miss Glenwood's gesture must have been instinctive. She only reached for the ribbons, and her small gloved hand touched his.

Then she blushed . . . and bit her lip . . . and hastily folded her hands in her lap.

Lord Robert looked at her pink, downcast profile and at the soft, full lip caught between her perfect white teeth, then at the dainty gloved hands.

While he was looking, the ribbons somehow transferred to one hand while the other took hers.

Her long lashes swept up slowly.

"Oh, Lord," he said.

"You should not be holding my hand," she said softly.

"I know," he said. "I can't help it. Miss Glenwood."

"Yes?" Her face was lifted to his, her lips slightly parted. There was an odd ringing in his ears, and Lord Robert had a curious sensation of falling — which, in a manner of speaking, he *was*, because his own face lowered to meet hers . . . and before he knew what he'd done, he'd kissed her.

Being a level-headed miss, the young lady ought to have boxed his ears. She did not. Thus the kiss continued a deal longer than it should have done. Long enough so that, when he finally remembered to stop, he could not possibly pretend it had been a mere friendly token of goodwill.

"Oh, my," she said.

"Miss Glenwood, I do beg your pardon. I don't know — "

She gazed at him in admiration. "Oh, but I think you *do*. That was ever so lovely. Really, it was a revelation. Rodger has never kissed me like that. All I ever get from him or James is a peck on the cheek, and only when they're in exceedingly good humour."

"Yes, Miss Glenwood, but I'm not your brother. I wouldn't be your brother," he added vehemently, "for anything in this world."

"Wouldn't you? What would you like to be?"

Lord Robert took a deep breath, tore his gaze from her blue, unwinking one, and stared fixedly at the horses.

"I don't mean to be forward, but I do wish you'd settle it in your mind," she said. "You can't be in love with two women at the same time, you know, and if you're not in love with me, it would be most unkind to confuse me with such agreeable kisses. I can't afford to be muddled at present. I have too many responsibilities."

With the matter thus set so plainly before him, Lord Robert could hardly fail to grasp it. In fact, he was mortified. He could not understand how he could have been so obtuse.

"I'm afraid I'm very much in love with you, Miss Glen — Cecily," he said, his face scarlet.

"I'm glad to hear it," she said. "I was beginning to feel quite ridiculous. I've been in love with you ever so long."

Relief quickly succeeded astonishment. He opened his mouth to speak, then changed his mind. There could be no other response to such a sweet, frank avowal but another fervent kiss. But as he drew away, the reality of his situation hurtled upon Lord Robert like a runaway carriage. Her disapproving aunt, bound to throw obstacles in their way . . . as though his own family wouldn't be quick enough to do that, though she was hardly in the same category as Elise — Good God! Elise!

"Egad!" he blurted out. "Now I'm in a devil of a fix."

"Not at all," came the confident response. "So long as we've got matters straight between us, we can mend everything else — because two heads are ever so much better than one, aren't they?"

16

Whatever other problems two heads might solve, that of Elise was Lord Robert's alone. No gentleman could possibly expect a gently bred innocent to advise him how to be rid of his mistress, especially when he'd solemnly pledged to marry that mistress in two months' time.

Accordingly, feeling like the lowest species of cur, Lord Robert drove to his lodgings.

As he opened the door, the scented atmosphere nearly turned a stomach that was already in knots. His mistress's affectionate greeting sent his conscience into screaming fits. He thought perhaps his confession could wait until tomorrow, but he'd no sooner thought it than he remembered Cecily's sweet, innocent mouth. He backed away as Elise moved to embrace him.

"What is this?" she cried. "You cannot be angry with me. What has your poor Lise done to make you so cold?" She retreated as well. "Ah, but you are often so, I find. I think so much time in grand company makes you despise me."

He swallowed. "I don't despise you. Not at all. You've been — you've been wonderful to me. Better than I deserve. That is to say, I don't know why you've stuck it out so long."

She turned glistening eyes upon him. "So long? But I told you *forever*. Have I not promised? Have I not pledged myself to you?"

"Yes, well, maybe you shouldn't have." Lord Robert took another deep breath, made himself look her in the eye, and said, "I'm afraid I've fallen in love with someone else."

Her dark eyes opened wide in shock. He turned away and moved to the mantel.

"I didn't mean to," he said, picking up one of the framed silhouettes that stood there. "It just happened. I think it happened weeks ago, but it never occurred to me. I never dreamed I could love anyone else. But I do, and — and so I came to ask you to let me go. You can't want to marry a man who's in love with another woman."

He replaced the picture and waited.

There was a long silence. Then she said, her voice hurt but gentle, "Ah, my poor Robin. You have some infatuation, I comprehend. Well, I must be patient. It will fade, and you will find me still waiting."

"Elise, I'm sorry, but it's not like that," he

answered, vexed at her humouring him. "I'm going to marry her — as soon as I can."

Mademoiselle Fourgette promptly swooned.

An hour later, Robert drove away, in worse case than when he'd arrived. He'd talked until he was blue in the face, and Elise — usually so perceptive — had been utterly unable to understand him. She was thoroughly convinced his new passion was but a whim.

At length, torn with guilt and not a little frustrated, he'd tried to buy his mistress off. Half his trust fund he'd promised. It would be hers forever. He'd have papers drawn up immediately.

Then she'd fainted again, and when she revived, there was no talking to her at all, because she was hysterical. She could not think, she told him. Her head was spinning. It was too much to take in at once. He must give her time to recover from the shock. He could not be so cruel as to press her now — and to speak of money!

Still, Robert told himself as he brought the carriage to the mews, he would press, because she must be got to go away peaceably. Good God — what if she took to haunting him, as Lady Caroline had haunted Byron all last year? What if they met up in public and Elise created a scene?

She very well might. Julian had warned about that only the other day. Cecily might understand, but her aunt — Gad, if Elise enacted any scenes in front of the widow, he and Cecily would be done for.

Julian. Of course. Julian always knew what to do. First, unfortunately, there'd be hell to pay about borrowing the curricle. Still, he'd only rip up fierce for a while, and after, he'd order brandy. Then Robert would ask his advice.

Accordingly, when Julian had returned to the house to change for the evening, Lord Robert squared his shoulders, marched up the stairs, and knocked at the door.

He found the marquess standing by the window, staring out. "What do you want now?" Julian asked.

Stammering a good deal, Robert made his confession to his cousin's back.

"Sims would not have let you take the curricle if he did not trust your skill," was the dispassionate response. "Feel free to drive yourself to perdition."

"Yes, well, that's very kind of you," Robert said nervously.

"Indeed, I am a model of every Christian value."

Julian turned round. His face was its usual

mask of boredom. Obviously, then, he could not be miserable, regardless what Cecily believed. Tired, perhaps.

"I hate to bother you," Robert said, trying for airiness, "but I'm in a devil of a fix, don't you know? You see, I borrowed the curricle so I could take Miss Glenwood driving — "

The black eyebrows rose slightly. "Her aunt permitted the girl to drive with you?"

"Well, not exactly — though I don't see why she shouldn't. Anyhow, she'd gone to Lady Enders's. Still, Mrs. Wellwicke didn't raise any sort of fuss. Don't see why she should. No harm in a fellow taking a girl out for a drive in an open — "

"Good God."

"I beg your pardon?"

The marquess turned back to the window. "Get out," he said.

"But, Julian, I have to speak with you. It's very important. Elise — "

"Go to hell."

Man of honour or no, Lord Robert saw no alternative but to confide these latest developments to Cecily. Julian clearly was not going to be any help. He was apparently in a perfectly hideous fit of the blue devils. Even Hillard had quietly advised Robert to keep out of his cousin's way.

If Julian wouldn't help pacify Elise, the poor distracted woman might very well do something rash. It was only fair to prepare Cecily for that eventuality.

The information was relayed that night in short bursts while they danced.

Cecily accepted the news with her usual imperturbability, and told him not to worry about *that*. The major problem at present was Aunt Lilith.

"She was terribly disappointed in me because I went driving with you," said Cecily. "And so we had another heart-to-heart talk, and now you and I must be exceedingly cautious."

Caution, it turned out, meant that Lord Robert was not to attend every single affair she did. Cecily had promised her aunt she'd not spend so much time with him.

Cecily had not promised anything else, which must have made her conscience perfectly easy regarding the notes which thereafter travelled surreptitiously between the marquess's and the widow's town houses.

While these letters were being exchanged, the owner of a few dozen far more torrid ones was weighing her prospects.

Elise suspected within three days of the event that the widow had given Lord Brandon his *congé*. Elise heard of his reappearances at several of his old haunts, and saw him herself at the performance of *Othello*.

Therefore, she put off Lord Robert, visited with her friends, and listened to the shop girls' talk. Before a week had passed, her suspicions were confirmed: Society noted with disappointment that Lord Brandon had once again vanished into the depths of the *demi-monde*.

Little more than a fortnight remained of the stipulated seduction period. He would lose, as Elise had been certain he would. She was equally certain his pride would not permit him to revert to his previous threats.

Perhaps he no longer cared what became of the letters or of Robert. On the other hand, what of the girl Robert was so eager to marry? Surely the marquess would wish to forward this oh-so-suitable match. In that case, he was bound to offer more than a mere half of Robert's paltry trust fund — and more likely to pay. Once wed, Robert might conveniently forget what he owed his mistress for two years' fidelity. Besides, Robert could not legally promise any portion of his trust fund until he was twenty-five. He might be wed before then.

Mlle. Fourgette concluded that, of her two options, the marquess was the lesser risk. She would gamble on him.

When, at the end of her week's recovery, Lord Robert called to renew his pleas, Elise was adamant: she would *never* give him up. He'd made a terrible mistake, but she'd forgive him, and would wait until he came to his senses. She did not, however, promise to wait quietly.

My Darling Cecily,

I've done my best but it's just as you feared and I know we're bound to raise the very Devvil of a Dust but there's no Choice. Julian and your Aunt are too wrappt up in their own Troubbles. Do forgive me Dearest Darling Cecily because I should of known better and been Patiant, you are always so Level-Headed. Now I only wait for you to give the Word only please let it be Soon as possibble, we can't wait much longer and don't dare. I know I can't wait much longer to make you Mine.

Your Adoring

Robert

Miss Glenwood did not, as was her custom, tear this missive to tiny pieces and burn it.

She only smiled and murmured to herself, "Dear Robert. How sweetly you write — and so cleverly to the purpose."

Susan entered a while later, looking for the reply she knew must be forthcoming. "You'd better make haste, miss," she warned. "Hobbs can't be lingering about much longer."

"There's no need for him to linger," said Miss Glenwood. "Tell him the answer is *Tuesday*."

On Tuesday evening, Lord Brandon stood before his glass and stabbed an emerald pin into his cravat. The pin set off admirably the green embroidery of his satin waistcoat, and the combined effect drew riveting attention to his eyes.

This effect might not have been altogether desirable, considering his eyes were edged with deep shadows, the lines at the corners clearly evident, even in the flattering candlelight of his dressing room. In a few years, the lines would set deeply, and the furrow between his dark eyebrows would harden and deepen too. His face, like those of his older acquaintances, would reflect the empty, corrupt life he lived. In another few years, he'd look like every other aging roué.

Still, so long as he had money, he'd never lack for company. Even a troll could find some trollop to warm his bed, so long as he had the gold to persuade her.

Not that this night's harlot would require any great expenditure, he reflected. He was not decrepit yet, and though he'd not troubled to exert his notorious charm, the woman was willing. Another actress — but then, weren't they all?

He turned from the glass as Hillard entered.

"I've conquered the thing at last," his lordship said, with a brief glance at the heap of discarded neck-cloths he'd flung onto a chair. "Still, even Brummell has his share of failures."

"So he does, m'lud," said the valet, taking up his master's black evening coat. As the marquess thrust his arm into the left sleeve, a folded piece of thick stationery fell out. Hillard picked it up and handed it to him.

Five minutes later, Lord Brandon was running down the stairs, shouting for his curricle.

"The bloody fool!" he raged as he stomped to the vestibule. "I'll hang him myself! Where the devil is my curricle?"

A trembling footman wrenched open the front door. His lordship thundered through, and stormed round the corner to the stables.

"He's taken it?" Lord Brandon repeated,

glaring at his tiger.

"I was just comin' to tell you, my lord. I was out, enjoyin' a pint with Hobbs and Jem, and these others," Sims said indignantly, glaring at two much-abashed stable lads, "didn't know any better."

"Never mind. I'll take the other carriage. Only, be quick, will you?"

While he waited for the carriage to be readied, Lord Brandon considered his options. He could go after them himself — now. They could not have more than an hour's start of him, more likely less. But Lilith — did she know yet? He hoped not. That idiot Bexley would be no help. His plodding nags would be better employed behind a plough.

"Had Hobbs any word for me?" he asked his tiger.

"He only said his mistress was going to Lady Jersey's, and the young lady — Miss Glenwood, that is — was sick at home. The other lady was staying with her. I meant to tell you, lord, but I come back and these *numskulls* —"

"It doesn't matter. Where's Ezra?"

"You gave him the night off, my lord."

"Damn." The marquess briefly considered taking his horse, but quickly discarded that idea. The closed carriage was best. More discreet.

"Cover the crest," he told Sims. "And I'm sorry to offend your dignity, but you must serve as coachman this night."

When they reached the Jerseys', Lord Brandon remained within the vehicle and sent Sims round to the servants' entrance with a few gold coins and a message.

A quarter hour later, Mrs. Davenant was hurrying out the door and up the carriage steps.

She stopped short when she saw who was within.

Quickly he yanked her inside, and the carriage rumbled into motion.

"You — you — "

He put his hand over her mouth. "It's not a trick, and I'm not abducting you. Your niece is in trouble." Then he took his hand away and gave her Robert's note.

"What is this?" she cried. "How am I to read it in the dark?"

"I'll tell you what it says, but you may read it later if you don't believe me. They've eloped — my blasted fool of a cousin and your niece. That's why you were strongly advised to come alone. How did you keep your loyal fiancé from following, by the way."

"He was talking with the Prince of Orange. I only repeated the message: that Cecily had taken a bad turn and Emma had sent Mary in

300

a carriage for me. He offered to come, but I could not see what use he would be."

"Quite right. Men are useless when it comes to illness. I shall take you home, so that we can make certain Miss Glenwood is gone, and then — "

"She can't be," Lilith insisted. "I can't believe Cecily would do such a thing."

"Judging by Robert's purple prose, they consider themselves in desperate case."

She stared blindly at him a moment. "Oh no," she said faintly, dropping back against the thick squabs. "It's my fault. I had no idea there was any — any serious feeling between them. I warned her repeatedly against him — but it was only to prevent her discouraging her other suitors. Oh, she couldn't have run away with him. She couldn't have misunderstood me so. I'm sure I never expressed any dislike of him."

"I'm sure you didn't," he said while inwardly cursing his cousin and Miss Glenwood. Desperate or no, couldn't they have considered how this woman would suffer?

"Still, I lectured. Too much, I see now. To think how the poor child must have wanted to confide the true state of her feelings — and didn't dare. She must have suffered terribly, or she would never, never do such a shocking thing."

Lord Brandon decided to keep his own counsel on the subject of Cecily's sufferings. His cousin, he was convinced, had neither the forethought nor the intelligence to plan an elopement. This had obviously been planned. Had he known sooner about Miss Glenwood's "illness," the marquess would have smelled a rat. Cecily Glenwood was the type of girl who never took ill. Left naked in a monsoon, she'd come away without so much as a sniffle. Furthermore, unless he was very much mistaken in her character, Miss Glenwood had planned everything, down to the last detail.

Except perhaps the note. The girl would not have been so careless as to leave clues. The note must have been Robert's own fevered piece of work. Quite the correspondent that boy was.

Miss Glenwood, as the marquess had predicted, was not in her room, or anywhere in the house.

All that turned up after a frantic search was one crumpled note — again Lord Robert's. Emma found it by the wardrobe door, where Cecily must have accidentally dropped it.

Lilith read it, then handed it to Lord Brandon.

His lip curled as he glanced over it. "It only confirms the obvious. They've been planning this some time," he said, thrusting the note into his pocket. "I'd better be off. They've nearly two hours' start by now, and a speedier vehicle. Still, I have no doubt Sims will make up the time. With any luck, I'll have them back before morning."

"*We* shall have them back," Lilith corrected. "You can't believe I'd stay behind. My niece will need me."

He paused at the doorway and turned around.

Lilith had been too overwrought to spare him more than a glance. Now, she was taken aback by the grim set of his countenance and the deep shadows round his eyes. He looked ill — as he had when she'd first met him. Or more ill, perhaps. His face was thinner, older, and his green eyes were dull with fatigue.

"You can't come," he said. "You'll be jolted to pieces for hours on end. Besides, there's always the chance I *won't* be in luck, and you must be here to keep off the scandal-mongers."

Lilith turned to Emma. "You'll see to that, won't you?"

The plump lady nodded. "Certainly. I've only to mention the ailment is contagious, and everyone will keep away." She threw Lilith a reassuring smile. "I'll see to everything here. Naturally, you must go. If nothing else, Cecily must come back chaperoned."

As she spoke, Emma was opening drawers.
"I'll put together a few things for Cecily —
and you must take some necessaries yourself.
You don't know how long you'll be upon the
road."

The marquess glanced from one woman to
the other. "I'll wait downstairs," he said.

17

They sat in opposite corners of the coach, staring out the windows. Not until they were well out of London did Lord Brandon break the silence.

"I'm sorry," he said.

"It's hardly your fault," Lilith made herself answer. "If anyone's to blame in this, it's I — "

"That's not what I meant. Or at least, it's not all. My aunt — Robert's mother — has no high opinion of the men in our family. A lot of contemptible rogues, she thinks us. Some weeks ago she told me . . . well, it doesn't matter — but I do wish it hadn't been my own cousin, of all men, to bring you such trouble. You've been injured enough. By God, Lilith, I'm sorry."

Her throat ached. She waited until she could control her voice, then said, "They will have to stop to change horses. Cecily will not let him abuse your cattle. I shall pray the ostlers are very slow."

"Lilith."

"She packed very little. Perhaps they'll have to stop to purchase — "

"Lilith, please. I'm not asking you to forgive me — but there's something you must know."

She returned her gaze to the window. "We shall likely be journeying together many hours, my lord. You had meant to travel alone. Perhaps it would be best to behave as though you were doing so."

There was a moment's heavy silence in the dark carriage. Then he said wearily, "Yes, perhaps, as always, I am."

Though the carriage stopped frequently so that Lord Brandon could make enquiries, he had by sunrise still no word of Cecily and Robert.

"I don't understand it," the marquess said as he climbed back in for what seemed the hundredth time. "How is it possible no tollgate keeper, no innkeeper, has seen them? Robert could not possibly have had sufficient funds to bribe every human being en route."

The widow's hand was pressed to her temples. Her head must be aching horribly.

"I begin to think they may not be headed for Gretna after all," she said. "Perhaps the note was written to mislead."

"But where else would they go? I doubt my

306

cousin could have obtained a special license. It's not as though the bishops hand them out to every hot-headed young idiot who comes along."

"You're right. Very likely they've merely made a few detours. But they must return to the Great North Road at some point, mustn't they?"

Her voice, as always, was evenly modulated, low and controlled. Another woman would have spent the journey in complaints or hysterics. Not Lilith Davenant. For hours she'd sat mute, staring into the darkness. This was the longest conversation they'd had since his abortive attempt to . . . to what? Apologise? Explain? As though there could be any apology, or explanation.

He'd had ample time to reflect, and thus to wonder why he'd believed it could signify in any way that he'd wanted her from the first, and wanted her yet. Regardless the motive, his aim had always been seduction. He'd never had her best interests at heart. All that had moved him was Desire.

He'd struggled, all these hours, to keep from looking at her. He'd been trying, all these last endless days, to banish her image from his mind. Now he must begin all over again.

All the same, in spite of his resolutions, his

glance stole to her white, still face. She had not wept — not once. But her fine, slate-blue eyes were red-rimmed, her proud countenance tired and drawn. She'd seemed exhausted even before they started out, yet she refused to rest, and she'd scarcely touched a morsel when they stopped. She remained calm and upright by sheer force of will.

"You're tired," he said. "We'll make a longer stop next time."

"There will be time enough to rest when we've found them," she murmured. "If you traveled alone, you would not wish any delays."

"Don't be obstinate, Lilith," he answered briskly. "You won't be of any use to your niece if you collapse at her feet. In any case, we must endeavour to spare Sims. To enact the role of coachman is beneath his dignity, you know. In his view, coachmen are common servants. A tiger, on the other hand, is a professional — an artist, if you will."

This elicited a weak smile, and Julian felt a queer tugging at his heart as he recollected warmer smiles, and the rich, haunting sound of her laughter. He slumped back into his corner.

Emma Wellwicke was at the breakfast table, perusing a letter. Her husband had written it while in Spain, four months before, but it had arrived only this morning. While the letter was old, the sentiments Colonel Wellwicke expressed were eternal, and sufficiently heartening to take the lady's mind off present domestic anxieties.

Emma looked up at the sound of light footsteps. Then her mouth dropped open. "Cecily!" she gasped.

"Good morning," said Cecily. She dropped a light kiss upon the thunderstruck Emma's forehead. "Aunt is not down yet? How odd. Normally, she is up with the servants. Was she very late at Lady Jersey's?"

"Cecily!"

Miss Glenwood, who'd immediately headed for the sideboard, paused and peered at the companion's round face. "Good heavens, Emma, you look as though you've seen a ghost. I do hope you've not had bad news in that letter."

"Cecily Glenwood, where have you been?" Mrs. Wellwicke demanded.

"In my bed, of course," was the puzzled response. "Where else should I be?"

"Where else? Where else? On the Great North Road, I should think. Where your poor aunt is at this moment, searching for you, and worried half to death."

Cecily pulled out the chair next to Emma

and sat down. "Oh, dear," she said.

"Cecily Glenwood — "

"Oh, dear."

"Where were you last night? And don't say 'in my bed' because you weren't. Your aunt and I turned the house upside down. Now the poor woman is racing off to Scotland after you."

"Good gracious! You don't mean to say my aunt went alone?"

"She left with Lord Brandon. To prevent an elopement." In a few curt sentences, Mrs. Wellwicke described the previous night's excitement, closing with the demand, "Where *were* you?"

"Oh, dear. I shall explain everything, Emma. What a dreadful muddle! But first, don't you think we'd better send someone to bring them back?"

Half an hour later, Harris was tearing his way out of London, and Mrs. Wellwicke and Cecily had retired to the latter's sitting room.

"Yes, I did promise to go away with Lord Robert," Cecily was confessing calmly. "But when it came to the point, I couldn't do it. I only crept out to tell him so, but he was ever so stubborn. We argued — oh, for hours, I think. I expect he's still very cross with me. He said he was going to get drunk. I expect he's at his cousin's, sleeping off the aftereffects, poor man. Still, I'd rather have him on my conscience than Aunt Lilith, as I told him. I just couldn't pay her back so cruelly, after all she's done for me, even if she doesn't understand — "

"She *might* have understood," Emma reproved, "if you'd done her the courtesy of telling the truth, instead of sneaking about behind her back."

"Yes, of course you're right. But you see, I'm so dreadfully fond of Lord Robert, and she seemed to take him in such dislike. Well, I'm lamentably ignorant. If I weren't, I wouldn't have been so confused. But it's very confusing to be in love. Everyone says so." Cecily sighed. "Poor Aunt. Even *she's* confused, and she's so much older and more sophisticated. Still, we mustn't be overanxious. I'm certain Lord Brandon is taking very good care of her."

Mrs. Wellwicke studied the innocent, blue-eyed countenance in silence for a moment. Then she rose and left the room, wondering why she felt so very certain that Cecily had not quite explained everything.

Julian had at length persuaded his companion to take some refreshment when they stopped, but he could not persuade her to rest. So long as Sims declared himself perfectly satisfied with a quarter hour's nap snatched here and there, Lilith refused to admit she wanted any naps at all.

It was not until late morning, when the clouds began mounding into black thunderheads, that either of these two would consent to be reasonable. Sims had no taste for driving through thunderstorms, and Lilith, at this point, could scarce sit upright.

They reached a large inn just as the first heavy drops began to fall. As soon as the coach had rattled to a stop, Lord Brandon sprang out.

Lilith had declined his hand every other time. This time, when he saw her stumble to the carriage door, he ignored her protests and swung her down.

Her feet had no sooner touched the ground than her knees gave way.

"I knew it," he muttered as he lifted her in his arms. "Obstinate, pigheaded — "

"Put me down."

"Be quiet, or I shall drop you into the trough."

He carried her into the inn, shouted for a room, and began trudging up the stairs, the landlord scurrying after.

The latter had discerned no recognisable marking on the carriage, and his imperious guest had not deigned to mention his name.

Nonetheless, Mine Host knew nobility when he saw it and the voice of authority when he heard it. In minutes, Mrs. Davenant was tucked into the hostelry's most luxurious chamber, surrounded by servants whose sole aim in life, apparently, was to make the lady comfortable.

While Lilith rested, Julian made the rounds of the inn, questioning everybody everywhere, from tap-room to stables. Though he dropped coins wherever he went, he could obtain no word of the eloping couple.

The storm exploded into a fury of fiery flashes and deafening thunder. The inn quickly filled with soaked travellers, all of whom the marquess questioned. No one had noticed the distinctive black curricle. No one had glimpsed the young pair. It was as though they'd vanished.

Lord Brandon sat alone in a corner of the public dining room, nursing a mug of ale and thinking. More than ever, he was convinced he was on the wrong trail. The trouble was, he had no idea what the right one might be. At length, he decided to leave it to Lilith. If she wished to continue to Scotland, they would do so. If not — well, he would do as she wished. After all, the elopement promised only minor problems for Robert. It was the girl who'd most to lose. As always.

The women always paid dearly, he reflected. He should not have allowed Lilith to come. She would pay as well, to have been gone overnight with neither maid nor companion — and with him, of all men.

Yet how his heart had leapt when she'd insisted on accompanying him. How he'd wanted her company, even despising him as she did. Even cold and silent, shut off to him as irrevocably as if she'd been sealed in the vault beside her husband.

Lord Brandon pushed the mug away and stood up. He might as well take advantage of the bed he'd procured for himself, since the storm offered no sign of slackening. While sleep was the furthest thing from his mind, he could at least lie down. He had not slept in days. The strain would tell eventually if he was not careful.

His chamber was at the opposite end of the hall from Lilith's. As he reached her door, he paused. Even as he was telling himself to keep on to his room, his hand covered the doorknob.

It opened easily. Julian frowned. She should have locked it. He'd better wake her and tell her.

Noiselessly, he moved to the bed. She lay, fully dressed but shoeless, on top of the bedclothes. She slept soundly, her breathing slow and even. Better to let her sleep, he thought. He would have the door locked from outside.

Yet he stood, watching her. The thick, curling hair streamed over the pillow in fire-tinted waves. One tangled strand had fallen over her eye. He reached out and gently brushed it away.

She seemed so young and vulnerable, curled up on her side, one hand tucked under the pillow, the other across her breast. "My beautiful girl," he murmured. He kissed her forehead.

It was only a feather touch, but the long, sooty lashes swept up, and he found himself gazing into dazed, blue-grey eyes.

"Julian," she breathed sleepily. Then she blinked. "Oh. What is it? What time is it? Did I sleep?" She pulled herself upright, her eyes wary now.

"It doesn't matter what time it is," he answered unsteadily. "We can't leave until the storm abates."

A resounding boom shook the window.

"As you can hear," he went on, "it's raging like all the furies of Hades."

"Then they must have stopped as well."

"No doubt. Only . . . " He hesitated.

"What is it? Have you heard anything?

"No — and that's the trouble." He turned away from her worried gaze. "Lilith, I think that note of Robert's was meant to put me on

315

the wrong track. Not a hint of them, after all these hours. It doesn't make sense. Robert wouldn't have taken detours and back roads. He doesn't know the countryside well enough, and he's too impatient. I can only conclude your suspicions were correct, and Gretna wasn't their destination. The problem is — "

"I know," she said. "The problem is, we have no idea where they *have* gone." She glanced up at him. "Do you wish to return to London?"

"Only if that's *your* wish. Your niece is the main concern. My cousin may go to the devil who spawned him. Confounded, rattle-brained moron that he is," he went on heatedly. "Damn him! Oh, damn me as well. It was my fault his path crossed your niece's in the first place. If I'd left him to his tart — if I'd never met the scheming — Well, it scarcely matters, does it? What's done is done."

"Yes."

He saw her face close against him then, and scarcely thinking what he did, he clasped her hands in his. "Lilith, please believe me, I never meant what you think. No, that isn't right. I meant it at the start, perhaps — and to my shame — but not at the last."

She snatched her hands away. "Always *you*," she said. "What do I care what you meant, at first or at last? Whatever your game

— your wager — whatever you intended — it was *I* let you play it. You have only behaved according to your nature, while I — I," she repeated, pressing her fist to her breast, "have behaved in every way contrary to mine. That you cannot explain. That you cannot excuse. I am not your — your damned puppet or pet, you conceited, selfish man! How dare you apologise to me!"

A moment passed, while he took in the furious beauty of her countenance and all the imperious passion blazing in her eyes, and in that moment he was lost.

"Because I want you," he said helplessly. "I want you still. I miss you. I've thought of nothing but you all these days and nights, all the while I willed myself to think of anything else. I've never wanted anyone, anything, so much in my whole life as I want you, Lilith Davenant. How I wish I'd never met you."

"And how I wish," she retorted fiercely, "I'd left you in the ditch that day."

"Lilith — "

"Don't. Not another word. I made up my mind I would not stoop to question you. There is nothing you can say I wish to hear. It's all lies — always lies, and easy speeches." She scrambled to the other side of the high bed and pushed herself off.

He watched her ransack the contents of the

small bag Emma had packed for her, and disentangle a hairbrush from a chemise. He ought to leave, but he could not. He'd never felt so lonely, so utterly shut out, yet somehow it seemed worse, far worse, to leave the room.

The brush tore into her scalp, and Julian winced.

He crossed the room to her. "Let me," he said as he tried to pry the brush from her rigid fingers. "There's no need to rip your hair out just because I'm a conceited, selfish beast."

She pushed him away. "Leave me alone."

"Lilith."

She hurled the brush across the room. It flew past him, narrowly missing his shoulder, and struck the bed-post.

"I hate you! I hate you!" she cried. "How could you say those things to me? How could you be so unfair, so unkind, Julian? What had I ever done to be used so? How could you talk of love to me, and then laugh with that woman — at me, at the fool I was? How could you?"

He caught her in his arms and pressed her tense, stiff body close. "Not a fool, my love," he said. "Never that. Ah, if you only knew how that woman has laughed at me. But never you, my beautiful girl. She knew you'd break my heart."

318

"You haven't got a heart," she returned in a watery voice. "Or a conscience . . . or morals —"

"Then it was only indigestion," he said gently. "That's why I can't sleep or eat. That's why I can't bear to speak to anyone. That's why my staff is half terrified to death."

"It was only your pride was hurt. Because you lost your wager."

"That was all? My pride?"

"Yes." She stirred a bit. "And indigestion."

He glanced down at her bent head. A tumble of copper-tinted curls hid her face. She didn't try to break free, but her body remained taut, unyielding.

His fingers moved to her hair, to stroke it tenderly, as one would soothe a troubled child. He'd never meant to hurt her, but how could he have helped it? She was not like his other women.

Her head dropped a little lower to lay wearily against his chest. His heart ricocheted against his ribs. He bent to kiss the top of her head. "I've missed you," he whispered. "God, how I've missed you."

His hands slid to her back and tightened about her. He felt the slight shudder that ran through her. "Lilith."

She raised her head at last. The anger and hurt was gone from her eyes, and something sadder and gentler there called to him, making his thrashing heart ache.

He breathed her name once more. Then his mouth closed over hers, and the storm without was nothing to the tempest unleashed within.

Lightning seared the room in blinding white. The heavens roared and rattled the window-panes, but it was a mere zephyr to what raged between them as they clung to each other.

In minutes, he'd swept her to the bed and torn off his coat, neck-cloth, waistcoat. Frantic, hurried, desperate, wild to press her close again, to taste and touch . . . and above all, to *possess*. *His*. His at last, he thought, as she pulled him down to her and her lips sought his again.

He felt her hands upon his chest, and the touch scorched and chilled at the same time. He heard his own voice, murmuring urgently, but it was unintelligible, lost in the crash of thunder and the blood pounding in his ears.

His shaking fingers finally found the row of tiny buttons at her back. He nearly screamed with frustration.

Merely buttons, he pacified himself. There was no need for haste. Brandon was never hasty. Yet his fingers seemed to thicken to thrice their normal size, while the buttons simultaneously shrank to tiny, obstate nails imbedded in armour.

I'll rip the damned thing open, he raged silently. *I'll buy her a hundred frocks — what does one matter?*

He raised his head from her neck and looked at her.

"What is it?" she whispered. Her eyes slowly widened, searching his. That was when he saw it.

Or perhaps he'd seen it before, but refused to recognise it. He recognised it now.

He caught his breath and looked away . . . and was ashamed.

18

"We'll be back before midnight," Julian said as he turned away from the carriage window, "even if we stop for dinner."

They were returning to London.

Lilith was not hungry, but she agreed to the dinner. It would give Sims time for rest and nourishment. He ought to be considered, regardless how desperate she was to be home again. These last few hours had been torture.

Oh, Julian had apologised. He could not have been kinder, and, as usual, he must take all the blame. He had cursed himself a hundred times for his thoughtlessness and selfishness. He'd injured her enough, he said. He would never forgive himself for so abusing her trust. Angry and hurt, anxious for her niece, she'd been worried to death, utterly distracted. He'd behaved abominably, to take advantage of her confusion, her need for comforting. He'd very nearly ravished her. Thank heaven she'd brought him to his senses.

Indeed, it would have been a sweet apology, if Lilith hadn't known better. It was he who'd stopped it. He'd come to his senses all on his own.

He'd only wanted what he couldn't have. Once it was offered — She stifled a shudder of embarrassment. Still, there was no hiding from the truth. She'd heard the tenderness and sorrow in his voice, seen the regret in his eyes, and believed, because she could not do otherwise. She'd offered herself shamelessly. Yet for all his coaxing words, he'd found her wanting, just as Charles had. She'd bored him — or disgusted him, perhaps.

Very well. She'd made a fool of herself. Contemplating her stupidity served nothing. She had far graver matters to consider: her niece, first and foremost. Scandal was unavoidable. Good society would be closed to Cecily for years, if not forever. Nonetheless, the families could and must be appeased.

Julian had promised to help. Lord Brandon, Lilith amended. He would deal with his aunt, uncle, and cousins, while she dealt with her in-laws. The young couple must at least be accepted by their families.

Thomas would have to be dealt with as well, but that would be simple enough. Naturally, given the scandal, he'd wish to cry off. That scarcely mattered now, since her nieces would never be trusted to her again.

In a short while, the vehicle slowed and turned into the courtyard of yet another in the endless succession of inns.

Lilith allowed Lord Brandon to assist her from the carriage, though she wished he wouldn't press her hand so tightly, or hold it so long after she'd alighted. The warm, firm clasp made her want to weep. She was trying to swallow the lump in her throat when she heard the shout.

Lilith turned towards the sound. A small, thin man was running at them. She blinked. Harris? But this filthy, wet creature, his cap a sodden lump upon his head, could not be Cecily's groom. He stumbled to a stop before her.

"Oh, missus," he gasped. "Thank God I found you — "

There was a buzzing in her ears, and an odd, numb feeling in her spine. Lilith clutched Julian's arm for support as the world about her glared yellow, then faded to black.

Lilith opened her eyes to anxious green ones. A warm, strong hand held hers.

"Do you mean to remain with us this time?" Julian asked.

"I — I fainted, didn't I?"

"Repeatedly. We've had a confounded time bringing you round."

A pillow supported her head, but the settle she lay upon was narrow and hard. Gingerly, Lilith began to pull herself up to a sitting position. He released her hand to help her. Then he did not take it again.

"I should give your groom a sound thrashing," he said. "I can't imagine what he was thinking of, to spring at you in that outrageous way. I've never beheld so hideous a spectacle — and stinking to high heaven as well. No wonder you swooned."

"It *was* Harris," she gasped. "Is it about Cecily? Is she hurt?"

"Cecily is perfectly well. You may be quite easy. We've been off on a precious wild-goose chase. The girl never left London."

"Never left?" she echoed weakly.

"Never left, never eloped. It was all a hum." Julian rose from his chair. "I mean to say, it was a misunderstanding. From what Harris babbled, I gather Robert intended to run away with her, but your niece must have developed qualms at the last minute. She must have sneaked back after we'd gone."

He'd not much else to tell her. Harris was exhausted, having ridden hard since early morning. In any case, the groom had not been given many details.

"It doesn't matter," Lilith said as the news truly penetrated and relief washed over her.

"So long as she's safe at home. I should have known. I should have trusted her. She has far too much sense to do such a thing. I wish I'd been more confident at the start. I might have spared you — "

"Not at all. I told you I'd keep an eye on Robert, and I failed you. Naturally, I must have gone after him, regardless your confidence in your niece. I only regret that several hours must pass before I can wring his neck." He moved to the door. "I shall order a large dinner, which we may consume at our leisure. Then, we have but to return you discreetly in the dead of night, bribe Harris to hold his tongue, and all is well with the world."

"Yes," she said. No, she thought. Nothing would ever be altogether well again.

Considering he'd expected to be murdered, Lord Robert ought to have been grateful his cousin merely threw him against the library wall and half throttled him before turning away in disgust.

Lord Robert was relieved to escape with so negligible a physical punishment. He was not, however, sufficiently appreciative to keep silent.

"Go home?" he bleated, rubbing his aching throat. "You can't send me home. You haven't any authority over me, Julian."

"Don't test my patience, Cousin. That commodity is in short supply at present."

"I'm not going home. Cecily needs me. I'm not going anywhere without her. We're going to be married — I don't care what anyone says. She doesn't care, either."

Julian poured himself a glass of wine.

"In that you are sadly mistaken," he answered. "Or lamentably ignorant. I'm afraid you don't understand precisely the sort of predicament you've gotten yourself into."

He dropped his weary body into a large overstuffed chair, sipped his wine, leaned back, and proceeded to explain Robert's predicament in numbing detail.

When the marquess was done, Robert stumbled to the chair opposite and fell into it.

"Twenty-five thousand pounds," he said dazedly. "Breach of promise. She couldn't. She wouldn't." He turned a pleading countenance to his cousin. "She can't, Julian. She'll ruin everything. I could never marry Cecily. I couldn't do that to her."

"Naturally not. Her family wouldn't let you. In fact, if you have any feeling for her, you'll not venture into Miss Glenwood's general vicinity. I warned you the sort of scenes you might expect from your discarded mistress."

"But Julian, there has to be some way.

Surely if *you* talked to Elise. Gad, give her what she wants — the whole trust fund."

"She wants a title or revenge, the latter in the form of a scandalous, expensive, interminable, but eventually highly profitable lawsuit."

"I won't marry her. I can't believe I ever thought I loved her, when all this time she's only been planning how to ruin me."

"Yes, you were a great help to her in that."

Robert groaned. "How could I have been so stupid — stupid, stupid, stupid, and blind? Gad, I wish you *had* killed me. What am I going to do?"

The marquess stared into his wineglass. After a moment, he asked, "Are you quite certain you wish to marry Miss Glenwood? Are you *positive* you're truly in love with the girl?"

Robert's sinking head shot up. "How can you ask?" he demanded indignantly. "I adore her. I've been crazy about her since the moment I met her."

"You never mentioned it."

The younger man squirmed. "I didn't realise at first. I only thought of her as a . . . well, a friend, I suppose. Then, when I finally figured it out, I did come to you. Don't you remember? That day when I told you about the curricle?"

Julian only stared at him.

"I tried after that, but you were never home. Or when you were, you stayed locked in your room, or in the library, or somewhere. And you just ignored me, even when I pounded on the door. Or you told me to go to blazes. Well, it was obvious enough what your —" He caught himself up short. "That is to say, a man has to deal with his own problems. You're not my nurse, as you've told me a hundred times."

"Indeed. You've dealt with your problem marvelously, I see."

"I never pretended to be as clever as you," Robert shot back angrily. "You can sneer if you like. You don't know what it is to be half crazy about a girl — while everyone else makes it completely hopeless for you. It's all right if *you* go into the ugliest sulk there ever was and treat me like a pesky infant. But I'm not. I'm a grown man. I'm sorry I'm not as wise and blasé as you — but I couldn't just sit down to a card game and brandy and forget. I had to do *something*."

"So you did," was the dispassionate answer. "What amazes me is Miss Glenwood's consenting to such a hare-brained plan."

"Well, it was her — that is to say, I had a devil of a time persuading her."

Julian eyed him consideringly. "Why, I wonder, do I suspect it was the other way round?"

Robert squirmed again. "What nonsense."

"Naturally, you will not betray your beloved," said the other with a sardonic smile. "I know you're lying to me. Still, she *is* your beloved, evidently." He stood up. "I'm going out for a while."

"Now?" Robert shrieked.

"There's no need to agitate yourself, Cousin. You and Miss Glenwood have made your point. Attention has been called to your plight — though I'm not certain what you think Nurse can do with this unmitigated disaster. Really, Robin, you have quite the knack. Thank heaven you never went for the military. England could not possibly have withstood the blow."

With that, he left the room.

The sun shone brightly in the neat, tiny parlour. Its beams shot through the sparkling decanter, turning the wine to a glowing garnet. Elise handed her guest his glass.

"A toast," Lord Brandon said, touching his goblet lightly to hers, "to your victory, *mademoiselle*."

Her fine, dark eyebrows rose a fraction.

"Our wager," he explained. "You've won. I congratulate you."

"You are precipitate, milord. More than a week remains to you," she answered cautiously.

"By that time, I shall be gone," he said. He moved to the plain, shabby mantel to examine the two small silhouettes displayed there. The profiles — one of Robert, one of Elise — faced opposite directions. "To Paris," he added after a moment.

"Ah, the pursuit palls. You are bored."

"No, I've failed. You chose your champion well."

"I had no doubt of that."

He turned back to her. "I agreed to cease troubling you on Robert's account, and honour demands I abide by our terms. On the other hand, honour demands I do no injury to innocent persons. If I keep silent, I do such an injury."

"English honour," she said. "Such difficulties it makes."

"I think you are aware of this particular difficulty," he said quietly. "You know Robert wishes to marry a certain young lady. You know, then, you can't keep him. That you can make trouble for him I won't deny. His future is in your hands. Perhaps that's no more than he deserves. All the same, the young lady — "

"Yes, the young lady who has destroyed my future, milord. Do you come to plead on her behalf? Do you think to soften my heart towards my rival?"

All this time his face had been its customary

331

bored, impassive mask, his voice cool, expressionless. Nonetheless, there was a shadow upon him. Elise perceived it in his eyes and in the set of his mouth. She had suspected. Now she was almost certain. She waited while he turned the wineglass slowly in his hand.

"You have no more heart, my dear, than I do," he answered. "We are two of a kind, untroubled by heart or conscience. I will speak to your intellect." He met her gaze. "Lawsuits are time-consuming, expensive, and often exceedingly unpleasant matters. I can spare you the ordeal. I am prepared to settle an annuity upon you. In addition, I have a comfortable house in Kensington. You are welcome to inhabit it until such time as you find a replacement for my cousin. The annuity, naturally, would continue regardless. One thousand a year is not twenty-five thousand in a lump, but you know as well as I what will remain of a court's award . . . if, that is, you win."

She had expected an offer. She had not dared imagine one so generous. She said, "Two thousand."

A pause. "Two thousand, then."

"I begin to think you have a conscience after all," she said smiling.

The green eyes flickered. "I have a responsibility," he corrected.

"Oh, *certainement*. To your family. To your honour."

"To the girl. I should be happy to let Robert pay for his mistakes. I cannot permit an innocent young lady to pay for mine. Had it not been for our wager, I doubt she would have met my cousin, let alone fallen in love with him."

"Ah, *love*. The English are so romantic — and the men worse than the women." She shook her head. *"Pauvre homme,* I think she has dealt you the death-blow, the proud widow. I was wiser than I guessed."

His face had frozen, but he made no answer.

"A moment, milord, if you please."

She stepped out of the room briefly. When she returned, she carried a small enameled box. She handed it to him.

"Robert's letters," she said. "All of them. On top, you will find the letter you so much desired from me. It suits the purpose, I believe. One does not require many words to refuse one's hand."

He opened the box and read the topmost letter. Then he refolded it and tucked it into his pocket. "Thank you," he said. "You are most gracious, *mademoiselle.*"

She laughed. "I am merely a common slut, not gracious at all. I have but lost a lover. I

333

will find another — and better. When one has money, one may be more selective. Your generous recompense will ease my little pride's ache."

"I am gratified to hear it."

"But there will be no ease for you, I think," she went on, not troubling to conceal the triumph she felt. "You say you have no heart. But my champion, she has found yours — and cut it to pieces — has she not?"

He smiled faintly. "Now it is *you* who wax romantic."

"I see what I see."

"Do you? What is it you see, I wonder? Is my neck-cloth askew? Perhaps a dust mote upon my boots leads to the conclusion I am in romantic extremity?" He placed his wineglass upon a small table. "Naturally, one cannot be altogether pleased with failure. That is a new experience, but not so amusing that I plan to make a habit of it."

"Of course. To lose is not agreeable. Still, you will go to Paris, and you will forget."

"Yes." He took up his hat and gloves and walked to the door. Then he paused. "We *are* two of a kind, you know — a pair of precious knaves."

"So we are," she said. "*Âmes damnées*. Fortunately, we are beautiful, and still young enough."

"I leave for Dover on Sunday," he said as he drew on his gloves. "Perhaps you would join me. It has been many years since you visited the land of your birth, I believe."

Elise eyed him with critical appreciation. He was a beautiful man. Not golden, like Robert, but far more striking was the marquess, with his dark, arrogant looks. Tall and strong, his hair thick and black, and his eyes — ah, they were calculated to make a woman's heart drum to wild music. But not hers.

"*Merci*, milord, but I think not."

"As you wish. If you change your mind, feel free to send me word."

When he'd gone, Elise walked to the table and picked up the glass he'd left there. He'd scarcely touched it. She shook her head. "I will not pity you," she said softly. "The revenge is too sweet, my great and powerful lord. You would have crushed me if you could. No, it is just as you deserve."

At four o'clock Bella Martin arrived, to show off her new chaise and patronise her less fortunate friend with a drive in Hyde Park.

It was there Elise spied the widow, riding in a carriage with her betrothed and his relations.

"How ill she looks. The widow," she explained as Bella peered curiously about her at the parade of vehicles.

"Oh, *her*. I expect she should. Reggie said she and the girl — that blonde dab of a thing he's so taken with, you know."

"Miss Glenwood."

"Yes. Sick in bed for two days, and the house shut up tight. So Reggie sends enough flowers for six funerals." She gave the widow another contemptuous glance. "Appropriate, I'd say. I always thought she looked like a corpse anyhow."

"Her complexion is very fair," Elise said thoughtfully, "but she never looked so ill before, I think."

"Maybe someone's been keeping her up late nights," was the sly retort.

"Lord Brandon was here?" Lilith said as she took the package from her butler.

"He said it wasn't a call, madam. He wished simply to leave that for you. He seemed to be in rather a hurry."

"Yes. Yes, I expect he was," she mumbled. She turned and headed up the stairs to her room.

She'd hardly taken off her bonnet when Mary appeared.

"There, now," the maid said disapprovingly, "didn't I warn you to keep to your bed? You're tired to death. You'd better take a nap

336

if you mean to go out tonight."

"I'm not going out," said Lilith. "I've asked Lady Enders to take Cecily to the Gowerbys'. If you'll just undo the buttons, I'll manage the rest myself."

The abigail opened her mouth to protest, then shut it tightly, did as she was bid, and quietly left the room.

Her hands shaking, Lilith undressed and wrapped herself in an old cotton robe. Then she sat in the chair by the window and stared a long while at the package.

An hour passed before she could bring herself to unwrap it. As the paper fluttered to the floor, her lower lip began to tremble.

Mansfield Park. The book she'd been reading that day at Hookham's . . . and dropped, in her agitation.

"Oh, Julian," she murmured. She opened the first volume to the fly-leaf. The handwriting was black and bold, as arrogant as its owner. The words were simple: "May life with your 'Edmund Bertram' be, truly, happily ever after. Brandon."

There was something more, however. In the middle of the volume, pressed between a piece of silver paper and a note, was a small, white orchid, tinged with mauve.

The note informed her that Mr. Higginbottom had been instructed to deposit all her payments towards Davenant's debt into a separate account at her bank. Lord Brandon hoped she would make use of these funds as she required — as wedding gifts for her nieces, if she liked, or for any other estimable purpose.

Lilith lay note and orchid upon the table beside her, opened to the first chapter, and began to read.

19

Though Lord Brandon did not return to his town house until sunrise, he found his cousin waiting up for him. The marquess had scarcely stepped through the front door when Lord Robert burst into the hall.

"Gad, Julian, you're enough to drive a chap to Bedlam. Where the devil have you been?"

"Oh, here and there." The marquess calmly strode past him into the library, dropped his hat and gloves onto a chair, then headed for the tray of decanters. He poured himself a glass of brandy and proceeded to make himself quite comfortable in his favourite chair.

"I say, Julian, I do believe you're doing this just to punish me. I know I've lost two stone from the suspense. What's happened? Have you talked to her? Have you been talking all this time?"

"No."

"Julian!"

"I do wish you would not jump about like a frantic puppy, Robin. I am tempted to swat

339

you with a newspaper. Really, you are very tiresome. A puppy would be less trouble, I am certain. Thank heaven I shall not have the house-training of you."

"Julian!"

"There is writing paper in the upper left drawer of my desk," Lord Brandon said, waving his glass in that direction. "You'd be wiser to occupy your time composing a letter to your father-in-law-to-be. No, on second thought, *I* shall compose it. Your grammar is shocking, your punctuation and spelling execrable."

Robert gazed blankly at him for a moment. Then he rushed to his cousin and began pumping his free hand up and down. "Oh, good show, Julian. Good show. Gad, but you're amazing. You can do anything!"

"I doubt I shall be able to restore my arm to its socket."

Robert abruptly released him. "Yes, of course. Carried away. You can't know how — how — Gad, I'm so relieved. I just kept sinking lower and lower the longer you were gone, until I thought I'd just better hang myself."

" 'Men have died from time to time, and worms have eaten them, but not for love.' "

"Well, if you say so. But I thought I *would* die. I don't know when I've spent a worse night."

"I'm tired, Robin. I want to go to bed. Can

we just get this letter done?"

"Yes, yes, absolutely. This minute." Robert plunked himself down at the desk, tore out a stack of paper, picked up a pen, and waited.

"Mind you don't spoil all my pens. And no blots."

"Yes, Julian," was the docile reply.

As it turned out, Lord Robert spoiled a dozen quills, because not one but two letters needed to be written. After Julian had examined the first and pronounced it tolerable, he had gone into a queer sort of trance. Then, in an equally queer voice, he had reminded Robert of Cecily's aunt.

Though the young pair had not eloped, they had caused the widow considerable distress. She deserved a personal apology, of course, but an advance note — properly penitent — would be needed, if Robert expected to be admitted to speak to her at all.

This note turned out to be far more difficult than the first, with Julian revising every word a hundred times and ordering sheet after sheet torn up. At last the thing was done.

It was sent to the widow midmorning, with a request for an appointment in the early afternoon.

Shortly after noon, a frantic Robert received word that Mrs. Davenant would await him at two o'clock.

He arrived at one-thirty, and was left to cool his heels the full remaining half hour before he was shown into the drawing room.

"You intend to seek Lord Glenwood's consent, I trust?" the widow asked after she'd listened composedly to Robert's incoherent apologies.

"Yes, ma'am. That is, if you don't object. I know I've given you every reason to dislike me, but you must know — "

"I don't dislike you," she said coolly. "I've never disliked you, Lord Robert. That was an unfortunate misunderstanding. If you truly care for my niece — "

"Oh, I *do*. Believe me, I'd die to make her happy. Really, I would. She's the finest girl in the world!"

"Yes. Well." She paused and Robert waited anxiously.

Really, he thought, she was as bad as Julian for dragging a thing out and driving a man distracted.

"Are your parents aware of your intentions?" she asked finally.

He assured her there would be no trouble with his family. They'd be delighted. Julian had written this very day — a wonderful letter. "But he's so clever," Robert went on. "The words just come to him, you know.

342

That is . . . well, he spoke so highly of Cec —
of Miss Glenwood. And when they meet her,
I know they'll love her. They can't help it.
No one could," he said fervently.

That earned a small smile. "Very well," she
said. "I shall ask Cecily to step down to speak
with you."

"Oh, Mrs. Davenant." Robert shot up out
of his chair, and forgetting altogether who she
was, yanked her up from hers and hugged
her. "Thank you," he cried. "You really are
splendid. Julian was quite right. That is — "
Hastily, he let go and blushed. "I beg your
pardon."

She flushed a bit as well, but she nodded
with her customary cool politeness, then turned
away to summon her niece.

Lord Robert was given a very generous half
hour alone with his darling, though the door
to the drawing room was left open and a servant hovered nearby. When the young man finally took his leave, Cecily ran upstairs to her
aunt's sitting room, hugged her a dozen times,
and told her she was the sweetest, kindest,
most understanding aunt a girl could ever
want — even a horribly ill-bred, ungrateful
girl like herself.

"I only want you to be happy, Cecily," said
Lilith.

"Yes, Aunt, and I shall be," said Cecily. She dropped onto the footstool and gazed thoughtfully at her aunt. "Though I do wish you'd be happy as well."

"Naturally, I am, dear. You have been a great success, and now you will marry a very suitable young man who loves you dearly. That is all I could wish for."

"Is it?" Cecily took her aunt's hand and squeezed it. "Is it *all* you wish for? Don't you ever wish for yourself?"

The aunt's posture grew more rigid.

"Don't you ever wish to be with someone who loves you dearly? Even if he doesn't quite know it. Because they never do, do they?" she asked, half to herself. "We have to tell them *everything.*"

She came out of her abstraction with a grin. "I must tell you, Aunt, this Season has been extremely educational. I had no idea men could be so confused and impractical. They will wander about aimlessly, making themselves cross and unhappy, and it never occurs to them what the trouble is. Or if it does, they won't speak of it, because it isn't dignified — or something. Do you know, Lord Robert was thoroughly astounded when I told him I cared for him?"

"Was he?" Lilith asked faintly.

Cecily nodded. "Did you ever hear anything so ridiculous? Almost as ridiculous as his not knowing he cared for me." She stood up. "Thank heaven *that's* over. He's much more sensible now."

"I'm glad to hear it, dear."

"Well, I should like to speak more with you, Aunt, but I know Sir Thomas is coming, and you probably have a great deal to discuss with him. I suppose he'll want to set a date at last, now I'm off your hands. But we can talk tonight, can't we, after we come home?"

"Yes, of course we can. As much as you like, dear."

"Downs?" Sir Thomas repeated as he took the cup and saucer Lilith held out to him. "Well, that is very good, I suppose. Excellent family, of course. He has been a bit wild, but he is young. I daresay he'll settle down soon enough. Married life is marvelously settling — when, that is, the characters are well-suited."

"And when there is deep affection."

"Indeed, yes. Mutual regard and respect — that is the foundation."

"Oh, Thomas." Lilith put down her cup and rose from the sofa.

He jumped up. "My dear, what is it? Have you qualms about the match? If so — "

"No. That is, not about Cecily." She folded

345

her hands before her and raised her chin. "It's about us, Thomas. There's no way to work up to it tactfully, I'm afraid. I cannot marry you."

"Lilith! What is this?" Angry scarlet mounted his neck and ears.

"I cannot," she said. "I cannot be your wife. I married once without love. I shall not make that mistake again."

He was obviously striving for patience. "Come now, Lilith. We are not a pair of moonstruck children. Infatuation is no basis for a marriage — not a sound one. You know that as well as I, surely."

"I know our basis is not a sound one — not for me, at least. I'm not what I thought I was — or what you think me. I know I'll make you unhappy, and myself as well. To marry you is to injure us both."

With an effort he regained his self-restraint, and the angry colour subsided. "You have been ill," he said, more judiciously. "You are overwrought, and a few natural anxieties — perfectly natural, my dear — seem insurmountable obstacles. You want more rest. It is all these late nights, hurrying from one noisy place to another, and too much rich food."

"I have been . . . unwell," she said slowly, "but I am not so now. I have been troubled, but it's my conscience troubles me. In my heart of hearts, I knew I was wrong to accept you. I pray you will forgive me for having done so. I did not know my own heart."

"You didn't know Brandon then, is what you mean," he snapped.

Her features hardened to marble.

His hands clamped together behind his back, Thomas began to pace the carpet.

"You think I'm blind," he said heatedly. "I'm not. I'd heard enough of him. He must make a conquest of every woman he meets. Yet I saw no great harm in my future bride's cultivating one who has the ear of the world's most powerful men: Castlereagh, Wellington, Metternich, and not only our own Regent, but half the monarchs of Europe. Knowing you, I saw no danger in the acquaintance. And so I told my sister. Lilith Davenant, I told her, would never lose her head over such a man. But you have, it seems." He paused to glare at her. "Now you will throw your life away. For what? A libertine who'll make love to you at ten o'clock and lie in the arms of a ballet dancer at twelve."

Lilith let him rage on. He was entitled. She had insulted him deeply, betrayed him repeatedly. He could devise no words harsher than those with which she'd already flogged herself. Nevertheless, no words either could produce would ever change her heart. She stood, and endured, and when it was done and he'd gone at last, she ordered a bath and calmly walked up to her room to prepare for the evening ahead.

The letter was delivered shortly after Lilith had arisen from her bath. It lay on the tray next to the cup of herbal tea Emma had prepared. The handwriting was unfamiliar. It was, however, a woman's hand.

Within a few sentences, the sender's identity became painfully clear. Lilith turned the page over.

"I tell you, Madame, for him I care nothing. If he is in misery all his days, I should not be troubled. But you, I think, suffer as well, and I prefer you did not, for you have done me so much good."

Then it came, all of it, the entire story of the "knaves' wager," as Elise titled it: Lord Brandon's efforts to keep Robert from disgrace, and Elise's refusal to yield her so-easily-managed lover. The letter continued:

"You will wonder what wicked devil inspired me to so vile a game with another's virtue. I answer, Madame, that I never believed your virtue in danger. Ah, and how I wished to see the noble marquess taught a lesson — to see him thwarted, just once. For I must tell you he was abominably insolent. To be humbled by such a man was more than my pride could bear. *Alors,* I perceive his strong attraction to you. I see as well he is doomed to fail, and so I goad and challenge him.

What would you have me do? Plead and weep? Throw myself at his feet? Beg for mercy from a man who thinks women weak and mindless, like infants?

In my place, you would have defied him. But you are a great lady — his social equal — and I am merely *une fille publique.* So I put you in my place, as my champion. And you did defy him.

Today he tells me I have won. But I see I have won more than our wager. He is not so arrogant now. This time it is the great lord who seeks mercy. Well, I have given him what he wishes — not for his sake, or Robert's, or even for the girl's — but for yours. You have given me better revenge than I hoped. I will not repay you by bringing shame upon you and your family. Also, to tell you frankly, I am paid well for my forbearance.

There is but one matter more. Not important, perhaps, for you may be happy to see the last of him. He leaves in two days' time for Paris. This time, I do not think he will return.

The room was spacious and luxurious, yet not ornate. Golden threads glistened in the green draperies and in the chair coverings; otherwise, gilt was at a minimum. Several choice landscape paintings hung in elegantly simple frames upon the walls.

Above the large marble fireplace loomed a man's portrait. Tall, stern, forbidding, he glared down his hawklike nose at the woman who stared defiantly back.

Beneath the wig, Lilith thought, his hair would be thick and raven black — perhaps streaked with grey at the temples, for this was not the portrait of a young man. The mouth was thinner, and the lines there and at the corners of the eyes were more deeply etched. The eyes themselves were not quite the same green — but what artist could capture that colour?

An intimidating figure he must have been, the late Marquess of Brandon. What would he have made of the woman who stood in his drawing room, her hair unbound, streaming down her back, her tall, slim body draped — and scarcely concealed in slate-blue silk?

Lilith heard footsteps approaching. She turned to the door, straightened her spine, and raised her chin.

350

The man she awaited burst through the door, then stopped short, visibly composed himself, and proceeded more slowly into the room. He halted some distance from her.

Lord Brandon had been dressing — and was not altogether done, she thought wryly. His neck-cloth was crooked, and the knot was loose, clumsily tied.

"This is an unlooked-for honour," he said. He sounded short of breath.

"I should hope so," she said. "I don't know many ladies who are in the habit of paying late-night calls."

"Not to single gentlemen." He glanced about the quiet room. "And certainly not without escort. Have you taken leave of your senses, Mrs. Davenant?"

"I have come to take leave of you," she answered frostily. "Since you are far too busy to take proper leave of me. I suppose you meant to depart without a word. Paris, I understand."

"You are well-informed."

"Not so well as I could wish. I wanted to satisfy my curiosity."

She moved past the fireplace in a rustle of silk, and paused at the sofa. No, it was better not to sit down. She felt stronger upright. She let her fingers trail lightly over the silken embroidery.

"Women are excessively curious, are they not?" she continued. "It is a known failing of our gender. We have a regrettable need to be enlightened on every matter that appears to concern us. For instance, I have been the object of a wager."

She threw him a glance from under her lashes, and saw his colour deepen. "It is very tiresome of me, I know, but I long to be apprised of the details," she added.

"Lilith, don't — "

"Have you truly lost? You see, I have no idea how much time you had to seduce me. Perhaps you'd be so kind as to tell me the truth."

"Eight weeks," came the low reply.

"Good heavens! So much? And how odd." She calculated rapidly. "I thought you'd been in London but *seven*. Unless my addition is at fault, you might have seduced me the other day and won your wager. I realise, of course, you were anxious about the children. Yet we were already delayed by the storm. Another few minutes could not have made a great difference."

"A few minutes?" he asked with something like his customary coolness. "Please consider my reputation."

"All you had to do was bed me," she shot back. "Surely you hadn't bargained how long you'd be about it. I do not recollect, in any case, making any effort to prevent you. On the contrary — "

"Stop it!" He moved a few steps nearer. "I know well enough what I've done and what I am."

"I don't," she said. "It seems I know nothing about you."

"That's true. You knew a stranger, a man I created for the occasion." He turned away to the fireplace and took up a poker. There was no fire, but he thrust angrily at the coals laid in the grate while he went on. "You said the other day my words were always lies and easy speeches. It was worse than you know. You asked for truth. If you can bear it, I suppose I can bear to tell it."

"I want the truth," she said.

He told her. He explained how he'd employed two of her servants to apprise him of all her plans. That was how he'd happened to be at Hookham's — and everywhere else she went. He told how he'd bribed the clerk to block the aisle, ordered Ezra to ply the Enderses' coachman with drink, maneuvered their walk at Redley Park. All this and more — all his strategems.

"I was awake to every opportunity, you see," he said. "I would have said anything, done anything. Scarcely a word or gesture escaped me but was deliberately intended to weaken you. Every wile and guile I ever learned, Lilith — and new ones I invented. Never was there such a calculated siege," he finished, his voice weary.

She had not suspected — not the half of it — and was mortified at her naïveté. Still, he'd gone to considerable lengths. Any woman must be flattered by so painstaking a pursuit.

"So *that* is why I succumbed. No wonder. What mere female could be proof against such an onslaught? My conscience is quite clear, then," she said, glaring at him. "But *you*, after putting yourself to such trouble — why did you not reap the fruits of your labours the other day?"

"I could not." His gaze was still locked upon the grate.

"Why was that? An attack of conscience? But you haven't any, as you've just explained. Was I not sufficiently eager? Or was there some other way you found me . . . inadequate?" she asked, her chin determinedly aloft.

He turned round. "Good God, woman. How can you imagine such a thing? The one matter I never lied about was wanting you. In that I was never false."

"Then why, Julian? And don't repeat your ludicrous speech about my vulnerability. Pray have some respect for my intelligence."

She waited through a long silence. He would tell her the truth. He must. And she would bear it, whatever it was, because she must.

"It was what I saw in your eyes," he said at last. "Or what I thought I saw — but that was enough."

"What was it?" He must have felt her gaze hard upon him, but he wouldn't meet it.

"I thought it was love."

She stood proudly still while hot embarrassment swept her face. "Oh."

"Naturally, I was delighted. I had only connived for your person, not your heart. Indeed, I was in raptures." He struck the coals savagely, once, then replaced the poker in its rack. "Overjoyed to discover I'd made you love a man who didn't exist."

"I can see that must have been a blow to your pride," she said evenly, though her heart lightened within her. "Still, was it worth losing your wager? Was it worth sacrificing your cousin?"

He threw her a surprised glance, then looked away again. "What do you know of that?"

"I had a letter from Miss Fourgette. I must admit there was some consolation in learning the stake was not money or property. My honour for your cousin's. Abstract, but equitable, perhaps. Why did you deliberately lose?" she asked.

He stood, one hand resting on the mantel, his gaze still avoiding hers. His arrogant, handsome face was drawn into tight lines, his mouth set, his green eyes clouded. Yes, he was unhappy, genuinely so. Perhaps that was no more than he deserved.

"Why, Julian?"

"You won't believe it. Too romantic by half."

"Tell me."

"I could not go to that woman and tell her I had won," he said quietly. "It was too precious a treasure you offered me. I would not have it debased into a common, sordid episode."

She ought to let him suffer some little for all the suffering he'd cost her. At least something for the high price she'd paid to come here: her reputation, honour . . . her pride. Yet she'd come needing answers, honest ones, and this at least was not the humiliation she'd steeled herself to meet.

"That was . . . noble of you," she said.

He uttered one short, contemptuous laugh. "Hardly. Robert was in no danger. I knew I could buy her off."

"Still, it would have been cheaper to seduce me."

"I've behaved cheaply enough, I think. I refused to admit how deeply I cared for you, because my vanity would not bear it. My heart had always been quite safe. It was insupportable to admit that you'd seduced *me*, body and soul. Gad — to admit I liked talking with you of *farming?* To admit I delighted in your quick-witted responses to my sophistries? To acknowledge I'd rather argue with you about books, music, art than hear another accept my every word as a jewel of wisdom? Worst of all was to admit I wanted your good opinion — nearly as much as I wanted your person. No, my dear — too mortifying for words," he said, his voice edged with bitterness. "I would admit none of these until the damage was done, when it was too late to woo you honestly. Why should you accept as truth speeches so like their false predecessors?"

"Why, indeed?" she returned. "I am a paragon in so many ways, according to you — yet far too stupid to distinguish fact from seductive fiction. I swallowed every lie. Naturally, it follows I must disregard every truth. Your logic is astonishing, my lord. Nearly as remarkable as your courage. You repent your wickedness — or so you imply. You admit you care for me — or so it seems. And you promptly prepare to flee for Paris."

That jolted him. His sinking head shot up and the eyes he turned to her blazed with anger and hurt.

"Did you think I'd remain to dance at your wedding, Lilith?" he snapped. "Is it not enough I lie awake nights, seeing you in Bexley's arms? Lie alone, except for the agreeable voice of my conscience. Yes, *that* keeps me company with its pleasant refrain: how it might have been *me*," he went on furiously. "How I might be holding you . . . if I had not been such a bloody *fool*."

She folded her trembling hands tightly before her. "There will be no wedding," she said. "I have jilted Thomas. I, too, lied to myself. I thought I could be a good wife to him, even after my heart was stolen from me." The knuckles of her clamped hands turned white with the pressure of her grip as she added, "You went to a deal of trouble to make me love you, Julian. I think you'll have a devil of a time making me stop."

He stared at her, his green eyes wide with disbelief. Then it penetrated . . . at last.

"By God," he said hoarsely. "By God, but you are extraordinary."

She shook her head. "Afraid, perhaps — or stubborn — I don't know. Yet I had to come — shameless, brazen as it was of me — because you meant to go away and . . . " She drew a steadying breath. "And I — I could not let you go without a fight, Julian. I can't. It doesn't matter what you've done. Don't

leave me," she said, almost inaudibly. "Not
. . . not yet."

"Lilith."

Strong arms reached for her and drew her
up against him. "Not yet," he repeated, bury-
ing his face in her hair. "Oh, not *yet*."

His fingers threaded through her hair,
stroking, soothing. With a shudder of relief,
she relaxed at last in the familiar scent of sandalwood, the comforting strength of his arms,
and rested her head against his pounding
heart.

"I love you," he said.

"Yes."

"I can't lose you now, Lilith. I won't." He
drew her head back to look at her. "You're
mine. *Mine*," he whispered fiercely.

"Yes."

"You don't understand." He bit his lip.
"Oh, Lord. Lilith?"

"Yes."

"I have something rather shocking to tell
you. Perhaps you'd better sit down."

20

"Aunt has gone?" Cecily repeated.

"Yes, miss. Ordered a hackney and flew out of the house — and her hair not even done up. That was almost an hour ago, and she's not back yet — and Lord Robert is downstairs waiting."

"Then you must go to Mrs. Wellwicke and help her dress quickly. I can't go without a chaperon, even if I am engaged."

"But, miss, hadn't you better wait for your aunt?"

"No, I think I'd better not. I shall entertain Lord Robert until Mrs. Wellwicke comes down."

"But, miss — "

"Good heavens, Susan. If Aunt had wanted me to wait, she would have said so, wouldn't she?" Miss Glenwood responded ingenuously as she slipped past her maid and through the door.

With Cawble's keen eye upon him, Lord

Robert dared no more than drop a light kiss on his beloved's forehead. When, a moment later, he learned she intended to go out without her aunt, he was sorely tempted to shake the dear girl.

"She'll kill us!" he whispered harshly. "She'll banish me, she'll write your father and — "

"She'll do no such thing," Cecily answered. "Mary said she had on her nicest gown and her hair was all unpinned. Besides, I saw the book your cousin gave her. She's gone to him, of course — so naturally, it's absurd to expect her to return in time for the party. Thank heaven! When she came back the other day so gloomy, I was at my wits' end. I was so certain they'd have made it up by then. After all, they were on the road together at least twenty-four hours."

Lord Robert drew her farther into the room. "That was a terrible scheme, darling. When I saw your aunt this afternoon — gad, I've never felt so guilty in my whole life. And she never scolded — not once. I wanted to crawl into a hole, really I did."

"Well, we hadn't any choice, had we?" was the unrepentant answer as Miss Glenwood plopped down onto the sofa. "There's nothing like an elopement for getting the concentrated attention of one's elders, is there? And there's nothing to feel guilty about, because we didn't run away, did we? Besides, haven't they worried us half to death, the two of them? The nightmares I've had of that tiresome Sir Thomas married to my splendid aunt and turning her into a prim, fussy, miserable old woman. With her hair in those nasty coils. And a lot of bald little fussy children whining at her." She shuddered.

Lord Robert glanced at the door outside which the butler hovered, then took a seat beside his darling girl. "Don't get your hopes up about any other sort of children," he warned *sotto voce*. "Hillard said Julian was packing for Paris."

"Then he'll just have to unpack, I daresay," Cecily retorted. "When it comes to obstinacy, he's no match for my aunt."

"You don't know Julian."

She smiled up at him. "Don't I? Would you care to place a wager, my lord?"

"I think you're labouring under a misapprehension," Lord Brandon said slowly. "I *was* preparing to flee the country, like a coward — but it wasn't because I despaired of making you my mistress. I couldn't — that is, I can't — " He realised he was fiddling nervously with his neck-cloth. Abruptly, his hand dropped to his side. "I don't want you as my mistress."

Her gaze fell to the carpet and the colour rose to her fine, high cheekbones.

"Damn! That's not how I meant — By God, why must this be so curst impossible! That imbecile Bexley did better, I'll warrant," he muttered, clenching his fists and glaring at his evening slippers. "I want — I love you, with — with all my heart. I think I've loved you from the moment I first clapped eyes on you. Lord, why the devil should you believe that? Another of my confounded treacle speeches." He gritted his teeth. "Lilith Davenant, would you — Drat it! I'm a thorough wretch and I couldn't have treated you more shabbily — and I know I deserve to be miserable all my days — but I wish you'd let me try to be better, as . . . as your husband. I know there can't be a worse prospect in all the United Kingdom," he added hurriedly, "but I *swear* I'll be a good one — or die trying."

Slowly her head rose, and two slate-blue eyes fixed wonderingly upon his flushed countenance. "My hearing is failing me," she said breathlessly. "It sounded as though you just asked me to marry you."

"I did," he said, appalled at the wretched state of his nerves. "You wonder how I can have the temerity, but the fact is, I haven't any choice."

"Well. Indeed." Her gaze reverted to her hands, folded in her lap. "I'm struck all of a heap."

"No more than I."

"That's because you're overwrought. This is what comes of giving rein to one's emotions. We have descended into melodrama. Later, when you're cooler, you'll think better of it."

"I most certainly will not!" Panic abruptly superseded indignation. "Or do you mean *you* don't think much of it? No, of course you wouldn't," he answered miserably. "What a fool I am. Irresistible as a lover, perhaps, but as a husband — heaven forbid. You've already had one of my ilk, haven't you? You're hardly likely to make the same experiment twice."

"I'm older and wiser now," she said, "yet I love you."

"Yes, but what's the good of that if you won't marry me?" he complained ungraciously, scarcely heeding her through the black gloom overpowering him. "*Now*, naturally, after you've cursed me with this fiendish ogre of a conscience. Oh, it doesn't matter. I'm behaving abominably. Robin isn't half so infantile. I suppose I should take my punishment like a man."

"I wish you would not always be ramming thoughts into my head and words into my mouth, Julian," she said with a touch of impatience. "I didn't say I wouldn't marry you."

He gazed blankly at her.

"Well, did I?" she asked.

"Didn't you?"

"I was only trying to allow you time for second thoughts. I was sure you'd taken leave of your wits momentarily. Unfortunately, since you seem to persist in the ailment — "

"You wicked, teasing, *cruel* girl." He moved nearer to drop to one knee before her.

"Very likely I am. I hope you're prepared for a lifetime of it."

"I'll gladly endure all the torments of the damned," he joyfully assured her. "The question is, Are *you* prepared, my love?" He captured both her hands in his. "I want to parade you about in public and make my friends die of envy. I want to snatch you from your dancing partners and hold you as close as I like when we whirl about the room. I want to live with you. I want to rattle my newspaper at you during breakfast and quarrel with you about politics and the servants and the rearing of our children. I want to talk with you and tease you and care for you. I even want to trudge with you through muddy fields, to worry about the rain and the crops and the cattle."

"That may be your best speech yet," she said softly. Her cool blue gaze had softened too. "I'm afraid you're in a very bad way, my lord. Still, if ours is a *long* engagement, perhaps you'll come to your senses in time."

He uncoiled his long form from its position of supplication to take a more satisfactory place beside her on the sofa.

"It's true I feel rather giddy at the moment," he answered, "but I strongly doubt I shall ever come to my senses. Or perhaps I have at last. I don't know. I really am quite confused, weak, and dizzy. I had better take hold of something."

He gathered her close to him. Then his fingers crept into the gleaming, copper-lit curls framing her face. His gaze lingered on the haughty countenance that had so entranced and intrigued him from the start — the cool alabaster of her skin, the smouldering blue smoke of her eyes, the wanton ripeness of her generous mouth.

"I love you," he whispered.

Her mouth curled into a wicked smile that made his heart thump like a legion of marching infantry.

"So you do," she answered. "A costly mistake, I think."

"Indeed, I hadn't expected so high a price as marriage, madam. But what else is one to do? A mistress may be lost on a wager — or led astray by the next good-looking, sweet-talking rogue to cross her path. Marriage it is, then," he said, his voice low, fierce, possessive.

His kiss was fierce too, hungry, demanding. Yet there was at last peace of a sort within. And so, when she drew away after a moment or two, Julian quieted himself with the reflection that there would be time and time enough. Against every odd, Lilith Davenant would be his. Lady Brandon. His marchioness. The thought threw his heart crashing against his ribs.

"There's just one thing," she said, her fingers playing with the curls at his ear.

"Anything," he answered hoarsely.

"Well, actually, three things. There is Diana next year, then Emily the year after, and Barbara the next. Oh, and Claire — that makes four. But she will not be ready for a few years after *that*. Four more nieces, Julian."

"*Four* of them?" He sat back abruptly. "Perhaps I have been hasty. I don't believe I can survive any more of your nieces, Mrs. Davenant."

"They're very sweet girls," Lilith defended. "Darling girls, just like Cecily."

He shuddered theatrically. "No, not like Cecily. Anything but that."

"You can't be provoked with Cecily. Recollect she did come to her senses in time."

"She was never out of her senses," he retorted. "Not for a moment. I've never heard of such a coolly calculating little minx as that one. If her cousins are anything like her, I shall advise England's entire male population to make for the South Seas *at once.*"

"I'm sorry you feel that way, because she likes you immensely. She was taken with you from the start, you know," Lilith said. She reached up again, this time to stroke his stubborn jaw.

He brought her hand to his lips. "Was she?"

"Oh, yes. Because you were dark and devilish-looking. 'A bad, beautiful angel,' she called you — although she was comparing you to a horse at the time. All my nieces will dote upon you and make me jealous."

"Will they, just goddess? It seems the managing has begun already." He pressed another kiss upon her hand. "I see what our marriage will be like. You'll lead me about by the nose. What a pathetic prospect."

"Ah, yes, my lord, but such a *seductive* one. And poor me — I'm so susceptible to seduction."

He grasped the back of her head and brought her mouth to within an inch of his. "Indeed. Thank you for reminding me. In all my horror of impending nieces, I'd very nearly forgotten about *that*."

"Not until after we're wed, Julian," she said primly.

"Oh, no. Of course not."

"Your reformation must begin at once. There is not a minute to be lost. I am resolved."

Resolved or no, a devilish promise lurked in smoky blue depths.

"Yes, my love. And I respect you for it, indeed I do," he said. "Naturally, I can wait."

"Deceitful knave," she said.

"Yes," he breathed as his mouth covered hers.

Author's note: For the story's purposes, the debut of *Mansfield Park* has been advanced a few weeks. Miss Austen's novel was published in three volumes on 9 May 1814.★

★Source: *Jane Austen: Her Life*, by Park Honan. St. Martin's Press. New York. 1988.